Bello:

hidden talent red

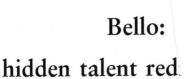

Bello is a digital only imprint of Pan Macmillan,
established to breathe new life into previously published,
classic books.

At Bello we believe in the timeless power of the imagination,
of good story, narrative and entertainment and we want to use
digital technology to ensure that many more readers
can enjoy these books into the future.

We publish in ebook and Print on Demand formats
to bring these wonderful books to new audiences.

www.panmacmillan.co.uk/bello

Winston Graham

Winston Mawdsley Graham OBE was an English novelist, best known for the series of historical novels about the Poldarks. Graham was born in Manchester in 1908, but moved to Perranporth, Cornwall when he was seventeen. His first novel, *The House with the Stained Glass Windows* was published in 1933. His first 'Poldark' novel, *Ross Poldark*, was published in 1945, and was followed by eleven further titles, the last of which, *Bella Poldark*, came out in 2002. The novels were set in Cornwall, especially in and around Perranporth, where Graham spent much of his life, and were made into a BBC television series in the 1970s. It was so successful that vicars moved or cancelled church services rather than try to hold them when Poldark was showing.

Aside from the Poldark series, Graham's most successful work was *Marnie*, a thriller which was filmed by Alfred Hitchcock in 1964. Hitchcock had originally hoped that Grace Kelly would return to films to play the lead and she had agreed in principle, but the plan failed when the principality of Monaco realised that the heroine was a thief and sexually repressed. The leads were eventually taken by Tippi Hedren and Sean Connery. Five of Graham's other books were filmed, including *The Walking Stick*, *Night Without Stars* and *Take My Life*. Graham wrote a history of the Spanish Armadas and an historical novel, *The Grove of Eagles*, based in that period. He was also an accomplished writer of suspense novels. His autobiography, *Memoirs of a Private Man*, was published by Macmillan in 2003. He had completed work on it just weeks before he died. Graham was a Fellow of the Royal Society of Literature, and in 1983 was honoured with the OBE.

Winston Graham

THE JAPANESE
GIRL

BELL◉

First published in 1971 by Collins

This edition published 2013 by Bello
an imprint of Pan Macmillan, a division of Macmillan Publishers Limited
Pan Macmillan, 20 New Wharf Road, London N1 9RR
Basingstoke and Oxford
Associated companies throughout the world

www.panmacmillan.co.uk/bello

ISBN 978-1-4472-5681-6 EPUB
ISBN 978-1-4472-5680-9 POD

The Japanese Girl

I didn't notice anything special about her at first. I didn't even notice she was foreign. You get in a crowded train and think yourself lucky to find a corner seat, and it doesn't occur to you to take any particular notice of the person opposite.

So I'd been sitting there maybe twenty minutes before I noticed this book she was reading. I'd been looking through the evening paper looking at the cricket scores and wondering if Surrey would have time to win, when I happened to glance up and look at her eyes. You couldn't tell what the book was because it had one of these fancy leather holders on it like you hardly ever see now; but the peculiar thing was her eyes weren't going from side to side, they were going up and down.

I watched for a bit, and it occurred to me to wonder if she was adding up figures, the way I do all day Song; but it didn't look like that. You can tell when people are calculating. And then she turned over a page, and I wondered if she was left-handed or I was going crackers and was seeing things in a mirror because she turned back instead of forwards. In other words she was reading the book from back to front.

Just at that minute she happened to glance up, and she met my eyes and I looked away, and I realized then she was an oriental. It wasn't much: so many girls pencil their eyes that way these days; and her skin was just pale, a bit sallow; but again make-up hardly allowed it to show.

I'd never seen anyone read a book like that, and didn't even know they did read that way, and I couldn't keep my eyes from going up every now and then and watching her.

So we were in Brighton almost before I knew it, and the train was emptying. She had a lot of parcels and getting out she dropped one and I picked it up for her and she thanked me. Then I followed her down the platform and out into the street.

It was a windy day, with a lot of April cloud scudding across the sky. I'd not been to Brighton since I was a kid, so I had to ask my way, and presently I found myself queueing for a bus about three people behind her.

She was a small girl, and quite slight but not thin, and her hair was black, but not that dead blackness you often see in the East; in fact when the wind lifted it it seemed to shine and glisten like it might have been wet. You couldn't call her good-looking but just something about her appealed to me and made me feel queer, and God knows I'm no womanizer: usually these days I've no time to bother looking around. But it just happened with this girl just then.

And getting into the bus she dropped the same parcel, so I trod on the toe of the fat man in front of me trying to get to it, and he thought I was attempting to get on the bus ahead of him and was quite nasty about it. This time she gave me a very nice smile indeed with a little personality about it. The first time it had been a lifting of the lips and a 'Thank you' with eyes that didn't properly look. This time they looked and recognized, and they smiled too and she said 'Please excuse me.' She didn't actually say 'prease' but it was half way between an R and an L.

I took the seat next to her in the bus and tried hard to think of something to say, and while I was still thinking and nothing coming at all the conductor came up and I asked him for Melton Street, and would he tell me when we got there. Then she said: 'Oh, I'm getting out there. I'll tell you.' All I could think to say was 'Thank you,' and I sweated and took off my glasses to polish them and put them back, and the bus jolted along and we sat in silence.

Then it was time to get off and this did give me a chance. I said: 'Perhaps you'd let me – as I've . . .' and took hold of the parcel I'd picked up twice already, and she smiled and let me.

Off the bus I said: 'I'm a stranger to Brighton, but if we're going the same way, perhaps I could carry it for you,' and she said: 'Well, yes, partly the same way. Melton Street is nearer to the sea.'

We walked along in the afternoon sunlight with the wind blowing strong between the houses and smelling sweet and salty. I'm not exactly a he-man to look at but I was a lot bigger than her, and it gave me a good feeling to be walking beside her. Good, did I call it? Wonderful. But mentally I was tearing my hair out how to capitalize on this bit of luck.

'D'you live in Brighton?' I asked.

'Yes. Yes, I work here. Do you? But of course not – you are not knowing it.'

'I live in London,' I said. 'I work in the City. I'm just here for the afternoon to visit a sick colleague. He's just been taken ill. *He's* lived here for years. Lucky man.'

'Yes, it's a nice place,' she said. 'I have only been here four years but it's a nice place.'

'England, d'you mean or – or d'you mean Brighton?'

'I was born in England.'

'Oh,' I said. 'Sorry.' I had to go on then. 'You see, I just noticed on the train. I noticed that book you were reading. It wasn't English, was it?'

'No . . . No, it was Japanese. My mother and father were both Japanese.'

'Oh,' I said. 'I see. I couldn't think. That book, you see. You were reading it from back to front. And up and down. I never knew Japanese was like that,'

She laughed. A little tinkling laugh. 'I have never been to Japan, but that was the first language I ever spoke.'

We had come to a stop. Just a bit of a conversation but it was the most important thing that had happened to me in a very long time.

'That's your way,' she said. 'To the end of the street where the traffic lights are, and Melton Street is next on your left.'

'I'm in no hurry,' I said. 'Can I carry this parcel home for you?'

'This is where I live.'

'Oh, well . . .' I hung on to the parcel and then had to give it up. 'Do you often go to London?'

'No. It is my half day. I go to visit my brother about once a month, that's all.'

'Well, I expect I may be visiting Mr Armitage again. Next week or the week after. It'll be a Saturday afternoon again. I'll look out for you on the train – see if I can carry another parcel.'

She laughed again and we separated. I watched her go up the steps to her house. I waited and saw her let herself in. She didn't turn round. I went on to call on Mr Armitage.

When I got home to Islington Hettie was looking fagged out. She nearly always did now.

It's a funny thing. It's funny how fate treats you. As a young chap I was as fond of girls as the average fellow, but I never was a Don Juan, either in looks or in carrying on. For one thing I was short-sighted and for another I was shy. Yet I married one of the prettiest girls in the district. One of the prettiest I've ever seen. Hettie at 19 was a real pretty one: dark curly hair, big eyes, beautiful skin. Perhaps a shade delicate looking; but there were lots of boys after her and I was delighted and flattered when she chose me.

And we were married and we were quite happy for a time. Setting up house, making love in an inexpert fashion; me in quite a good job that didn't then look as dead-end as it was going to be, she still going out to work herself. I think it was as good as most people's lives. And then she began to fade. There's no other word for it. Just like a flower out of water. She was anaemic, the doctor said, but none of his pills made any difference. She wasn't really ever seriously ill – it was just that her looks began to go at twenty-two instead of at forty-two. Her hair hung lank instead of curling, her eyes lost their lustre, her skin took on a sort of freckled look, only they weren't natural freckles, it was more like a change in the skin. Not that this all happened in a year, but it happened in five years. She was like a may-fly or something, beautiful for a day.

We didn't have children. First it was because she wanted to go

4

on working, then it was because she was too delicate. Of course I was still fond of her in a way, but it was in an anaemic way, as if her anaemia made it impossible for you to have strong feelings about her. Sometimes I felt trapped, shackled, pinned down by her and by my dead-end job. When I was a kid I'd had all sorts of dreams and ambitions – thought I'd travel, see life, make good. And I'm determined and a hard worker – with a break I *could* have made good. But the break didn't come and I was on a tread-mill, tied to a quiet, mousy, delicate wife, who never complained but who made a virtue of not complaining. She was rather religious: it maddened me sometimes when she did voluntary work and neglected her own home.

Of course it wouldn't be true to say I felt this all the time, or even a large part of the time. Most days, most weeks, I hardly thought about it at all. Routine is deadening. And in the end comforting. You still have dreams but you – what's the word? – sublimate them by filling up the pools and watching the telly.

But I came home this night really swimming with excitement. Meeting this girl was the most stimulating thing that had happened to me in a year. Because since I married Hettie, and that was fourteen years ago, I'd hardly looked at another woman seriously. And suddenly out of the blue it was as if I had been stung.

I slept badly. We slept in separate beds which we'd changed to three years ago because Hettie said my restlessness kept her awake. Tonight I was glad because I could toss and turn just as much as I pleased. Half awake and half asleep I went over my brief meeting with the Japanese girl and made up extra conversation that would have convinced her what a charming man I was.

The thing was that I thought from the way she looked at me that she was attracted to me too. It was only in the light of morning when the pale sunlight began to show in nicks through the thin green chintz curtains that I faced up to the fact that I would probably never see her again.

I worked for Annerton's, the big London dock firm. I was assistant cashier, under Mr Armitage (who had just been taken ill). It had looked a fair enough prospect when I joined the firm at 17: reasonable pay with good prospects of promotion. But although I'd moved up I'd not for some reason made the grade with them. Twice I'd been passed over and twice I'd nearly left. But somewhere at bottom in me is a streak of self-distrust – a dislike of anything new and a fear that the new may turn out worse than the old. I'm obstinate, people say, determined and ambitious. But they don't understand the fear I have of the unknown.

And Hettie always discouraged me from trying a new job. She really hadn't any confidence in my initiative, and I suppose, God help her, she was reasonably comfortable in our shared house, knowing her neighbours, not wanting to move.

The following Friday I went to see Mr Head and suggested he might like me to call on Mr Armitage again on the next Saturday. He seemed surprised, because Armitage and I had never got on specially well; but he said all right, if I *felt* like going down perhaps I could take these bank papers for Armitage to approve. I needn't wait for them: Armitage could post them back at his leisure.

I didn't wait for them. I was in and out of Armitage's house in twenty minutes, and then for three hours I moved around in the neighbourhood of the girl's home.

She looked quite startled when she saw me.

'Oh,' I said, 'well I said it *might* happen but I never thought it *would*. Haven't you any parcels I can carry this evening?'

She half laughed but didn't look displeased and we stood there a minute or so. I said I had been seeing my sick colleague again and she said she had been to the afternoon showing of a movie and had stayed out for supper.

I said: 'Well, it's a bit cold here. Would you like a drink? That looks quite a nice pub.'

She hesitated, and I knew this was the moment of decision. I'd planned this all beforehand, but it all fell to pieces if she said no.

She didn't say no, and that's how it all began.

We began to meet once a week, each Saturday afternoon. Her name was Yodi Okuma. Her parents were both dead. Her father had been a Japanese seaman whose ship had been unloading in Liverpool in 1941 and he had been interned. After the war he had come to London and married a Japanese girl and they had two children, Yodi and Takemoto – or Taki, as she called him – her younger brother. Taki was training to be a teacher at London University; Yodi worked in an upholstery firm in Brighton and with her wages was helping to support her brother through his college days. Taki, she said, was much more Japanese looking than she was, but he loved England and never wanted to leave it. His ambition was to become a tutor of Japanese at Oxford or Cambridge. Yodi on the contrary wanted to travel. She didn't care how soon she could get away from England. She wanted to see Japan and all the world.

This was an immediate bond between us. Her talk of travel lit up all my old ambitions. We went to the pictures three or four times, always to see travel films or movies set against glamorous backgrounds, such as *Hawaii*. We talked and talked, and always found more in common.

And of course it wasn't just talk. Every time we met the attraction grew, and soon I was kissing her goodbye. Then in no time it became a question not of how we could spend the afternoon but where we could spend it. The place she lived in was a hostel for girls, and the rules were still fairly strict.

One day I took a half day off from the office and went to Brighton unknown to her and took a room in a block of flats in Kemptown. It was only a tiny bed-sitter and it cost £5 a week, but it was modern and light and private, right on the top floor. I'd got £300 in the Post Office and Hettie would never know I had drawn it out. Just spending the capital it would go a long way. I didn't see beyond the end of the year.

So I took her to the flat the next Saturday afternoon and we made love. She was quite different from Hettie – I didn't know two women could be so different. She was so impulsively warm, so welcoming, that it made all the difference to me; I felt I was discovering a woman for the first time.

Of course I had told her I was married, and she didn't seem to mind that. She was a submissive little creature in some ways, as if generations of her forebears had left this as a mark on her, a mark of the inferior sex. Yet she had a distinct personality, quite strong, quite wayward, full of warmth and high spirits. She took things lightly, amiably, even ill-health. We hardly spoke of Hettie and she hardly spoke of her life before she met me. We both lived in the present, and we both talked of the future. She seemed to have no special friends among the girls she worked with or those she boarded with. She was devoted to her brother and wrote him every week. I don't know if she had had boy friends, I was only happy that she had none now.

All these weeks I had not, of course, been visiting Mr Armitage. He was still ill, and getting no better, but this news came by letter to the firm; there was no need for his assistant to go down. Him being away made a lot more work for me but I didn't mind because every week was just a preparation for Saturday.

I told Hettie I was still seeing Mr Armitage, but after a bit I thought, she's just not going to swallow this much longer, so I told her one night I was going to the races in Plumpton on the next Saturday. I knew it would shock her because she didn't approve of gambling, so I knew there was no risk of her wanting to come with me. I'd chosen racing partly for that reason and partly because I thought if she ever does find out about the £300, saying I'd lost it at the races was an easy way out.

Because I still hadn't really thought of leaving her.

Well, she was shocked, in her quiet rather listless way; but she also said: 'How long have you been going?'

'Going?' I stared at her. 'Why this is . . .' and then I sensed that it was better not to say it was the first time. 'This will be the third Saturday. Before that I went to see Armitage every week – honestly.'

'I knew there was something different,' she said. 'There was something different about you. There has been – even for longer than three weeks.'

'What d'you mean?' I laughed. 'I don't feel any different.'

'Well, you are. More excited, like. Excitable. Edgy.'

'Not bad-tempered. You can't say I've been bad-tempered.'

'No, no. I wouldn't say that. But edgy. Half the time you don't listen when I talk to you. You don't read the evening paper the way you used to. It's – something I can't describe. Oh, Jack . . .'

'Yes?' I was fearful then that she might have guessed.

'How much are you *betting* on the races? It's the craziest way of losing money. You get nothing for it – nothing at all. You might as well throw it down a drain!'

I laughed again. 'You can set your mind easy about that! I never put more than ten bob on any race – more often it's five! Honestly, Hettie, since Armitage was taken ill I've been working late nearly every night, you know that. I've been at a stretch. And I find this going off and watching horses, it's a sort of relaxation. You ought to come sometime.'

She shook her head dubiously, as I hoped she would. 'It's such a *bad* habit. There are such awful people at race meetings. And anyway, even if you only put ten shillings on a race, it might mean you losing three or four pounds in an afternoon.'

'Oh, really!' I patted her hand, almost in affection, though now she meant nothing, nothing to me. 'I've never lost more than two pounds yet. And I win sometimes. So far I'm not a pound down on three meetings.'

'Three meetings,' she said quietly. 'You told me it had only been two.'

The next day, the next afternoon, Yodi and I went and sat on the beach for an hour or two before we went back to the little room in Kemptown. We talked about beaches. Neither of us had ever been out of England, but these days everybody has a good idea what foreign places look like: the Mediterranean towns, the surfs of Australia and Honolulu, the glimmering domes of Venice, the temples and magnolias of Kyoto, the painted fishes of the Caribbean. We talked about them and wished we could visit them together. She was mad keen to travel – even keener than I was – and as soon as her brother was earning his own keep she meant to get a job, if she could, which would enable her to. Japanese airlines, she thought, might welcome a girl who could speak good English.

But of course at heart that was not the way she wanted to travel, whisked by jets from place to place, boarded at hostels, on a rigorous time-schedule. Nor did I. The essence of travel as I saw it, even if only perhaps for two holidays a year, was leisure to enjoy the places one visited and money to visit them in comfort.

Just then I began to see a tremendous opportunity ahead. Armitage was no better and was not going to get any better. The fiction was still put about but nobody believed in it any more. Armitage had not been appointed head cashier until he was 47. I was only 35. But I was his second man. If he retired – as he must very soon – there was every prospect of me taking his place. That meant nearly double what I was making now – and four weeks' holiday a year, instead of two. If that happened, I thought, I'd have the courage to tell Hettie about Yodi. Whether I left Hettie might depend on her, but I would be able to keep Yodi in a really pleasant little flat somewhere and we could spend all our spare time together and all my holidays. If Hettie would divorce me, so much the better: then I could make a clean break. Also as head cashier at Annerton's I would be in a good position to apply for a still better position somewhere and one that would give me a chance to travel.

I was very excited when I told Yodi all this, and she quickly caught on to the idea. 'You mean if you could you would marry me, Jack?'

'Of course! It's the one thing I'd like most in the world. Didn't you know?'

'Well . . . Between this and being married – there is a gap. I was not so sure.'

'Why are you so modest, Yodi, so sort of self-effacing?'

'If I am, it is the way of Japanese women.'

'But you've been brought up in the West, brought up in our ways.'

She was silent. 'When I was small the Japanese were not popular in England. Some of the little girls I went to school with, their fathers had been in the prison camps – So it was not very nice for me. Since I grew up, young men . . . well, they have not wanted marriage. Perhaps it has given me a sense of inferiority.'

'I've got to put that to rights,' I said.

All the next two weeks I was on tenterhooks. I heard Armitage had sent in his resignation. I knew the board would be thinking about his successor – probably had been for some time. I worked furiously, wondering when the call would come and if it would come. Rumours of all sorts flew about, but I didn't believe half of them. I knew Armitage hadn't liked me, but I thought my work was good enough. I was ripe for the big move. Because of Yodi I had to have it.

Then one Friday afternoon Mr Head sent for me. I went in, mouth dry, hands hot, but cool in the head, not nervous so that anyone could see, not shaking.

He said: 'Ah, Jack, sit down. You know of course that Mr Armitage has resigned. Poor chap, I think he's about done for. The result of the latest tests he's had could hardly have been worse.'

I said: 'I'm sorry. Of course I knew he was leaving.'

'Yes, well, there it is, there it is. A good and loyal servant. Naturally the board have been considering his successor.'

'Yes,' I said, 'I expect they have.'

'They've interviewed a number of candidates and yesterday they appointed a new man. His name is Cassell, and he comes from Palmer's, the textile combine. I hope you'll get on well with him. He comes with the highest references.'

Hettie, of course, was not surprised and not too upset. 'After all, dear, you are a bit young, aren't you?'

'The new man's 39,' I said.

'Well, he's had a lot of other experience, I expect.'

'What's other experience to do with it? I know Annerton's business through and through! D'you know, this new fellow will have to lean on me for *months* before he knows whether he's coming or going! *I'*ll have to teach him what *I* know before he can begin to do his job properly! It's just too damned unfair. That bastard Ward! And I expect Armitage had his say!'

'Don't be so angry, Jack. It'll upset me. What's the use of carrying on? They've made their choice. You – maybe you . . .'

'Well, go on: what were you going to say?'

'Well, maybe they wanted somebody . . . better educated or something. Or with different interests. I should hope they don't know you go racing every week!'

It was typical of her, I thought, to show she felt I didn't measure up to the job. How can anyone do well in life with a wife like that? I asked Yodi this and she said: 'Jack, don't think about her. I see why you are unhappy with her but don't let that sort of talk put you down. Let us plan what *we* are going to do now. Do you now look for another job?'

'Not yet,' I said. 'I've had a pretty drastic idea. But first I want to see how the new man measures up.'

In the night I *had* had drastic ideas, ideas that had frightened me, yet often as I rejected them during the next two weeks they kept coming back. And the longer I considered them, the more solid and feasible and acceptable they became.

Cassell arrived and confirmed my suspicion. He was an adequate sort of chap with a hearty public school manner that I could see would have impressed the board. I tested him out gingerly on one or two points and he knew his accountancy well enough, but he came from an entirely different firm from Annerton's and it would take him months to get the hang of things. Cassell was friendly to me because he needed my help, but when he had it all at his finger-tips he would be patronizing. I could see it coming. It would be Armitage all over again.

And I couldn't stand that. I wasn't prepared to stand that. There were only two alternatives: I could look for a new job – and what chance had I of getting a new position much different from the old – and if that happened how long could I keep the flat for Yodi? How long in fact could I keep Yodi's love and loyalty? The other alternative I stayed awake at nights considering. I had the guts to *do* it: I felt certain of that, because I was driven into a corner. But did I have the guts to carry it through? And, more important than all that, more important than anything I did, did Yodi have the courage and the love and the loyalty to play her part?

The third Saturday I determined to sound her out. Yet I didn't know how to begin. I plunged in suddenly, when we were lying in bed after our love, when we were sipping coffee and smoking.

'Yodi, I have a plan – for both of us. It's a way I think we can marry and travel and have money. But it needs – awful courage, and – and great loyalty – and patience. No, don't smile; this is serious. Dead serious. Let me tell you. Don't interrupt. Just let me tell you. But, right at the start, I want one promise, that's if you don't want to do this, if you won't do my plan, then we'll drop it and you forget I've ever spoken. Promise you'll forget.'

She looked at me with her jet-fringed eyes – misty after love the way I liked to see them. 'I promise Jack. Yes, I pledge that.' She didn't say 'predge', but the word was half way between the two.

I said: 'Just now,' and swallowed and stopped; began again. 'Just now I could steal money from Annerton's and nobody would know.'

She lay very still beside me.

I said: 'I could've done for the last three months but it never entered my *head*. I'm not – a thief. Not if I could choose I wouldn't be. But maybe this is the time when I must *choose* to be. Because the opportunity won't ever come again. This man, this new man Cassell, he's all at sea at present. All the time I'm handling big money – pay for the staff every Friday: there's 400 on the staff – other things. Any week, any week *at all*, a thousand pounds could drop into my lap, nobody would know.'

I waited then, drawing breath. A freckle of ash dropped off her cigarette. 'But somebody would find out, Jack, sooner or later they'd –'

'Wait. I'm coming to that. A thousand pounds any week, every week, for the next three or four months. Get me? We could make away with probably twenty thousand. Perhaps even more.'

'We?'

'Yes, we.'

'How do I . . .'

'Listen, Yodi. Sooner or later I'll get caught. That's for certain.

They'll want to know what I've done with the money. A lucky thing, just by chance, when Hettie wanted to know where I was going every Saturday I said I was going to the races. There was a reason for that, but now it fits in. I shall say I lost the money on the races. But all the time you'll have it.'

She sat up. 'Oh, Jack, this is not serious –'

'It is. It's a proposition. No one can prove I didn't gamble the money away. No one knows about you and me. People round here will recognize you because you're Japanese; but not me, I'm just anybody – a man. There's nothing to connect us. You said you never told anybody my name . . .'

'Of course not! I didn't wish to get you into trouble with your wife.'

'So.' Even while I spoke the proposition seemed to solidify. 'So the money will come to you. You will bank it. There's nothing to stop you opening half a dozen bank accounts. Banks never object to money being paid *in*. It's not their concern where it came from so long as their customer has respectable references. They only worry if you want an overdraft. So in a few months you could have £20,000 in your name, untouchable, safe. So long as no one knows about us, no one could ever query it.'

She was sitting up, holding the sheet to her throat. 'But, Jack, what good would that be to you? If they caught you, you would go to prison!'

'Yes,' I said. 'I know. That's what I've got to *face*. It's the only way we could make this scheme work.'

'But – but if we *really* did this – and it makes me tremble just the thought of it – if we did it, why couldn't we stop when you thought you were going to be found out – stop in time and then – then we'd leave the country together – go to South America, or even Japan!'

'Would you want to marry a wanted criminal?' I asked. 'And be a wanted criminal yourself? You would be, you know, then. And as for me, maybe I'm funny. It'd give me a real kick to steal this money – it really would, from Annerton's – I'd *enjoy* it. But I couldn't – couldn't – enjoy spending the money feeling every minute a policeman's hand might come on my shoulder. There isn't any peace of mind that way, I'd feel like a hunted rat!'

'But if you went to prison, how could you enjoy it? I don't understand –'

'Listen, Yodi. It would be my first offence. My lawyer would make a lot of me being tempted to gamble and being deeply sorry, etc., etc. I might get three years. I might get four. With good behaviour I shouldn't have to serve more than three at the outside. My wife'll be shocked to death. She's religious. Pretty certainly she'll be persuaded by her father and mother to divorce me. In three years I come out. I get some job found for me by the Prisoners' Aid or whatever they're called. I hold it down for three months, then I turn it in, take a job in Brighton, happen to meet you. We fall in love and get married. Presently we leave England. I've got a clean sheet, I've paid for my crime. We go to live somewhere else – France or Canada or Japan. Presently we begin to live a little better. Once we're out of England nobody will ever check. Then we travel as we want to travel, live as we want to live. Maybe it won't last us all our lives, but we'll have a wonderful time on it travelling everywhere we want – together.'

There was a long silence beside me. I couldn't hear her breathing but I could feel it Slow take in, then a tremulous give out. A clock struck, and I knew I should be going.

'Well?' I said at last.

She took my hand. 'Give me time, please. I have to think of this thing. Give me time.'

TWO

So we began to plan. It looked easy, but there were twenty ways of slipping up and I had to guard against them all.

Getting the money wasn't any trouble. When you have a pay-roll of four hundred. I didn't make up the pay envelopes, two clerks did that; but I made out the cheque for drawing the money, and nobody ever queried it. Nobody would ever query it until the audit at Christmas, which was five months off. Even then, accountancy firms being rushed off their feet, it would be at least another month after that before they tackled the accounts. I wasn't at all afraid of Cassell. He never concerned himself with the day-to-day working of the firm; he was dealing with jobs like the financing of development plans, the costing of new products. And there were other ways I could get money apart from the wages cheque.

But because it was easy I went along with infinite care. To be caught later on might not matter; to be caught at the beginning would ruin everything.

And getting the money was only the beginning. There must be no connection, no hint of a connection between me and Yodi. If there was we were done for – and she would be in trouble as well as me. The likelihood of me being recognized in the flat in Kempton was infinitely tiny; small-time embezzlers don't get their photos in the papers; those days are over; but I took to wearing dark clip-ons over my ordinary lenses, and I only went to the flat now and again. Every week from the week she agreed, instead of coming straight to meet her I went a race meeting. Sometimes it was Brighton, sometimes Plumpton or Lingfield. After I got there I put five or ten pounds on the first two races, stuffed the slips in my pockets, and after the horses had lost – as they usually did – I left and met Yodi by arrangement somewhere and handed her the money. I didn't buy a car myself but I bought her a second hand Morris 1000 so that she could get about in it to meet me. Sometimes I went farther afield when there was no racing in Sussex or Kent, and then I would not see her but would keep the money till the following week. At home I ordered the racing papers and kept them upstairs, marking them heavily in blue pencil as if I'd been studying form. Hettie complained about them cluttering up the bedroom, but I took no notice and one day when I found she'd burned some I made such a row that she burst into tears.

I was building up the picture, and every suit I had carried a pocket half full of old betting slips.

Passing the money to Yodi was no problem; a thousand pounds in fivers and tenners will easily go in a big envelope; but she did seem unnecessarily scared about opening so many bank accounts and she seemed to feel the money was safer from prying eyes in a suitcase under the bed. In the end she opened five accounts: two in Brighton in different banks, one in Hove, one in Worthing, one in Eastbourne. They were all under her own name. I didn't want *any* irregularity to exist, so that anyone could get at her. After all there's no law against having money. Banks love you if you have money. So does almost everybody, I've found.

But even with five accounts it's a bit much to pay in £200 in cash every week. Even with five accounts the suitcases under the bed began to get full. Where money was concerned she was sharp and yet she was timid. She latched on quickly enough to all my ideas and followed them to the letter; but she was terrified of paying the money into the banks, of opening a deposit account so that the money could earn interest, of chatting naturally to the bank cashier and perhaps asking his advice.

One evening when we had been able to go back to the flat and make love she said: 'Supposing – you say we have to make plans for everything – supposing I was asked where all this money came from – nothing to do with you, but somebody said: "Miss Okuma, please tell me where all this cash comes from. I demand to know." '

I said: 'Tell them you're a prostitute.'

She stared at me, eyes wider than they were ever meant to go. Then she laughed. 'Oh, you are funny!'

'No, I'm serious. I don't know much about it, but the tales they tell, some of these high-class girls make a fantastic amount, and all in cash.'

Her eyes clouded. 'You would have me say that?'

I patted her arm. 'I wouldn't have you *be* that. But if you *were* asked – if you were ever in a corner – it would be an explanation, a way out. They couldn't ever prove different.'

She was silent quite a while, and I thought maybe I'd offended her. But after a while she went on: 'Jack, while we are talking like this, do you realize how much you are trusting me?'

'We discussed all that when you agreed to the plan.'

'Yes, but think again. Think now. You are giving this to me –

all this money. You have no *hold* over me – we are not even married. What if I let you go to prison and then betrayed you?'

'You wouldn't. I just know you wouldn't.'

'But what if I *did*, Jack? You said prepare for everything. What if I did?'

These weeks I had grown up, aged, matured; it was queer: I could feel it myself. At her question I looked deep into the darkness of my own nature. It was as if I'd opened a door that hadn't ever been opened before.

I said: 'Then, Yodi, I think if you betrayed me, if all this went for nothing, then I think I should kill you.'

She took my hand. 'But I could disappear, go and live in Tokyo. There there are millions of girls who look like me. If I changed my name – Oh, I know I *won't*; but you have to realize the risk, the *trust* . . .'

'If I couldn't find you,' I said, 'then I think I would kill your brother.'

I felt her shrink as if she had been touched by a hot iron. 'Jack . . . you couldn't – you wouldn't.'

I took her hand again: it was very clammy. 'No, I wouldn't; I couldn't. But if you betrayed me in this it would be the end of the world. You wouldn't – you couldn't do that.'

No more was said then; but if that conversation brought a sort of chill between us for the rest of the evening, it also some-how served to cement the pact. Now we quite understood each other.

The weeks passed and the plan continued to run smoothly. I dreaded a sudden illness which would keep me away from the office for a week or more. So long as I was there to superintend the figures we were perfectly safe. Yodi was due for a week's holiday from her firm, and I sent her to Switzerland. In that week in two journeys she took out nearly ten thousand pounds.

Of course this was risky: smuggling currency out of the country is a penal offence, and she would have had a bad time had she been caught. But in the late holiday season the numbers passing through the air terminals are still great, and she was so inconspicuous: small, quiet, pretty, poorly dressed. The only thing that distinguished her was the Japanese name on a British passport; but this apparently only brought a friendly question from the officials.

I began to breathe more freely now. With £17,000 safely put away, at least the scheme couldn't totally fail. There was really only one big risk still, and that was the connection between her and me. Hettie might become suspicious and have me followed, or someone in the firm might notice the discrepancies and not tell me but they'd set detectives on me without me knowing.

But Hettie wasn't the type. She probably didn't think I had it in me to take up with another woman, and even if she suspected she wouldn't ever go about it that way. And as for the firm, there was really only the two clerks and I kept them always in their place. As for Cassell, he was a non-starter.

Mind, as the money went on building up, the tension grew. All the time, quietly, like an iron band it tightened. After a couple of short flaming rows which showed the strain between us, Yodi adopted the plan of bringing with her every week a bunch of travel books and brochures. Then, if we met in the flat, after making love we made plans, if not in the flat we sat in her car in some by-way or dropped in at a pub and looked over the brochures together.

When I came out I'd be thirty-eight or thirty-nine; and it was going to be a long wait, three to four years. So it would be a help while I was in to be able to dwell on the exact plans we had as soon as we met again.

The first plan, when we got married, was to go on a honeymoon to the South of France. We'd buy a little car and drive along stopping at whatever beach took our fancy and stay just as long as we liked and then move on again. After that we'd go into Italy, to Pisa, to Florence and then across to Venice. There we would park our little car and stay in Venice exploring all its beauty and having gondola rides until we wanted to move on again. So we would take a boat down the Jugoslav coast of the Adriatic, stopping off wherever we fancied and so slowly reach Greece. Here we would explore Athens and Mycenae and Delphi and presently take the train on to Istanbul. We had read up all about the covered markets and sailing up the Bosphorous and the great beautiful unused Mosques. And so we would stay there until the last of the summer faded. Then we would fly back to Venice and from there drive slowly home.

This was our first itinerary. The very first. The second, undertaken the second year, would be to Hong Kong, Bangkok and Japan ...

This planning helped a lot. It gave us an escape. It justified what we were doing. It made the future real – this life at present was just a preparation.

Hettie was ailing when Christmas came: the chills of November brought on a bronchial catarrh, and she asked me to stay home Saturdays to keep her company. I said I was sorry I couldn't. She said it was crazy: how much money had I lost up to now? I said I hadn't lost, I'd made a profit. She said surely there can't be racing in this weather. I said I was going to point-to-point; they were just as exciting to me.

At Christmas I had to stay at home because she took to her bed for a few days – that is, I missed one Saturday. Sitting by the fire that evening I thought: where shall I be next Christmas? Not as comfortable and warm as this. Cold and lonely and locked up. And the Christmas after and the Christmas after. But the next. The next one we could spend in the Bahamas ...

When I met her on the Saturday following Yodi wanted to break our plan. 'Jack,' she said. 'I can't stand it; I can't stand it any more! This waiting; this feeling as if an axe is going to fall! I can't bear it! Let's go!'

'Go?'

'Yes, go. What have we got now? We had £26,000 before this week. Now this week you bring £1,500. That means £27,500. It is enough. Why wait for this terrible blow to fall? Could we not be lost in South America? There are all mixtures of races there. A Japanese would be nothing unusual, neither would an Englishman. In three or four years anything could happen. It is too *long*! There could be another war by then. We could escape somewhere *now* and be happy!'

The same thoughts had not been absent from my mind. It was well to plan, all right in theory to say you'd wait until you were caught, pay the penalty, go to prison, take the punishment and come out clean. But who likes the prospect of three years in jail? Youth doesn't last for ever. Three of my best years gone for ever. What you could do with them. Three years without touching Yodi's soft body, hearing her voice, even reading a letter from her. Sometimes in the night I couldn't sleep, turning and tossing until even Hettie in the other bed was wakened.

Yet to run now completely destroyed the scheme. All my life I've been a coward, always I've been afraid of being pursued – perhaps it's what happened when I was a kid once and a whole baying pack of older boys came after me racing through the streets. Perhaps it's just the way I was born. If I ran now I'd perhaps get right away, but should I ever have another moment's peace? I'd read the story of the Train Robbers. What sort of a life had they had, hounded, tracked down, changing names, places, never at rest? In the end they'd nearly all given themselves up or been caught. If I stuck to the plan and it worked, I paid my penalty and came out free. I met Yodi as if I'd never known her before. I fell in love with her. Where her money came from was nobody's business.

I took her face in my hands. 'Let's wait,' I said. 'Let's take a chance for another two or three weeks. I'm taking more every week now. If we get up to £35,000 we'll think again.'

'I do not believe I can stand it,' she said, beginning to weep. 'If you leave me, if you go to prison, I shall have all this money! I shall be too terrified!'

'Nobody can touch *you*,' I said. 'So long as no one discovers that we know each other, you'll be absolutely safe.'

'But all those years I shall lose you. All those years and we can't even – even write.'

'I know,' I said. 'Don't weaken me now, dear. I know how you must feel – but understand how *I* feel. Just the same.'

'Let us go,' she said. 'Let us make plans to leave early next month.'

The following week, plunging now, I took three thousand. I knew it couldn't be long now because of the auditors. It was a question of weeks, perhaps even days. Yet they were all so blind. They didn't seem to *want* to find out. I realized I could have taken two thousand a week all the time and nobody would have questioned it. They didn't *deserve* to catch me. I *should* slip away, I could slip away while there was still time.

The next week I took another three thousand. I began to feel fatalistic about it. Nobody could expect this luck to last. I began to make preparations. Dover to Calais, you were over in an hour. Train to Paris. Hire a car there, drive to Geneva. Leave the car, train to Berne. Whom should I meet in a café but Miss Yodi Okuma who happened to have flown over to Zürich on a holiday. There was £10,000 in Zürich. That would last till the hue and cry died down. We were not Train Robbers. They wouldn't go on pursuing me endlessly the way they had them.

So I decided it was my last week. Another three thousand and then I was off. I promised Yodi this. I promised myself this. The Tuesday and the Wednesday went by, and I thought, if I am really going to bolt, why limit myself to £3,000? Why not five? Why not six? So I made plans, and on the Thursday morning when Mr Head called me in for his usual morning chat I had the whole scoop in line. Tomorrow when I left I would carry a bag. This would be the one big scoop.

But when I went into his office Mr Cassell was there too, and with them were two grave-faced men I knew by sight. They were the auditors.

So it all happened as planned. First questioned by them, then tackled, then challenged. I finally broke down and confessed what I had done. It was a nasty time, especially when they brought in two of the firm's directors. But it gave me an opportunity I'd never had before to tell them just what I thought of them, why I'd broken out like this, why I'd defrauded them, why I'd lost thousands of pounds of their money on the races. Because I had been a loyal servant of theirs for eighteen years, had joined them straight from school, had wanted only to work for them and work my way up the firm for the rest of my life. Instead I had been treated as a cog not as a human being, overworked, underpaid and disregarded when any promotion was going. I was expected to work for another twenty-five years and then I'd be retired with a gold watch and a miserly pension and told to enjoy my old age! It was time they woke up, I told them, and realized that the days of slavery were past, and if their treatment of their staff was oppressive and dishonest, they couldn't expect loyalty and honesty in return.

I fairly let myself go. I said the same things again when the police arrived. Maybe I overdid it a bit, because it seemed such a good line. God knows it was the truth, and maybe it sounded like the truth. But possibly I overdid it.

It was all worse than I thought. That's the trouble with imagination: you can't trust it. You go to the dentist and think he's going to torture you and you don't feel a thing. You go to a doctor for a simple pain somewhere and his examination gives you hell. Well, this was hell.

They took me away, and the next day I was up before a magistrate and was remanded in custody. Remanded in custody, mark you. It means I was shoved in prison like an old lag in a cell with two other men who'd been caught shop-breaking. It was grim, just that to begin, and I can tell you my heart was in my boots. Because this was the very beginning and I couldn't see all the time ahead.

I didn't want to see Hettie but she came just the same. 'Oh, Jack, why did you *do* it? Why? Why? Why? Weren't we happy together? Did you want for anything? What was *wrong*?'

'I wanted for *everything*,' I said passionately. 'Everything that makes life worth living!'

She burst into fresh tears. 'I told you. Oh, I told you. That racing! All the betting! I can't *believe* you lost, wasted so much!'

This was a point of interest to the police too. One day Inspector Lawrence came to me and said: 'Look, tell me a bit about this racing. Who did you go with?'

'Nobody. I went on my own.'

'Every week? No pals? You must have had pals.'

'I didn't. I went on my own. I didn't need anyone else.'

'And all this money. How much did you lose?'

'The lot. Every penny. Every week.'

'You never won at all?'

'Oh, yes, sometimes! It was great then! Sometimes I nearly got back what I'd lost.'

'And what did you spend it on?'

'Spend it on? I went next week and put it on the horses again.'

'Look,' said Inspector Lawrence again. 'I know you've lost a lot. But you *must* have some left. Well, I tell you, if you hand this over it will mitigate your sentence. If you are able to return even five or six thousand pounds. Restitution. That's what they call it. It might mean a year off your sentence. You've been very straightforward about everything else. This would help.'

'I'm sorry,' said. 'If I had it they could have it back. Honest. It isn't going to be any use to me where I'm going.'

The Inspector looked at me. 'Too true,' he said.

The trial didn't last very long. After all, I admitted everything so they had nothing to prove. The judge gave me seven years.

I *couldn't* believe it at first. That thin old crow with the haggard face and the dirty grey wig. I'd thought when he was addressing me he sounded pretty harsh, but I thought that was part of the drill.

Something I'd said to the police about getting back at Annerton's for treating me like a cypher, that somehow rubbed him up wrong. I suppose judges have to think about society. I suppose he thought if I don't make an example of this chap, every little downtrodden clerk will think he's entitled to pinch the week's takings.

But seven years. It hit me like a blow in the face and I nearly fainted before they took me down below. I know they fetched a doctor to me so I must have looked pretty sick.

'Never mind,' said one of the warders grimly, trying to comfort me. 'It's only five really – that's if you behave yourself.'

I've said about imagination not matching up. Well, it didn't match up. I say to all those people who think of taking a risk, well don't. And all this talk about improving prisons. All I can say is if the prison I was in was an improved one, then God help it before.

The humiliation, the degradation, maybe you expect that too, but it takes a greater grip on you than you ever thought, making you feel like something that crawls and isn't even fit again to see the light. I regretted then, God, how I regretted not having made a run for it while there was still time! Now I should be sunning myself on the Copacabana Beach in Rio instead of shut in four narrow walls with a bucket seat for a lavatory in the corner and a tiny window with six bars. And with Yodi. With Yodi! Yodi I would see no more for five long years. Yodi with the sloe eyes and the casual, easy smile, the dark glinty hair and the welcoming arms.

Because of course it had to be a part of our scheme that she should never come to see me. Never, whatever the emergency. And I could never write to her. Never. We had arranged it that once every three months she would send me a copy of *Sporting Life*, for the first day of the month she sent it. This would show that she was keeping to our plan and waiting for me and that all was well. I'd specially forbidden her even to enclose a message or try to underline a passage in it. And I'd told her always to post it from London, never from Brighton.

I was absolutely determined that we should be safe.

It drove me mad that the wrong woman could visit me at regular intervals. This was the first snag. Hettie's religion made her react the wrong way, and she said stoutly she was going to stick by me whatever the cost to herself, and meet me when I came out. She gave up our place and went to live with her parents. At first I tried to be gentle with her, acting the remorseful husband and saying that she must divorce me for her own sake: she was pretty, I said, and still young; she could marry again; my life was finished, I said; when I came out I'd be no use – no one would ever offer me a decent job again, I could never support a wife; for her own sake she must leave me and forget me.

She would have none of it. Sometimes I thought she actually enjoyed her nobility; she saw herself in the role; the disgrace, the near-poverty might kill her, but never should she be said to lack loyalty to her unhappy husband. I wrote to her father, telling him what I thought. Her father wrote back telling me what *he* thought, and it didn't make polite reading. But his views didn't sway her.

After six months in London they took me up to the midlands and there I stayed for two years. At the beginning I used to do what I told Yodi I'd do, which was go over in my mind every night one of the six wonderful holidays we'd planned down to the last detail. It worked for a while and I used to go to sleep lulled by a sense of anticipation, with sensuous thoughts of marriage to her and travel in the most beautiful lands in the world. And if it had been only three years to wait the plan might have lasted longer. But by the time nine months had gone by, with an absolute minimum of another fifty months ahead before I could *hope* to begin the first journey, the anodyne was wearing thin. Then often I would lie sleepless for hours on end wondering what I had done to myself. When I got out I would be forty. I wasn't quite thirty-six yet. To middle aged people forty is quite young; to someone still only thirty-five it looks like the beginning of old age.

Perhaps if she had been able to visit me it would have been different. But only the wrong woman visited me.

One day after eighteen months, the accumulated bitterness of everything bubbled over in me and I told Hettie I was not coming back to her when I got out. I told her I was sick of the sight of her anaemic mottled face on the other side of the glass and that I had only stolen the money and gambled with it in the hope of getting away from her. I told her it was her fault all through and I never wanted to see her again and why didn't she leave me alone and I'd rather be dead than ever live with her again.

I told her a lot that I wasn't proud of afterwards, but it did the trick. I had no more visits from her, no more letters. Six months later she began divorce proceedings. I never saw her again.

It's a funny thing but a human being can gradually get used to anything. My life before I met Yodi had been all routine: now it was all routine again. Horrible routine, of course, but by the end of the second year just that bit more bearable. The warders you got to know and they got to know you. They were a grim lot and not much intelligence, but you knew which ones to avoid and how to stay out of trouble. The prisoners were nearly all long-term men like me and some were as nasty as they come, but others were friendly enough and generous when it came to the pinch. I came to be known as a quiet one, best left to myself, no trouble to anyone but no use to anyone.

I read a lot. First it was all travel books, but somehow that began to taste bad and I went on to history and biography. I read and read, everything I could get hold of, and the time passed. I learned to sew mail-bags and did some printing and carpentering. At the end of two and a half years, they moved me down south again – not exactly to an open prison but one where there was more liberty. I was put in the garden. I never knew the first thing about cabbages or how to grow potatoes but I learned now.

Every three months *Sporting Life* arrived regularly. But after I'd been moved it kept getting posted up to Leeds and then being forwarded on. There was no way of me letting her know that I'd moved. I just had to hope that some way she'd find out.

It's funny too how all the anger and the bitterness dies away with time. Or it doesn't so much die away as lose its reality. Like Yodi and the plans for travel, like Hettie and her sad thin face, like Annerton's and the feel of wads of five-pound notes. There's that song that I first heard about now: 'Sunrise, sunset, sunrise, sunset, quietly flow the years . . .' It was sunrise and sunset for me, with just the routine jobs in between, the hours in the garden, the crude meals, the recreation room, the library, the cinema, the shuffling back to the cells.

It was a monastic sort of life – steady work, plain food, mortification or deprivation of the flesh, time to think. Time to pray. Only no one prayed. And your companions didn't look like holy fathers.

I never made any real close friends. I knew all of them, talked sometimes, more often was talked to (usually out of the corners of their mouths). Grey-faced men. Wolf-faced. Weasel-faced.

Pig-faced. All with their tales to tell. All longing to get out, but many of them in for their second or third stretch. Many you could see were confirmed outlaws. As soon as their term inside was ended, they'd go out and be against the law straight away, fighting it until they were copped again.

Not like me – inside paying for my future in the sun.

The third year went and part of the fourth. I didn't have any visitors except prison visitors who did their best for me and talked about life outside. There was one cousin who came about every two months. He was the only relative.

The fourth year went and moved into the fifth. I had my thirty-ninth birthday. Sometimes I felt as if I'd never lived in the outside world at all, as if it was only something I had ever known from hearsay. I'd changed a lot, I thought, when I saw myself in a glass. My hair was going grey at the sides and my cheeks had sunken in. I hadn't really lost any weight but it was distributed differently. The skin of my body was ash-white like the underside of a stone. I suffered a lot from indigestion and constipation. The colour of my face and hands was not bad because of all the work in the garden, but my nails were broken and darkened with working with the soil. My thumbs had spread and the nails had flattened like little spades. I knew all about market gardening. One of my prison visitors suggested that when I came out I would easily get a job in market gardening. There were good opportunities, he said, and you were paid good money because labour was scarce. I thanked him and thought my own thoughts.

In the fifth year the only danger was that something might happen and I wouldn't earn myself full remission. There was a bit of trouble in the prison and I was lucky to be able to steer clear of it.

Sometimes I tried to picture what Yodi was like, and now and then I tried to remember the itineraries we had planned. But the dead silence of fifty months had sapped it all away. Of course I knew that it would all come back as soon as I was free, but I was anxious lest I should have changed so much that Yodi wouldn't any longer love me. And would I even *recognize* her?

And the fifth year neared its end, and one day, planting out some brussels sprouts, I realized that I would not be there to eat them. I looked round the garden with a new eye and decided that when we finally settled down after all our travels I would always have a garden of my own. Growing things, green things, seemed one of the few jobs in life really worth while.

And so at last the end. There is an end to everything. And so at last they let me out.

I came out used to the open air – in a way – but mentally it was as if I'd been five years underground. I blinked like an old dog; I came out into a world where the traffic had doubled and it seemed to me the pace of life had too. And no one cared, no one waited, no one met me. I learned that Hettie hadn't remarried but was still living with her mother and father. Perhaps that was how she always ought to have been; her one mistake had been ever to leave home.

They found me a job at a petrol station, but I moved soon from that and started work with a firm of garden contractors near Newbury. It was up my street, the sort of thing I'd grown used to now, and to like. The men were better, that was the chief difference. After a month I sent a copy of *Sporting Life* to an address in Brighton. On the back page I wrote my new address. Two weeks later a copy of *Sporting Life* came back to me. It didn't have any address on it or any message. It didn't have to. Not even a date. The date we'd arranged was to be two weeks after the date of the newspaper.

I began to be dead scared. Even just living in the world outside the prison, ordinary life, was bad enough: it rushed about me like a whirlwind; people were mad. But now I was approaching the climax of my whole scheme. I was scared that I should look so old, that I wouldn't recognize her, that we wouldn't like each other any more, that she or I would have forgotten the arrangements for meeting, that something had gone wrong outside I would know nothing about. Perhaps she was dead. Perhaps the police would be waiting for me.

I tried to freshen up, to make my hands look better, to get the ingrained dirt out of the nails; I put dye on my hair and then thought it looked worse than ever and tried to wash it out. I bought a fresh suit, a coloured shirt, a gay tie: they all looked wrong on me, as if you were dressing up a corpse.

It was to be a Saturday again.

Always, it seemed, everything happened on a Saturday. I left Newbury early, changed from Paddington to Victoria, took a fast train for Brighton. I didn't like crossing London, I was really *scared* of people, so many people. Even the train seemed fuller than usual for midday. People looked smarter, younger, took no notice of me. No girl sat opposite me in the train reading a book up and down and from back to front.

It was windy at Brighton as usual. My legs felt like jelly as I went down the hill. Maybe, I thought, even the café where we'd arranged to meet would have closed down, be an amusement arcade or a supermarket.

But no, it looked just the same, didn't look as if it had even had a coat of paint all these years. It was near the end of lunch time but the place was still crowded. I blinked on the threshold, afraid to plunge in. Then in a corner I saw a smartly dressed Japanese girl.

I almost didn't recognize her, she was so smart; and she looked much older, more sophisticated, her glinting hair quite short: she looked more Japanese; there was no mistaking her now. Somehow in five years she had grown up and her race you couldn't mistake.

She wasn't looking up – she was eating soup and had a copy of *Sporting Life* propped up against a sauce bottle. This was exactly as arranged. There was one empty four-table and an isolated seat here and there, but I went slowly across, shakily, could hardly stand.

'D'you mind,' I said, and cleared my throat, 'd'you mind if I share your table, miss?'

She glanced up briefly, eyes trying to be casual but strangely scared. 'Not at all.' She looked down again at her newspaper.

Nothing more was said. I sat down, the waitress came, and I ordered. This was as far as our arrangement had gone. We'd agreed that from here on we should go on with our playacting, pretending, in case anyone had followed me, that this was our first meeting, that we just casually got acquainted, liked each other, and arranged to meet again sometime.

But the separation had been too long; too much emotion, too much tension built up in half a meal. In any case I knew I had been too cautious in my planning here. Nobody followed me. Nobody ever would. Nobody cared twopence what happened to me or what I did from now on. I'd committed a crime and had paid for it, and that was it so far as the police were concerned. I was free.

Free but damaged. I was still locked, chained within an experience, could not shake off the fetters. I was not the same man. And I was scared. I was scared of not being satisfactory to her. At first when you are imprisoned sex is a big problem; but the months and the years simply sap away your vitality and your desires ...

Over the coffee we began to talk. Words came aridly, guardedly, bridging great gaps of time, turning back to try to fill in the gaps. Often it was like reaching for stepping-stones that were not there.

After coffee we got up, went to her place. She had long since left the little room we had had, lived now in a smart flat just off Bedford Square. It was an old-fashioned sort of house but the flat was very smart. On my money, I presumed. Did it matter? It was *our money*, jointly owned, to be jointly spent.

Sitting in this flat smoking and drinking another coffee I felt ill-at-ease, uncouth, a stranger. She too was ill-at-ease, restless, kept getting up and rearranging things, stubbing out one cigarette and lighting another. She had changed for the better – at least in looks – as much as I had changed for the worse. She wasn't any longer the lonely, meek, submissive, casual little girl whose parcel I'd picked up. She was so well tamed out, her nails painted, a rich perfume about her. I kept eyeing her. Her skirts were absurdly short, she was like a warm well-bred beautiful cat. The difference in our ages when we first met had hardly seemed to matter. Now it was a gulf.

She said: 'Dar-ling, do you remember those plans we made? To travel. To travel here and there.'

'Yes ... they kept me going – for the first year or so they kept me going.'

'And after that?'

'Oh, I remembered them all through.'

'I'm glad. So have I.'

'Well, it was our aim, wasn't it. One of our aims.'

'The first one was to go to Paris, wasn't it?'

'No, the South of France.'

'That's it. And then to Italy and Venice.'

'Then down the Adriatic by steamer.'

'Calling at Dubrovnik before going to Greece and Turkey.'

'You remember it all.'

'Yes, I remember it all.'

The afternoon passed. I felt I was visiting. Twice the telephone rang, but each time she answered it only briefly and immediately came back. Of course she was loving and attentive; but there wasn't any reality in it yet. We were still separated from each other, not now by prison bars but by the different lives we had led in the last five years. We were foreigners to each other, with only the shared memory of some months of stolen love and stolen money, which had happened in another age, a long life ago. Before that we had been strangers. Could the memory come alive within us and become a part of our present existence? Patience, there would have to be patience and understanding on both sides. It was early days yet: the very first hours of meeting. I told myself that very soon it would all be different, would be as before.

We were both waiting for the evening. She chain-smoked all the time. She constantly asked me questions about my life, about Hettie, about whether the newspaper had reached me regularly. How shocked she had been at the verdict. How long it had all seemed. When I asked her about her life she several times turned the question into a question about mine. At length, being pressed, she said a little sulkily that she had got through it somehow.

'How? What have you done? Have you been working?'

'Oh, yes, most of the time I was working. But three years ago – I have to tell you this, Jack – I had to go to Japan.'

'*Japan?*' I said.

'I had to, dar-ling. An uncle died. My brother – it was in his term-time and he couldn't go. I had to go. It was important.'

'So you have seen it without me.'

'A little.' She nestled close to me. 'Only a little. There is much more still to see.'

'You spent my money to go?'

'I had to. I thought you would not mind.'

'Where is your brother now?'

'At the University. He is teaching. He is very happy in England.'

'But you are not?'

'I am happier than I used to be, dearest Jack.'

In the early evening we made love. It was all right, I thought, after all. She was so easy, so sweet, so welcoming. That part was all right. But her bedroom was furnished like a Japanese room, with bright silks and a low bed and paintings of flowers and birds on hanging silk. I was oppressed by the perfume and the luxury. I would have been so much more at home in the bare little room where we had first been together. That would have had some connection with the past. This had not. The past was quite gone. She gave herself to me wantonly; it was beautiful but it was unreal.

In the late evening she got up and made a dish of fried chicken and rice and we had white wine and sat on stools at a low table in the living-room. She pressed the wine on me and I drank a lot, trying to disengage my past and to enter this new world that she now lived in. I was not used to the wine and it went to my head. Afterwards we made love again, and this time I met her wantonness with a sort of savagery of my own. This homecoming contained all the ingredients that I had so often pictured in my lonely cell, only the ingredients had changed their flavour.

Lying there in the dark, I said: 'How much of my money have you got left?'

'I haven't counted. For a long time I haven't counted, darling.'

'When are we going away?'

'To the South of France, to Italy, to Greece?'

'Yes.'

'It's too early yet. It will be cold there. May or June would be best.'

'When are we going to marry?'

'It is better to wait. You told me it would be unsafe for a year perhaps.'

'I think I was too cautious. Nobody will care.'

She lay silent in the darkness.

'Have you changed, Yodi?' I asked.

'Yes, in a way I have changed, dear Jack. Your money has changed me.'

'You don't love me?'

'It isn't that. Of course I love you. But we have to get used to each other again.'

There was a long silence. 'Tell me,' I said.

'I think you are going to be very angry.'

My heart began to thump. 'Tell me,' I said again.

'I was faithful to our plan, my darling. I was faithful to it, I swear. I stayed just the same for all of one year, oh, for more than one year. But I asked. They told me it would be at least six years before you got out. I waited but it seemed a lifetime. There was a threat of war. Do you know what that could mean? My father and mother suffered in the last war, were imprisoned, half their lives taken. But if there is another war, this time the world will end. All our chance of ever living, loving, seeing, tasting, enjoying. It will all be done.'

'What are you trying to tell me?'

'So I thought, I thought surely he will not *mind* if I see just a tiny few of the things we planned to see together, before it is too late.'

I lay there very quiet in the dark listening to the soft, gentle sweet voice. She was soft and sweet against me.

'So I went to the South of France in the second summer. I – I stopped there, but it was lovely and I was tempted to go farther. I – I wrestled with this temptation and I lost. So I went on.'

34

'Where did you go?'

'I went to Pisa, to Florence, to Venice. I lost my heart and my mind. I took a boat down the Adriatic to Athens. I went to Istanbul. I swear I did not intend any of this when I left; but the beauty of it, the – the travel went to my head. Your money corrupted me, Jack.'

I still lay very still, but now I was listening to the thump of my heart again. 'Go on,' I said.

'It was wonderful, dar-ling. I – I spent money. I bought clothes. Then I came home for the winter here living quietly, thinking of the horrible thing I had done to you.'

The only light in the room was the light coming from outside, through the curtains. It was different from the light in a cell. She wiped her mouth on a handkerchief, and her hand trembled as it moved against mine.

'It was – a terrible winter,' she said.

'Yes, it was a bad winter – even where I was.'

'Don't be angry with me, darling. Please, please. I couldn't bear that. It would make me cry.'

'What happened that winter?' I asked.

'In – in the February I could stand the cold no longer. I thought of all the beauty I had seen. I longed for it again. In the February I could stand it no longer. I – went to Japan.'

'And,' I said, 'and to Bangkok and Hong Kong?'

'Yes . . . then I came back through India. Bombay, Madras, up to Nepal, then Baghdad, Beirut. And home.'

'It would cost you a lot,' I said.

'Yes. It was more expensive than we planned.'

'But for one only. Or did you take your brother?'

'No.'

'Or some other man?'

'No, it was for one only! I swear to you!'

'And then?'

'Forgive me, darling Jack,' she said, beginning to cry. 'Each year it was the same. Every year when I came home I swore it would be the last time. But every year it was the same. I went across

America to Honolulu – two years ago, that was – and then to Tahiti. Then there was Mexico and South America. Chile is so beautiful I longed to stay there.'

'But you came back.'

'I came back. I'd promised you.'

'Because of the risk to your brother?'

She looked at me in sudden fear. 'Because I had promised *you*! Don't be too angry with me, Jack. I'll – I'll make it up to you. In time it will all be as you planned.'

'How much of my money have you got left?'

'I don't know. Really I don't know, darling.'

'Tell me.'

'Oh, don't. Don't, Jack.' I had grasped her wrist. 'I – have other things to tell you yet.'

'How much did you spend? How much is left?'

'Your money corrupted me! It made me think differently, act differently! I have never been the same. I should never have promised: I was too young to understand. You put too big a burden –' Her hand twisted in mine, trying to get free. 'Last year I had £3,000. I thought –'

'Three thousand pounds! Great God!'

'Wait! I have more now, darling. I knew then that somehow I must repay you. Somehow I must do something to help. I thought you might be out this year – I wasn't sure. Then something you had said to me once – when I asked you how I should explain having this money if ever I was asked – that came back to me. I had one last holiday. I had always wanted to see Egypt and South Africa . . . After it I bought this flat, furnished it, set myself up. It was the only way. I have already made money . . .'

My mind was groping in the dark bog that her words had created. Before I could speak she went on: 'I can make money again, Jack. This is very profitable. You cannot live here but we can often meet. You can come here as we arrange. And you can travel on *my* money – as I travelled on yours. When I can get away, if I can get away, we can still go together. Please, please try to understand what you did to me leaving me with all this money. I was only a child . . .'

I released her hand and got up. Doors were opening and shutting in my brain like cell doors clanging in prison. I saw lights where there were no lights, blundered over a chair, began to dress.

She slipped out beside me, put on a kimono, stood near to me, still gently talking, soft labial sounds, distressed, fearful, explaining, excusing, persuading. This must have been a terrible moment for her; yet she had faced it out of fear for her brother. She was very beautiful. I could see what a success she would be in her trade.

I thought of all I had done, of all I had suffered, of all I had planned, of the supreme success of the whole plan – utterly, utterly in vain because of her. I went insane with grief and rage. She had put on the bedside light and saw my face, and then she tried to turn and run.

I caught her at the door. Still pleading, still beautiful, she fought off my hands until they gripped her throat. Then she kicked and scratched while her heart still beat.

After a long while I was lying on the bed alone, and the insanity had passed, and she was on the floor. I got up slowly and went into the bathroom and sluiced my face and hands. Then I went back and looked at her and tried not to retch. My knees were like water, my hands trembling without control. I finished dressing and began to search her flat. The telephone went once but I ignored it. I found two hundred and twenty pounds in a wallet in a drawer. That was all I ever made out of my years in prison.

I put on my coat and went and had a last look at her. It was not until I was about to close the outer door of the flat that I thought of all the fingerprints.

So I went back in and dampened a tea-towel and spent half an hour wiping over all the surfaces I was likely to have touched.

'I caught a train back to London but missed the last train for Newbury so spent the night in a cheap hotel.

. . . On the Monday morning I went back to my market gardening. And now I am waiting. There is *no* connection at all between me and the murdered prostitute – no one knows we ever met or knew of each other's existence. The chances are that the police will find a fingerprint somewhere. If they do they'll soon catch on. If not, I am free.

If I stay free I shall stick to market gardening and the soil. Growing green things out of the good earth is one of the few worthwhile jobs left. It is real to me, one of the few things left that are real. And in doing it one does not need to meet people or have dealings with them or to travel far.

If the police do catch up with me, it will mean, perhaps three years in close confinement, and then no doubt I shall be moved to a prison where I can till and hoe the soil again.

I don't want to go back, but perhaps the end in either case is not very different.

These last few days, since that terrible visit to Brighton, some of the tension has been draining out of me. Five years in prison have quite unfitted me for the stress and strain of everyday life, the push and the pressure of people, the business of competing with other men, not merely for a living but for a foot on the pavement, a seat in a train, a place in a queue. Above all it has unfitted me for travel.

It is a relief now to know that all those grandiose schemes we thought up need never be implemented. It's a relief that I shall never have to travel far again.

The Medici Ear-Ring

Bob Loveridge owned this Medici ear-ring. It had been in his family for a long time, and it was one of the things he'd always bring out to show you if you gave him any encouragement. He was proud of it, liked telling the story.

Bob was a friend of mine, though he was 20 years older, and for a few months I'd courted his daughter. Bob was in shipping and lived in Hampstead and drove a Bentley. Lucille, his daughter, had the usual Mini. Bob's marriage had folded up about 12 years ago, and Lucille was now the only woman in his life.

I am an artist. That means I eke out life in patched jeans and a turtle-neck sweater and earn as much in a year, if I'm lucky, as a junior typist. This made the prospect of suggesting marriage to Lucille rather difficult. I had known the family all my life, and I got on well with Bob; and no doubt he had enough for three, but one doesn't *want* to be kept – nor, if painting really means something, does one want to drift into shipping as a means of keeping a family. Because coy little water-colours of a Saturday just won't do.

It was hard, as I say, because she was a pretty girl and we got on well – really well; she had the colouring I like: autumn-tinted hair and short-sighted sleepy eyes with umber depths to them. So when she took up with Peter Stevenson I was half jealous, half relieved. An artist can afford girls, and there are always girls in Chelsea who will share your bed and your gas stove; but marriage ... Peter's arrival took temptation out of my way, but made what I was losing all the more delectable.

I liked him too – perhaps all the better because he also was poor. But as a Grammar School junior teacher even his prospects, at twenty-three, were better than mine at thirty.

This time I'm talking about, they had been engaged three months, and Bob Loveridge rang me inviting me to his house for the evening.

Just then I'd rented a studio from an equally unsuccessful friend who was trying his luck for a change in Paris, and I was painting hard, having had luck with two things I'd sold to the Grantham Gallery and was feeling generally inspired. I dragged myself away from the easel reluctantly and put on my best suit and went along to the Loveridges expecting a good meal and probably an evening of bridge with him and Lucille and Peter Stevenson. Bob was mad on bridge, and I like it for its orderliness, its formality. But when I got there I was told there was to be an eight. The Mayhews and the Frenches were coming, and we were to play duplicate, which is always a bit more intense.

The Mayhews turned out to be an upper middle-aged, upper middle-income couple from out of town somewhere; she a Jewess, and he a tight-necked, red-faced man with a Battle of Britain scar on his cheek. The Frenches were late and when they came it was only Captain French, his sister having gone down with a migraine.

I disliked French at sight. Perhaps he couldn't be blamed for his defaulting sister mucking up the evening; but he was in a crack regiment, not long out of Sandhurst, and young and suave and far too sure of his own charm. He hardly bothered to apologize for being late or for not letting Bob Loveridge know in time to get an eighth. The fact that he had come himself was apparently in his view a more than adequate recompense.

And straight away he set his sights on Lucille and took a bearing. He talked so much to her at dinner that she might have been the general's daughter. Now Lucille is nobody's fool, and no doubt it had happened to her before; but I suppose his charm really did work for some people, and she was modest enough to be flattered. I could see rocks ahead. Peter Stevenson stood the onslaught on his girl pretty well. He was on his best behaviour, of course, but I had known times when he could be quick off the mark and bull-headed. Humphrey French – and in a way Lucille – were trying him high tonight.

After dinner we drifted into the drawing-room, and the two

tables were set for bridge; and all I could see – for three of us anyhow – was 'dummy' bridge, which is neither fish, flesh nor fowl, and I was beginning to yawn mentally when Captain French suggested couldn't we play poker instead? What business it was of his to suggest this I never knew, but anyway Bob Loveridge said, why not? if everyone was agreeable, we could make the stakes fairly small.

This we did, pulling the two tables together and settling down, French again beside Lucille; and Peter took the opposite side of the table. By now his face was tightening, like somebody's glove that's a size small.

A humorist once called poker a game of chance. Maybe he was a good player. I am not. Nor is Peter. Or he wasn't that night. But that night it became a sort of private war between him and French, and that made him reckless. French, of course, was cool as an ice-pack and knew his stuff – from long years of practice, no doubt. Anyway, he won all along the line. As for the others, the Mayhews lost a little, but in the good-humoured way of people having an inexpensive evening out. Bob Loveridge was just in pocket. Lucille was very lucky and won quite a lot. This made things more difficult for Peter. By eleven I was £18 down. Peter about £40.

At this stage, Peter said with deadly politeness that he was cleaned out, and the game, in spite of Humphrey French's offer to lend him a fiver, broke up. Well, I was livid both with French and with Bob Loveridge, because Bob must have known if he'd the gumption of a louse that neither of us could afford to lose that kind of money. In spite of my little run of prosperity £18 to me was more than £100 to him, and I could see it might mean me being late with the rent for the studio, an idea I wasn't wild about, seeing there was someone in Paris depending on it for his bread ticket.

And £40 to Peter at this stage must have been quite a fortune. A war orphan since he was three, he'd had a fairly tough life; and the thing that astonished me was that he had that sort of spare folding money spoiling the line of his jacket. (It came out later that an elderly aunt had just died and in the way of old ladies had kept a nest-egg in a tin box under the bed. This had been found by the district nurse and turned over to him that day. As he said to me afterwards, if the party had been a day later the money would all have been out of harm's way helping to reduce his overdraft.)

By this time a bit of the general embarrassment must have penetrated Bob Loveridge's thick skin, and there's no doubt he would later have tried some tactful and roundabout way of making it up to the boy – if it had ever got that far. So would Lucille; but for her it was already a little late. By now Peter's general dislike of the situation was centring not so much on Humphrey French as on her.

It wasn't unnatural. Anyone who's been in love knows that love is about as stable as the bubble in a spirit level. Give it the slightest tilt and you're way off centre and inclining at 45 degrees towards the milder forms of homicide.

So the fraternization between Peter and Lucille after the poker game was strictly nil. Humphrey French was still making a fuss of the girl, but she'd seen the red lights, and did some back-pedalling.

Then I heard Mrs Mayhew ask about the Medici Ear-ring. Bob Loveridge had mentioned it to her at supper, and this started a new trend of talk. He went across to his little safe in the wall and brought back the ear-ring for us to see.

Of course I'd seen it three or four times before, and watched the usual reactions, the exclamations of interest and admiration. I estimate Bob must have had more than his full repayment in entertainment, even if he had bought the thing and paid double its value in some casual sale; but in fact he swore it had been in his family a hundred and fifty years.

'My great-great-grandfather bought it in Naples from a broken-down nobleman. My great-grandfather in a letter to his brother refers to a parchment that went with the ear-ring, telling how it came to be made and giving a record of its owners, but, whatever it was, it's been lost. All we have is this letter which presumably tells the same story, the way one would write to one's brother about it. The date of the ear-ring is 1494.'

'Very exact,' said Mayhew, finishing his whisky. 'Would it be spring or autumn?'

'Well the exactness is not so silly as it sounds – that's if the story is really true. In fact it would be the autumn.' Bob really enjoyed being able to say this. 'A pair of ear-rings were made by a Florentine silversmith for one of the Medicis, Pietro the Second. Lorenzo – the great Lorenzo – had been dead only two years and his son Pietro was 23, a brilliant young man but unstable and dissolute. These ear-rings were made to his order for his current favourite, a girl called Giovanna Farenza, and the story is that when they were ready, Pietro insisted he should fit them in her ears himself. But while he was in her room doing this – and who knows what else besides! – news came that the French under Charles VIII were in Italy and advancing on Pisa and Leghorn with 40,000 trained soldiers. Florence was committed by treaty to oppose this invasion, so Pietro up and left Giovanna Farenza on the instant, with one ear-ring in her ear and the other still in his pocket. They never met again. Pietro was outnumbered and turned yellow. He gave in to his enemies and made a shameful bargain with them. When he returned to Florence he was thrown out for his treachery, and the long Medici rule was at an end. Pietro after a few attempts to regain power went south with the French and a few years later was drowned in a river crossing and buried at Monte Cassino ... This ear-ring ... this is the other one – the one that is supposed to have belonged to Giovanna Farenza ...'

It was a pretty trinket, heavy for the modern eye, of chased silver with a pearl inset. It was a pretty story too. Even if the thing had been dreamed up in some silversmith's shop in Naples, it was still picturesque. One felt it *ought* to be true.

'I should think this is worth quite a lot,' said Humphrey French. 'The pearl alone.'

'I've never had it valued,' said Bob. 'To me it's just an heirloom that I wouldn't want to be without.'

Captain French said: 'What do you think, Nora? You ought to have a pretty good idea.'

It was the first hint I'd got that he and Mrs Mayhew had met before. Nora Mayhew coloured and picked up the ear-ring again.

'Why you?' said Bob Loveridge, asking the natural question.

'I've studied antiques,' said Mrs Mayhew. 'I used to have a shop in Marylebone Lane. This ... Oh, I'd think it was worth ...' She felt the pearl between her fingers. 'Dreadfully difficult to know nowadays, but if the pearl's what it seems, I should say that is worth £300. The whole thing – as an antique – I think if you put it up at Sotheby's you'd be very unlucky to get less than £500 – even without the story.'

Loveridge said: 'Well, I should never sell it. It's got a sentimental feeling for me – as if Giovanna Farenza were an ancestor of mine.'

'Perhaps she was,' said Mayhew, chuckling into his tight collar.

'The other one has never been found, I suppose?' said French. 'Isn't it worth making a duplicate? You'd look wonderful in them,' he added to Lucille.

'I've never had my ears pierced. Anyway, I'm not the Italian type. One needs to be dark and tall, with sleek heavy hair.'

Loveridge was called away to the telephone and talk broke out generally. When Bob came back he gave us whiskies all round and under this warming influence things improved.

About midnight the Mayhews said they ought to be going: it was a long ride back, and Mayhew was flying to Paris in the morning. They got up, and others got up, and then Loveridge said:

'Oh, I'll put the ear-ring away,' and picked up the case and carried it to the safe. At the safe he stopped with his back to us, while Humphrey French told us about a marvellous yachting party he had been on last year. After a minute Loveridge turned and said: 'By the way, what did I *do* with the ear-ring?'

We all stared at him.

'What did you think you did with it?' Mayhew asked.

'Put it back in the case.'

'Yes, well ...'

'It isn't here,' said Bob. 'I happened to open it as I was going to lock it away and ...'

We all stared at the case which he held for us to see. It was lined with shiny blue silk and quite empty.

'It's only by chance I opened it,' he repeated. 'I was just going to put the case back in the safe and I clicked it open with my thumb . . .'

'You dropped it in your pocket, probably,' Lucille said.

'No.' He felt in his pockets. 'I never put it in a pocket because it's a bit delicate. Anyway, don't you remember, I was called away to the phone and left it in here.'

Nora Mayhew gave a brief laugh and said, 'My dear, let's turn out *our* pockets, then. Perhaps somebody here has been absent-minded . . .'

At once Bob Loveridge was apologetic. Of course, nothing was farther from his thoughts than that anyone here should have pocketed it. In fact, he thought perhaps someone might be joking. Obviously, nothing could be farther from his thoughts . . .

We searched. We searched the room, we turned out the loose cushions from the chairs, we lifted the rugs, we moved the tables, we searched the study, where the telephone was, we even shook out magazines and newspapers in that rather senseless way one does when all the sensible places have been explored. Nothing. We stood there dusting our knees, not quite sure what the next move was.

Eventually Bob said: 'D'you know I believe it *is* a joke. One of you is doing this to take the micky out of me.' He smiled. 'Honestly . . . it's the only explanation.'

There was an uncomfortable silence.

'Has anyone else been in the study?' I asked. 'The maid who served the coffee . . .'

'No, that was before I took the ear-ring out. And even if I had carried it in there, there's no way into the room except through this one. Violet only came in here to pick up the coffee things. She never went into the study at all.'

'You should come on one of these yachting parlies sometime.' Humphrey French said to Lucille in an undertone. 'Fabulous fun. Just people of our own age, you know. Quite a ball.'

45

Nora Mayhew picked up her bag. 'We've really got to go, Bob. I'm sorry, but it's a full hour's drive. I don't know what you think about this – this loss, I really don't. It's terribly unfortunate to happen like this –'

'I'm stumped. Completely and utterly –'

'But I think I know what I *want* to do,' Mrs Mayhew continued. 'Or what I *ought* to do, anyhow. What we all ought to do.' She laughed in embarrassment and went to the card table and cleared a space. Then she turned her handbag upside down and the contents fell out with a clatter – lipsticks, compact, hair grips, cigarettes, lighter, money, comb, aspirin, nail boards, eye shadow, safety-pins.

'My *dear* girl –'

'It's the only thing, Bob. Really the only thing. Unless you want to call in the police –'

'Of course not . . . At least, not in that way, and not yet –'

'Well, calling them in later won't be much use if one of us is to blame. Really, this is the only sensible thing to do – for our satisfaction, apart from yours. Darling, how *would* we feel if the ear-ring were never found?'

'It's on the *floor* somewhere,' said Loveridge in exasperation. 'It's been dropped, or slipped down . . .'

'Well, you do see we can't stay all night, and this is the only other way. The men can turn out their pockets too. Lucille, come and look through these things for me, will you. George, mere's another table over there. Empty your pockets and let everyone see you do it.'

With Loveridge still muttering and protesting, Nora Mayhew insisted that her husband should turn out everything in his pockets, and when Bob refused to search him, George Mayhew took off his coat, pulled it inside out and offered himself to French.

So after about five very awkward minutes, the two Mayhews had made it pretty plain to everyone in the room that, unless they were a couple of professional pickpockets, *they* were not responsible for any funny goings-on in Hampstead. They then prepared to take their leave, with over-assurances of undying friendship on both sides. In fact it was quite hard to tell which were the more embarrassed, the Loveridges or their out-of-town friends.

When Bob came back into the room again, French was talking earnestly and without apparent constraint to Lucille and to me, and Peter had sat on the settee idly flipping the pages of a magazine.

Bob blew out a breath: 'Phew! That was a difficult moment. God, I'm tired! Shall we call it a day?'

'The difficult moment hasn't entirely passed,' said Peter, staring at his magazine.

'Well,' said French, yawning. 'I have nothing to hide. Let's get it over and done with.'

'I've told you,' Loveridge said, 'this is *unnecessary*. The darned thing wasn't insured, but if it's gone, it's *gone*. I don't want to lose all my friends as a consequence.'

'You won't lose 'em if you let them clear themselves,' French said. 'Nora Mayhew was right. *They'll* be much happier to turn out their pockets and have it all above board.'

'Speak for yourself,' said Peter.

We all looked at him in surprise.

'What d'you mean?'

'I think Bob's right about this,' Peter said. 'He invited us here as his friends. Something has vanished. Disappeared down a hole, maybe. That's bad luck for everybody. But if we have to turn out our *pockets* just to prove that we haven't *stolen* the thing, then for God's sake . . .'

'Exactly –' Bob said.

'Not exactly at all,' French said. 'Nora Mayhew was right. It's plain common sense –'

'For Heaven's sake stop sheltering behind Nora Mayhew,' Peter snapped. 'If it's your opinion, say so!'

French was still as cool as he'd been at poker. 'All right, it's my opinion, then. If I go now, without any check, and the ear-ring's never found, then I could never come here again. Bob may be a trustful sort of chap, but he can't help his thoughts.'

Peter Stevenson looked at me, but, much as I disliked French, I really had to agree with him over this. If you got a clearance now, well, then you were in the clear. Of course, they were both right in a sense. How can you choose between trust and proof?

Peter put down the magazine. 'It so happens that I don't want to turn out my pockets. Right? The reason's unimportant. I just don't. You've known me for about nine months, Bob. You, Lucille, for about twelve. Well, I give you my word that I've never touched your ear-ring tonight. Will that be enough? Satisfactory? Or is it not enough?'

'Of course –'

'Of course,' Bob said slowly. 'I don't want to –'

'Well thanks,' said French. 'But I suppose you realize that it leaves us in a position of thinking anything we choose.'

He turned to the card table, which by now had been cleared of everything else and methodically emptied all his pockets. Having done that, he pulled his jacket inside out the way George Mayhew had done and then went towards Bob Loveridge in his shirt sleeves with his hands in the air.

Bob said: 'No, no,' so French then tamed to me, and to satisfy him I patted his trousers and under his arms. Then, because I certainly didn't want to be saddled with any of the blame, I did the same. God knows, there wasn't much in my pockets but an empty wallet, a handkerchief and a bunch of keys. When it was done and we had our coats on again French looked at Peter. I thought Peter was being an obstinate fool too and said, much to my later regret: 'Come on, it's nothing; get it over. Bob doesn't want it, but we ought to insist on it as a matter of common good manners. Then the whole thing can be dropped. Like the ear-ring. I think the bloody thing's still stuck in the springs of one of the arm-chairs.'

Peter looked at me, and the way he looked gave me the first qualm. Until then I had only been anxious to clear him of any suspicion of bad temper, nothing more.

He abruptly jerked round and looked at Lucille, then he turned to Bob Loveridge.

'*Well*, if you will have it you will have it! The reason I didn't want to empty my pockets is that I have an ear-ring I brought to show you that's just like the one that's disappeared.'

We looked back at him, feeling pretty stupid ourselves, while he put his hand in his pocket and fumbled about and then took out a Swan Vestas matchbox. He put it down on the card table with a bang and opened the box, took out an ear-ring and slapped it on the table beside the box.

'I've only just got hold of it,' he said angrily. 'It's been in my family apparently for a time, but I hadn't seen it before. I wondered if it was a match for the one you have, so I brought it along to show you and compare it. But as it happened I decided not to take it out when you showed us yours.'

Bob Loveridge was looking hard at Peter while he spoke. We all were some distance from the table. Nobody made a move.

Peter said irritably: 'For God's sake look at it! There it is. That's the one I brought. It isn't yours, Bob, but I think it makes a pair.'

Bob Loveridge walked slowly to the table and picked up – well, picked up – *the* ear-ring. He held it for us all to see, turned it round, smoothed a thumb and finger over the pearl. His face was quite white, like someone who'd had bad news. Then he suddenly offered it to his daughter. Lucille's hair shook in a violent negative.

Humphrey French moved across and stared at the ear-ring but didn't touch it. Then he shrugged and looked expressively across at Peter. I did not move.

Peter said again: 'I think it makes a pair. That's if we ever find the other one.'

Loveridge said slowly: 'I suppose you – meant it as a joke.'

'Daddy,' Lucille said, 'if we –'

'A joke?' said Peter. 'No, it was no joke.'

'I'm inclined to agree with you,' said Loveridge. 'I was only trying to find a – a reasonable excuse for you for trying on – such a – such a damned silly *trick*.'

'Silly trick!' Peter said between his teeth. 'That's my ear-ring!'

'Can you prove it?'

'Why the hell should I?'

'I'd like to hear you try.'

'Well, you're going to be disappointed! It's exactly what I said before – either you trust and believe in someone or you don't –'

'I'm sorry, Peter,' Bob said. 'We've got a little beyond that, I'm afraid. I don't like what's happened and I'm not going to pretend to.'

'I'm sorry, too,' said Peter, staring directly back at him.

Bob said: 'Can you find your own way out?'

Peter glanced around – at me, at Captain French, briefly at Lucille.

'*Right*,' he said. '*Right*. I'll go. Good night and be damned to the lot of you!'

And he went. As he moved I spoke his name, having some unformed impulse to try and save the complete break. But whatever I had said at that moment would have been useless. Maybe the only one who could have stopped him was Lucille, and she was as tongue-tied as any of us.

The front door slammed.

The following day I had a visitor. The place I'd rented from my friend was the top floor of a Victorian house in Fulham-pretending-to-be-Chelsea. It wasn't huge even by the standards of today: a poky bedroom with a shared bath, but the studio was big and had a north light, and one cooked one's meals on a gas-ring in the corner.

It was Lucille Loveridge, whom I might have expected but somehow hadn't. I'd never really reached the heart-missing-a-beat stage with her; but welcoming her there, stained shirt and brash in hand, I thought how exactly right she was for me, the shape, the colour, the smell, the grace of good moving and a personality that immediately went click-click with mine. She lit the whole place up.

We talked for a bit generally, and she drew her cheeks in over a nervous cigarette while she looked at some of my recent pictures. I'd recently gone through a Fauvist phase and was just coming out for air at the other side. I tried to explain this to her and she nodded and was dutifully intelligent, but I knew only about a third of it registered either way.

Eventually, when she'd corkscrewed the stub of her cigarette in a British Railways ashtray, she said: 'Well, Bill, *wasn't* that a mess last night!'

I tutted in sympathetic agreement. She said: 'I felt so *sick*. I could have been as sick as a dog. I got to sleep about five, but then only for a couple of hours.'

I said: 'You haven't heard anything from Peter?'

She shook her head. 'Nor will, if I know him. It's the *end* between us. And all because of a filthy little ear-ring that couldn't have mattered less!'

I looked at her cautiously. 'In a way, it *had* to matter. Because it worked out as a question of trust, didn't it?'

'But why should he *take* the ear-ring in the first place? He's not a *thief* – never could be! The money he lost was an awful lot, I know, but it wasn't *that* important. Good Heavens, I would have advanced it him out of my quarterly allowance if he had wanted it!'

'He didn't want it,' I said. 'He wanted trust, didn't he? And he didn't get it.'

'Should he have? With the thing in his pocket? Should we all have said absolutely *nothing* and let him take the ear-ring away? It's just *past* my comprehension! Why he should ever have done it!'

'You don't think there was any truth in his story?'

She blinked at me with her cloudy eyes and lit another cigarette. 'No. How could there be? It was such a *feeble* excuse. Nobody's born as young as that, Bill; not any more.'

I liked her every way. Even in her wooden-headed approach to this problem of Peter, which was so much like her father. I liked the look of her brassiere strap showing through the shoulder of her thin blouse. I liked her ankles and legs. I coveted them. I coveted her. I knew I could teach her so much about life without harming or altering the essential, obstinate but charming female who answered to the name of Lucille Loveridge.

And at that very moment I was very much tempted, because I knew just how she felt and how easy that spirit-level bubble of love could be given a tilt in my direction. 'Look, my sweet,' I'd say, and put my arm round her, 'forget it for a day or so. Have lunch with me and then come back here and we can make plans for the evening. I'm free as air, and the only way to face life when it kicks you in the face is to grin and kick back. Can't I help you to kick back?'

Something like that but a little less obvious. Maybe words wouldn't be necessary at all, once one had made the right gestures . . .

She was looking at me. Well, I was tempted like Hell. But what's always been wrong with me in my life is that I'm not a big-timer.

I said: 'Should I go and see Peter?'

No great smoker at normal times, she drew at this second cigarette as if she had a real grudge against it. 'It wouldn't do any *good*, would it? I mean, what good would it do? What could you say? What could he say?'

'I don't know. That's what we'd have to find out.'

'*You* don't think there's anything in his fantastic story, do you?'

'Seems very doubtful. But if we both agree that he's not the natural thieving type, I think we ought to try and find what the true explanation is.'

'Yes,' she said. 'Yes. If we only had *something* to go on.'

When Peter Stevenson came out of the school gates at Beckenham I fell into step beside him. He looked startled, and then hitched up his collar and walked on.

'I want a word with you,' I said casually.

'Go to Hell!'

It wasn't good advice considering how I'd felt a few hours ago, but I put it down to ignorance.

'Was that story you told last night the truth?'

'What does it matter!'

'I thought it did.'

It was beginning to rain. He turned into the car park.

'You must admit,' I said, 'that it was a pretty odd coincidence.'

We came up to his dingy Morris 1000 and he began to fumble in his pockets. 'Of course it was a coincidence,' he said. 'I'd never seen the damned thing until Tuesday.'

'Which? Yours or theirs?'

'So you do believe me?'

'Yes,' I said. 'You're a bit thick at times, Peter, but you're not a liar. You haven't got the right lobes to your ears.'

He didn't think much of my humour and bent to unlock the door of the car. 'Can I give you a lift somewhere?'

'Yes, the nearest tube station. I only came out to see you.'

He clicked my door and presently I got in. He put the key in the ignition but did not switch on. 'An old aunt of mine died,' he said. 'Last week. I was the only relative. I went down to the funeral and then again on Tuesday to look over some things. There's some good Meissen that will make a show in the sale rooms. No money except what was in a tin box under the bed. That was what I lost. Odd how these old ladies exist on a shoestring, with an old age pension and *no* capital, but with about a thousand pounds' worth of china in daily use. Her jewel box was full of trinkets but nothing valuable except this ear-ring. As soon as I saw it I thought, good Lord, that's exactly like the Loveridge's, and took it to show them and compare it. I knew Bob would be sure to bring his ear-ring out if there were strangers there, and I thought it would set him rocking on his heels if I matched it. As good as a straight flush at poker. The one I didn't quite get.' He brooded, staring at the pockmarks of rain on the windscreen.

'Then when it came to the time,' I said, 'when Bob took out his ear-ring you were feeling too bloody-minded to produce yours.'

He looked at me. 'How did you know?'

'The crystal ball never lets me down.'

'I suppose it was obvious, wasn't it?' He added quickly: 'It wasn't so much losing the money I minded.'

'Of course not. It was the man French making a pass at Lucille.'

'Yes ... Yes.' Peter switched on the engine and started the car. He backed carefully out of the car park and headed north. 'I have to go some way tonight, so I might as well take you farther into town.'

'Thanks.'

'D'you know,' he said after a minute or two, when the traffic had eased off, 'I've always thought you were my nearest rival for Lucille.'

'Good Lord. What gave you that idea?'

'Well, I don't know . . . Isn't it true?'

'I know when I'm out of the running,' I said. 'Lucille fell for you in a big way at the first meeting, and I've never been in the hunt since.'

He laughed shortly. 'But she still thinks I'm a liar and a thief, eh?'

'She doesn't *want* to, my dear man. She's still madly in love with you, but if you go stalking off in a tizzy without making any attempt to justify yourself, what on earth can she think? In fact you seemed almost to welcome the thing as a trial by faith.'

He stopped with a jerk at traffic lights, and the man behind gave a complaining toot. 'D'you think it's *my* fault, then? Good grief, if you're in love with someone you don't believe them cheats and pickpockets at the drop of a hat! What chance is there of making a go of marriage if that's the only way you can begin –'

'Oh, I know, I know. But this is a tough age. I understand exactly how you feel, but that doesn't mean I approve of your sitting back with the sulks and doing nothing to prove your point. Try to think how impossible your story looks from their point of view. Haven't you got some evidence of ownership of this ear-ring? Didn't your aunt have some record of it? When did she buy it and where? Have you been through all her things?'

'No, of course not. It's not a job I like, prying into some dead old lady's private life. I never knew her well, Aunt Maud. She was one of those stiff-backed old girls who never let themselves down. But there's a mountain of stuff . . .'

'I know what it's like. But have a shot. You don't want to lose a valuable trinket and a valuable woman as well.'

As we accelerated away I saw his face had gone clouded and

obstinate again. 'They're doubting the trinket; I'm doubting – well ... I was ordered out of their house like a common sneak thief. Isn't it up to them to do the next bit of thinking?'

I sighed. 'It seems to me nobody thinks in this. Except perhaps me. But I can't bring you together. I can't get you near enough even to bang your heads.'

He let me out at the next tube station.

I saw nothing of any of them for a couple of weeks. I was working hard, and I was putting on the canvas something I wanted to put there. It was exciting and absorbing – one of the fairly rare moments in an artist's life when there is a fusion between ambition and attainment. Rare, but it makes the rest worthwhile.

Then, just after the impulse had worked itself out, I got a card from Bob Loveridge asking me to go up and see him without delay. When I arrived, boy, they were in a fine state. A letter had come by the morning post. In it was a typewritten message, unheaded and unsigned. It read:

'It was not the thief's intention that someone else should be accused of the theft. Enclosed is a pawn-ticket. By taking this to the address given, your ear-ring may, on payment of £25, be redeemed. In future, when people offer to turn out their pockets, ask them also to take off their shoes.'

Over the rest, to coin a phrase, it would be kinder to draw a veil.

I went with Bob Loveridge to this shop in Dulwich, and there the ear-ring certainly was, and Bob coughed up £25, much to the disappointment of the pawnbroker, a Cockney with a fat tight little face that cracked every now and then into a smile that looked as if it was painful. The young man who pawned it, he said, was about seventeen or eighteen and was dressed like a messenger. He would never conceivably recognize him again. The anxiety went out of his smile when we stopped asking questions, but the disappointment remained.

The ear-ring was a bit bent, but otherwise sound enough. The odd thing was that when we got it home and compared it with Peter's ear-ring they were not an exact match, there being slight differences in the turning of the silver. Whether it was in fact the ear-ring that Pietro the Second carried off to war, or whether it was another one made by the same bright Neapolitan silversmith to sell the same story over again, we never knew. The pearl was a good one and the silver was old. Lucille, after getting her ears pierced, wore them both at her wedding.

Not that she came to that easily. Having let myself in for the dreary job of go-between I carried on, but before the end I began to feel like a U.N. conciliation officer in a border dispute.

Of course Bob Loveridge combined the handsome apologies he made to Peter with an absolute burning determination to smoke out the real thief. The fact that he'd been led to make such a bloomer was an extra goad.

From time to time he could be seen staring broodingly at Violet's bent back when she came into the room. But actually Nora Mayhew seemed the least unlikely suspect, since she it was who had made the most fuss and insisted on a superficial search being made. We knew she had been in antiques, and Bob dug out the fact that she had once been heavily fined in Italy for attempting to smuggle an old master out of the country without a permit. Captain French's association with her was cleared up when we found that Mrs Mayhew, who had been a Miss Cohen, was at school in Switzerland with Humphrey French's mother, who had been a Miss Blomberg, and that they frequently still ski-ed together. This sinister revelation did not help us at all. Nor particularly did the discovery that Humphrey French was heavily in debt – it seemed likely enough in a young soldier who could still afford to cling to old-fashioned habits.

Eventually we gave it up, but the problem still rankled. One of Bob's favourite questions was why the person who sent it to the pawnbroker had not asked much more than £25 for it, since, if it was someone in the room, or even Violet the maid, they must all have heard Nora Mayhew's estimate of its value. It didn't appear to occur to him that perhaps the thief urgently wanted some fairly small sum of money for a limited period and might have pawned the jewel intending later to redeem it and return it in any case. I've often wondered how Robert would take such a suggestion.

Anyway my friend in Paris hadn't to wait for the rent of the studio.

Cotty's Cove

It was in the seventies of last century that it began, when she lived with her father in the manor of Sawle. It was a grey, quiet time in Cornwall, for the mining slump had taken hold and miners were leaving the country by every ship. Quietness and an uneasy peace were creeping over the scarred countryside, though here and there a chimney still smoked and an engine discordantly clanged.

Her name was Lavinia Cotty and their house was a large one, a thick-set, square-shouldered, low-lying house built of weathered yellow stone and set in a green sandy fold of the hills quite close to the sea. From it you could see the grey cottages of the village climbing the hill-side a mile away.

Mr Cotty had been a widower for twenty years and Miss Cotty a spinster for thirty-five. Great-grandfather Cotty, a tough old man, had built the house and started the family off in roaring good style in the days when Napoleon was still an ambitious schoolboy, but he would not have been pleased now at the sight of either his house or his grandson. One hadn't the money to maintain the other, and they had reached old age together and would presently tumble down and be decently forgotten.

Miss Cotty was prim and quiet and tall. She had never been good-looking and so had changed very little, there being no special bloom to fade. But she was neat and ladylike and graceful, with a certain restrained charm. She kept the house in some sort of order with one maid; she did a little genteel weeding in the garden, hands carefully gloved; she read poetry – chiefly Mr Tennyson and Mr Wordsworth – and, when her father wasn't there, a little fiction; she knitted for herself and sewed for the house and helped the vicar and visited the poor; she read the local papers to her father, whose eyes were troubling him; and once a month she drove to Truro in the trap, with the maid to carry the larger parcels.

To look at Miss Cotty you would not have guessed at her one indulgence.

From the back door of the house it was a quarter of a mile rather difficult walking across soft, hairy sandhills to the cliff-edge and the sea and a beach of pale golden sand. Down the cliff there was a path and at the foot a cave with an arched roof like a Gothic church.

This was something Miss Cotty had never been able to resist; she came every fine day in the light weather and stayed an hour – or more if she could spare it. It had been an escape ever since her girlhood. Often she didn't open her book but sat quiet in the sun, with the noise of the sea in her ears, and thought of everything and nothing, drowsy in the sun, and warm and happy and relaxed.

And on good days, when the sea was high enough to cut off this cove from all the others, leaving only a crescent of dry sand, she would go back into the cave and take off her clothes and slip into the bathing costume she had made and would turn quickly and plunge into the sea. And the cold rush of it would catch at her throat and she would give little crows of anguished delight. It was the best thing in the day.

Although hardly anyone ever passed even when the tide was out, she never bathed when there was any way round from the larger bays, and she never got over a half-attractive sense of doing wrong and a fear of being seen. For a few minutes each day she was a child again.

And sometimes on very hot days when the tide was very high she would creep, after putting off her things, to the mouth of the cave and stand naked for a moment just within the eye of the sun, her hands pressed to her temples, shivering with happiness like a flower in the warmth and the light.

After the bathe she would sit and comb her long silky hair until it slithered and shone. Then, very soon, it was time to braid it and pin it up and go home.

She did not bring much on these visits, for she had found a high ledge in the cave where she left the things she needed from day to day. No one took much interest in her absences. Susie was a dull girl and courting. Mr Cotty was short-sighted and gouty and thought only of his own ease. He had long since come to look on his daughter's liking for lonely walks as a queer habit he could do nothing to check.

One day something took place that changed Miss Cotty's life. The vicar had been to call and had stayed on and on talking of the over-grown churchyard and the failing-off in the collection, so she had not been able to go for her jaunt at the right time. It was too bad, as the weather had been rough for a week but was now broken and smiling: intense sunshine, brilliant skies and islands of cloud. She hurried down just before seven, knowing she must be back soon for supper. It was June and the days at their longest, but by now the tide would have been ebbing an hour. The sun was full on her cave.

As she reached the last slope of the path she let her weight carry her and reached the sand with a rush of feet. But she stopped there because someone was in her cave.

A man. He was lying there sunning himself, impudent and at ease. She was angry at once. For years she had been undisturbed; people just didn't come here; it was Cotty land right to the cliff edge; everyone knew that. In this state of the tide the man *must* have trespassed.

She coughed. He took no notice and made no move. She walked nearer and stopped again. Something wrong. He was asleep – or unconscious – or . . .

His clothes were wet; round him the soft sand was still dark with it. A young man in blue drill trousers and the rags of a white shirt hanging. His feet were bare. He had a great mane of fair hair all clotted with sand, a straight nose, a young mouth. Hair grew low on each cheek but he had no beard or moustache except for a day or so's stubble. He was breathing.

Miss Cotty took a step back. Then she turned and looked out to sea, but there was nothing there; nothing but the waves like great white cities and the sun shining on the wet sand.

A sailor? Cast off . . . living. She looked back at him, and his twisted attitude touched her pity. She knelt on the sand beside him and gingerly, after a close look, pulled his head up to rest on her lap.

It took strength, for he was a big, solid man. The muscles of his shoulder gleamed white through the torn shirt. His head was heavy and the yellow hair clogged and matted and dank. Like the head of a young lion. Flotsam. Something stirred in her. Poor boy . . . She'd heard of a wreck at Padstow, but surely that was too far. Why was she sitting here? She should run and bring help.

And then the young lion began to stir, and at once she wanted to get up and stand away primly watching. But to drop his head with a thump on the sand would not be the act of a Christian, so she stayed where she was, not sure whether to be alarmed or compassionate.

He opened his eyes. They were large and quite hazel with little flecks of a darker brown floating in them. He stared at Miss Cotty. Miss Cotty blushed. He moved his head again and passed his tongue over each lip.

'I'm going to be sick,' he said.

That made her feel no better, nor the event when his prediction came true; but the language was a reassurance because she had thought him a foreigner, probably a Scandinavian. And afterwards, when he was on the mend, she saw he was older than she had thought. Expression always adds age – and sometimes charm.

He spoke fair English with a burr – but not a Cornish burr – and although still very exhausted his story came out at short intervals. It was not the Padstow shipwreck but the *King Lear*, a fore and aft, for Bristol with grain. She had been badly damaged in the gales of the last few days and had foundered ten miles out. He had been in the water eight hours clinging to a spar, and for a good time before that had touched no food. She brought him two pieces of cake from the ledge and some home-made toffee. It was all there was. He ate the cake slowly and with care, propped up against the rock drying in the sun, while she stood a white shadow at the other side of the cave and watched him. She knew she ought to be getting back.

'I'm grateful for your help,' he said. 'Really I am. Me name's Stephen Dawe. What is yours, ma'am, if I may ask?'

Miss Cotty told him. 'I think,' she said, 'if you're better I'll go and tell the coastguards. They will see you are well looked after.'

'How far is the village? Give me time and perhaps I could walk. A mile? Is it more?'

'A little. It would be unwise to go so far without help.'

To prove her wrong he got to his feet, and at once his legs gave way. With a gasp she ran to him and helped him into a sitting position. For a few moments he lolled dizzily against her shoulder, then he shook his head like a dog and straightened his back and looked at her. She took her arm from round his shoulders and stood up – because his face had an almost frightening closeness. She had never been quite so close to a strange man before. And each time she looked at him he seemed to grow more mature. This was no ship-wrecked cabin-boy.

'Thank you, ma'am,' he said. 'Sorry to be so foolish, like.'

The next time he tried he was all right. Much taller than the tall Miss Cotty, she found. Fine broad shoulders and long flanks. There was a tattoo of a speared fish on his left forearm, and his blue trousers had bell bottoms. He was still looking at her.

'I think,' she said quietly, 'the sea is far enough out for us to get round.'

'Us? You're very kind, ma'am. If you'd show me and aid me a little to begin you could leave me half-way.'

But the help offered, she would not qualify it. Her father would be furious, but this surely was a fair excuse. The sailor might have lain there for hours, might even have died.

They got on slowly, for he had to rest now and then, while the twilight caught them up like a slow tide. They hardly spoke, because he was too exhausted and she too shy. After a while he did without her arm.

Then, as they came to the inlet round which the village clustered he sighed faintly and sat down on the sand and said he was done, so she went on ahead. Pink in the face and feeling conspicuous, she found the landlord of the Tavern Inn, and very soon men were carrying Stephen Dawe into the village. She hovered for a few minutes near the tap-room, but when the doctor said he could find nothing much wrong she slipped away and hurried off up the tow-path towards home.

Her father wasn't easily softened, not even by the story she brought, and grunted and sulked through the hour before it was time to go to bed.

In her own room Miss Cotty stood for a long time at the window listening to the distant tramp of the sea. When after a while she climbed into her curtained bed it was to dream of blond Vikings and caves and wet sand and a man's eyes upon her.

When she went down to the beach next day after lunch he was waiting for her. Her heart began to beat. He'd bought or borrowed new clothing: a blue shirt open at the throat and long blue corduroy trousers. And the two-day stubble was shaved. He bent his head a little over her hand, very polite.

'How,' she said, '– how did you know? ... Did you know I should be here?'

'Well, I didn't quite like to call at your home. And I reckoned I had to say thank you.'

'I – sent down this morning to ask. I heard you were better. But there's nothing to thank me for.'

He smiled at her. 'I like to think different. But it's good luck us meeting like this again. Can you stay a while?'

She sat down at the mouth of the cave, not easily and gracefully as she did when alone, but primly and stiffly, like a spinster. She felt she had been a little familiar in her greeting, and she was angry with herself for still feeling embarrassed.

But he soon got over that. He had a way with him. The exposure and the exhaustion had done him no harm. Miss Cotty got that impression of his vitality. Always it would be able to throw off fatigue or depression. It bubbled. It effervesced. It affected her and fascinated her and threatened to swamp her.

He called her Miss Cotty and was soon talking to her as to a woman of his own age and class. At first she had thought he looked on her as older than himself, but she saw now that it wasn't so. She was curiously flattered.

He told her he was the illegitimate son of a Gloucestershire baronet by one of his servant girls. He told her this without shame, and before she had time to feel horrified he was on with his tale. At sixteen he had run away to sea, and for twelve years had gone all over the world. That makes him twenty-eight, she thought. She began to subtract twenty-eight from thirty-five and then stopped. I don't know why I should bother to work *that* out, she thought.

Perhaps it was because he seemed interested in her. His bright eyes were always on her. She didn't know whether to be flattered or amused or scornful. After all he was a sailor. And he wasn't being familiar in a familiar way. She found herself swayed by the sound of his voice, quick to be angry and quick to sympathize. Her mind was active all the time in resisting his taking ways, yet all the time step by step it was yielding.

They talked for an hour, and then she remembered herself and got up, and he asked if he might come again. Her tongue played a trick and she said yes. It didn't hesitate and it didn't qualify. He kissed her fingers and went off with vigorous rangey strides, leaving her standing quietly there on the sand.

It is the surprise. I didn't expect him. Tomorrow I shall know. Tomorrow will be different. Kept at a distance he can be – amusing . . . one or two days more. He can't be staying longer than that. I forgot to ask him. Perhaps he won't be there even tomorrow.

That was silly, because it weakened her. And he was there. Of course he was there. Distantly she asked him her questions, but he wasn't put out. He was going to stay a while yet. As for money, there had been some in a belt round his waist, and when that was done he'd walk to Plymouth. He was tired of the sea and wanted change.

That day, after her pride had been softened, he asked her about herself, and in short sentences she told him what he wanted to know. He didn't seem to have seen anyone like her before. She was not pretty, no. But she was tall, with that grace – like the frond of a fern – and so cool and composed – or so he thought. And above all she was a lady and as unspotted as a flower growing under glass. She was so unlike his podgy, unimaginative mother and his rip-roaring father. He had met all the women he wanted in the hundred ports of the world; but not Miss Cotty.

He came the next day and the next day and the next. It grew to be an assignation. Two o'clock or three o'clock or four. He began to call her Miss Lavinia. She never called him anything to his face. Her pride had gone down in defeat. She no longer thought of the conventions. In fact she hardly thought at all – at least not reasonably, dispassionately, not in the way she used to think.

An hour was the time they stopped. Sometimes he talked all the time, sometimes hardly at all. He told her of the sea. Of Marseilles, and the great lion rock of Gibraltar, of the islands of Greece and the sapphire blue Caribbean; of Malay and villages built out in the water on stilts; of the opium dens of Singapore; of hurricanes in the Strait of Macassar and typhoons in the China Sea; of rounding Cape Horn in the black of the night, and scudding down the Roaring Forties; of wrecks and comradeship and old sea shanties.

She listened most times leaning back against the rock with closed eyes, at ease now and her stiffness forgotten. And always he watched her. Now and then she would smile and sometimes she would laugh outright, which did not seem like Miss Cotty. Sometimes she would blush – it was queer how easily she blushed; he could make the colour come and go almost as he pleased. And sometimes she would open her eyes and look at him and say: 'I don't believe that!' And because her eyes had a new sparkle in them he was set on convincing her and would kneel up in front of her in a supplicating way. Sometimes her laughter would stop short at this and she would get up and walk down to the sea as if her feelings were too much for her.

One day he kissed her. How it came to that she didn't know. He had been playfully imploring her to believe in some story about a shark and she would not. Perhaps there was something in her eyes that should not have been there, because the next moment he was nearer her and his lips were on hers.

That changed everything. She pushed him away from her and ran breathless up the cliff-path. For three sunny days she did not go near the cove. But on the fourth she went and found him there.

At first he was penitent, bending his yellow head and saying he was sorry. But after she'd half relented she found things subtly different. She wasn't any longer in control, and she crossed the sandhills on her way home knowing that they had agreed to meet tomorrow and that she had listened to things no respectable lady should have stayed to hear.

After that there was no fixed hour. He crossed the beach with the incoming tide and left it with the ebb. Sometimes that meant two hours, sometimes three.

The weather had set fair, with a faint easterly breeze which turned the sand-dunes paler, and the sea was quiet and lapped at their feet. They were like days taken from an eternal summer.

Even Mr Cotty began to take note. These walks of Lavinia's grew longer and longer and could not seem to be put off for more urgent things, like reading to him. And the impulse took her at any awkward hour, sometimes soon after breakfast, sometimes late in the evening. She was absent-minded and jumpy and excitable; her cheeks would flush up at nothing, her eyes were queer and wayward. When she came in she was out of breath. At meals she was out of breath. It was all very trying. But she gave him no useful answers, and he did not see whom else he might ask. He had noticed the sailor once or twice in the village, a great tall fellow with tawny hair and a rolling seaman's walk. But nothing would ever have brought Mr Cotty to suppose that his daughter, his little Lavinia, rising thirty-five or six and devoted only to him could be carrying on with such a common fellow.

That was what it came to. Carrying on. The vulgar phrase brought the colour into her face, so after a time she refused to use it even in her private thoughts. She knew as well as her father that Lavinia Cotty wouldn't do what she was doing; some other woman had taken her place. Reason was there now and then, but it showed

66

like a half-tide rock, disappearing regularly with the flood of the tide.

And he, oddly, was in much the same state. Something withdrawn in her and untouched had turned his imagination into flame.

On the twentieth of July they separated at one in the afternoon and he said: 'Come tonight. At midnight the tide will be up and there'll be a fine moon.'

Without hesitation she said, *no*. But his last words were: 'I'll be here at midnight, waiting.'

She went up the cliff-path, hot and angry and afraid.

At eleven that night she stood at me window of her bedroom. She had fought the battle and won. Bad she had been – but not that. They loved each other; he had told her his own feelings often, and she – she knew what she felt about him.

But marriage was out of the question – even if he had suggested it, and he had not. Deep down there could be nothing between them except this strange passion. He had put in here like a ship into port, for rest and repair. Soon he'd be off again on his roving. Already perhaps he was privately dreaming of standing down the Channel in a stiff westerly breeze. Miss Cotty, sailor's wife. Futility before it began. Futility? Miss Cotty, sailor's mistress. That was what it came to, and here thirty-five years of strict upbringing was too strong for even Stephen Dawe.

She threw down the cloak she had picked up and went to the bed. Days of quiet work, nights of dreamless rest. Days and nights and years stretched behind her and stretching away ahead. Father asking for his spectacles. Susie crying when she is scolded and having to be petted up again. Sowing wall-flower seeds and layering carnations. Playing hymns on the piano. Knitting and sewing and reading. This is my life and I am happy in it, I am *happy* in it! Leave me alone! Go home, Stephen! Here in my own room I am too strong for you!

She left the house at eleven-thirty, slipping quietly from the back door and out at the gate in the tamarisk hedge. She wore her winter cloak, and the moon made silver streaks in her hair. The sandhills were a desert of salt with deep pools and ravines of shadow. Across them and through them she plunged, sometimes waist-deep in darkness, sometimes in full light, her shadow like a dog at her feet. She walked as if in a dream.

At the cliff she hesitated. The surf was a line of phantom cavalry dividing sand and sea. All that was fastidious in her urged her to go back, but her will would not bring itself to check her steps. Instead, her cloak fluttering, she went down.

At the bottom the sand was soft and pale and secret. The lightest of cool airs wafted, and she shivered, but it was not cold. Everything was different. It was not her friendly familiar cave. The rocks were sharp-edged like witches' faces and the shadows were monstrous and misshapen. It was a midsummer night's dream, all of it a dream, in which she walked lonely and afraid.

She went into the cave, knowing that at any moment a shadow would move to join her and turn this dream into a muted twilit reality, to drown her thoughts in a dark ecstasy for the duration of its stay.

But no shadow was there. And none came.

Next day she knew the truth. She had fled back soon after twelve, in humiliation, angry, thankful, sick at heart. She had been sleepwalking and had come awake. It was a hard blow that had roused her, but now she was thankful, hardly able to believe she had gone at all, desperately affronted. By morning she was too ill to get up. Her father was frightened by this odd turn and came to sit by her bed. He'd thought her a bit off colour for some time, he said. Sickening for something for some time. Only last night at supper ... Best thing was to send for old Tregarthen. It never did to let these things run on. Women were queer creatures ... Oh, by the way, had she heard? That fellow she found on the beach had been arrested in the Tavern last night. A rum-runner, or some such thing; captain of a schooner that had fallen foul of a government cutter and got itself sunk. He'd gone off to Bristol to stand his trial. You thought that sort of thing had died out nowadays. Now in his father's time – your grandfather's, my dear – the game had been worth the candle. Everyone was in the trade then – even the parson.

They gave him nine months, and it was all Miss Cotty could learn. After that the papers said nothing, it being neither news nor policy to report on the health and progress of petty criminals.

In the early spring of the following year she felt it grow in her that one day soon when she went down to the cave he would be there, with the sun shining on his yellow head. For a time then she never went without expectancy and hope, knowing that by now he would be free again, sure he would return to keep the appointment; but always the cave gaped at her and there was nothing but the mutter of the impersonal sea. Before, she had never needed company here; now her loneliness was intense and almost unendurable. All that summer and through the next winter she went daily, blaming herself now for not having got into some sort of communication with him while she could. She never expected him to write or to call at the house; if he came it would be as he'd first come and as she'd always met him.

But she never saw him again.

As time passed the continual ache in her breast grew less unbearable. She carried it about with her like the wound of a soldier, with a certain pride. We are the slaves of our temperaments, and hers, quietly tenacious in all things, grew more constant with the years. She forgot her old judgments and thought only of the fine things in his character. In her mind he grew into a legend. If he had turned up this might have been shattered, but he did not come, and the daily walk became a pilgrimage. She didn't stretch luxuriously in the sun or splash shyly in the water; she came to live over in her memory the hours of that summer.

At home, after the first week, she went on as usual, and no one noticed a lack of interest in the daily round. Susie was soon to marry the baker boy, and Mr Cotty was full of his gout. Little Lavinia, he thought, had tired of her long walks and now took short ones. She'd always been a wilful child, and if sometimes she came back soaked by the soft sou'westers he couldn't do anything to keep her in.

Her need to go down to the cove once every day came to be fanatical. Nothing must stop her. Even when her father died she was only away two days and then went dressed in sombre black to sit staring quietly out to sea with a feeling that her presence had been missed and resented.

After her father had gone the house began to go too. Doors creaked and wouldn't open, slates, rattled in the wind and some blew off and let in the drip of rain. Rooms smelt of mildew and dust, and often enough there were dead leaves lying in the hall. The sand crept round the front garden and slowly covered the soil and the rockery and the flowers.

She grew old, but not quite in the usual way. Her hair turned grey and then white, and her tall figure lost its straightness, but her face never took the lines of age. At fifty she looked young and strange.

They thought of her as queer, living alone in a rickety old house, and they left her alone; but she welcomed that. The important thing in her day was her visit to the shrine by the sea. She had dreamed there and loved there, and now she kept silent watch.

Twenty-three years after that summer she was found one morning by an old tin-streamer lying at the edge of the cliff where the path went down. She had known he was coming and had gone out at dawn but had not quite been able to manage the last few yards.

It's still there, the house, what's left of it, a crumbling ruin half buried in sand, eyeless and roofless and gaunt. And the cove is still there, unchanged as she was unchanged.

One day seventy years after, six people walked into the cove and settled to spend the afternoon in the sun. After bathing they sat in the mouth of the cave for lunch. After lunch they sun-bathed and kicked a ball about and sea-bathed again. After tea the girls began to gather up the things while the three men still lay indolently smoking. It had been a perfect day, and only the salesman was talkative.

'I bought an ordnance map this morning. It's interesting. The gap we're in is called Cotty's Cove.' He spread the map and pointed with a pencil. 'You can tell which it is by the way the rock juts out into the sea.'

'Every rock and every stump round here has a name,' said the young married man, peering. 'Pass my towel, would you, Dawe?'

The tall fair man roused himself. He'd been almost asleep, on the border-line of dreaming, yet hearing the talk of others.

'Personally,' he said, 'I don't care what it's called so long as they don't fence it in and say it belongs to someone called Cotty.' Curious name. 'The wind's getting up a bit.' Cotty, strange name. Cotty. His pipe was out.

'And the sea,' said the salesman. 'We shall have to move soon.'

'We're safe enough,' said Dawe. There's some sort of a path, I know.'

Silence fell then until one of the sisters came out of the cave.

'Look what I've found,' she said. 'I hung my bikini on a ledge and this caught in the strap.' She showed a comb.

It was old, sticky with sand, and the silver of the handle was badly corroded with rust.

'Looks pretty ancient,' said the salesman. 'Must have been there a few years.'

'More than a *few* years,' said the girl. 'More than a few years, by the shape of it.'

'Is it worth keeping? Take it back with you as a souvenir.'

'It's not much good. It might clean up, but . . .' She stopped and looked across at Robert Dawe, whose eyes were on it. Curious eyes he seemed to have just then, gold-specked on the pupils, and lambent and foreign and old.

'I should put it back,' he said. 'You never know. Someone may come to claim it.'

The sun had gone behind a cloud, and the cove was suddenly chill and colourless. The girl shivered slightly. Dawe's eyes were fixed with a puzzled frown on the horizon where the sea still shimmered. What had he been thinking of when he dozed off? Odd, broken thoughts not quite his own . . . He felt as if he had

71

just forgotten something and now would never remember. He was sad because something was lost to him for ever.

The girl made a move back towards the cave. 'All right,' she said. 'It's no use to me so I think I will.'

No one nowadays believes in ghosts. Like other superstitions, they have been explained away or gone out of fashion. And anyway the rusty comb on the ledge in the cave remains unclaimed.

But on some nights when the moon is up and the sea quiet – all but that thin line of muttering surf; and the sandhills are white and lumpy and the black rock edge alive with a hundred silhouette faces – then maybe something of Miss Cotty; not perhaps her ghost, but some impress of her vigil, some part of her maiden lonely spirit, broods over the cove like an echo of rapture and a memory of pain.

The Island

I am nine years old, and I live in the park three miles from the centre of the city. I have lived there all my life. My mother is a delicate woman with catarrh, a weak heart and a resolute will. My father is my mother's husband. He is a merchant, a small tubby vigorous man with a fair moustache, a bald head and keen twinkling eyes. They are both over forty when I am born and they have not much in common with my youth.

They have lived all their lives on an island. Although they are living in a city they are on an island. I too am on this island until I am nine.

We live in a tall semi-detached house with a long narrow garden. On the ground floor there is a drawing-room, a kitchen and a dining-room, connected by a long hall. The dining-room has a big square mahogany table covered between meals by a green velvet cloth with tassels. A white tablecloth is put over this for mid-day dinner, for high tea and for supper. There is a bookcase with Chambers' Encyclopaedia, Darwin's *Descent of Man* and Morley's *Life of Gladstone*. There is a cane-bottomed rocking-chair before the fire and almost always a fire. The walls are hung with a heavy crimson flock paper, and there are big paintings of cattle sitting beside lakes with dark mountains in the background.

The drawing-room is for entertaining and for Sundays. It is a lighter room with moquette velvet arm-chairs, casement curtains drawn in at the waist by a cord, and a 'cello and a piano. My mother and my father play together and they also sing. They sing 'The Keys of Heaven' and other duets. My mother sings 'The Indian Love Lyrics' and 'In the Gloaming'. My father sings 'I Hear You Calling Me' and 'Absent' and 'Sun of My Soul'.

It was another man, though, Alfred Highman, who sang 'Sun of

My Soul' at their wedding breakfast. His was a light tenor, and his voice echoed through the house as my mother changed out of her wedding dress and got ready to leave. On the train, as it was pulling out of Exchange Station, my father sat on his silk hat. They went to Llandudno and made gentle love together on the warm September nights.

I have one brother but he went to the war, and another brother, but he died. I am a child of their middle age. I do not belong on their island.

We have one maid, Patty, a Northumbrian girl, who worries my mother because she will not always wear a cap; and sometimes there are rumours that she meets men on her afternoons off. Patty is quite a problem, for she is pretty and knows it. Indeed I have sometimes stolen into her bedroom and found her standing in front of the mirror saying: 'Aren't I beautiful! Aren't I beautiful!' Once, too, I walked into the bathroom when the tumblers of the key had not turned and found her naked to the waist standing with arms raised holding up her hair and with plump high breasts like pale, pale oranges waiting to be plucked.

I am often ill and sit alone in the dark dining-room reading, and one day I pick up the paper and see this advertisement. 'Will the owner of the third largest trout please communicate with Wylde, 60 Dickinson Road, when he will hear something to his advantage.'

Now I know that I own the third largest trout. It swims round and round in the big glass bowl on the pedestal in front of the dining-room window. His scales glisten gold and silver in the evening gaslight and in the morning sun. There are two other fish with him, but he is the biggest I have, and the third biggest in all the world.

How can I take him? He is mine, but my mother would not let me go. She would say it was dangerous crossing the busy streets, though in fact Dickinson Road is the only busy one, with single-deck electric tram cars skidding rapidly over the sets. The Park, where we live, is a private enclave within the city, privately kept up, with soft bumpy roads and lodges at each entrance, and wooden bars like frontier posts to keep out unwanted traffic.

How can I go? But Wednesday is Patty's afternoon off, and my mother rests each day from two until four. I will have a sick headache and be unable to go to school. I do this, and the dark October day connives at secrecy.

I know exactly where 60 Dickinson Road is, for this is my grandfather's house. Or it was my grandfather's house until he died. Then we were going to move there ourselves, and had the bedrooms repapered, mine with bluebirds flying over silver trees; but at the last moment there was some dispute with an uncle and the house was publicly sold. I do not know who owns it now, but I feel I shall be recognized.

I cannot take the whole bowl for it is too heavy to carry, but there is a two-pound stone jamjar and this with water in it can just contain my fish. Once it has plopped in, slippery and a little greasy in my fingers, it moves round almost snout to tail. Such a lovely fish with under-hung bottom jaw and slow palpitating gills and eyes like the blind man down the road. Secret, silent friend, he knows me, he knows *his* friend, and shows it with little twitches of his fins and tails. I put a thin sheet of wrapping paper over the top and tie it with fine string the way I have seen my mother do with home-made marmalade.

School cap and a scarf, tuck the thick fair hair out of my eyes; jar under arm. The only risk is meeting rough lads who might play some trick. But mostly they will be at school, where I should be.

I slip down Scarsdale Road to the end of the Park, water flipping under my arm and darkening the paper cap. Across the rough ground opposite the Park and on to Dickinson Road. It is half a mile then.

The day has lowered, and there is a hint of frost. All sounds are clearer, more distinct, as if heard in an extra dimension. A dog's bark, the cry of a child, the hollow-tooth clop of horses' hooves, a city hooter, the bristling whisper of a broom among leaves, the noisy clanging bell of a distant tram.

No. 60. It looks different. There is a notice outside. Wylde's Photographers. It was Wylde's who advertised. This is a bigger, squarer house than ours; it is more middle-aged, more substantial.

The bay windows spread wide like an alderman's waistcoat. A crabbed oak tree, some thirty feet high and very powerful, stands in the front garden, its branches stretching towards the windows, which are just out of reach. The gate is big and wooden, not iron, the path loose-pebbled, and walking on it makes a noise like chewing nuts. The front door is green. There are no curtains at the front room windows, which I am not tall enough to see into.

(This is the house my mother was married from, in a white satin dress edged with lace and decorated with pale peach ribbons; she keeps it still, after 21 years, among tissue paper in a box in our attic.)

I knock at the front door. The knocker is of brass, and leaves a smell of metal polish on my fingers. A little movement in the jar tells me that my fish has stood the journey without harm. I wait.

At this stage for the first time I begin to feel afraid.

There is a long wait and then footsteps. The door opens cautiously a few inches and a boy of about fourteen peers out. He is dressed in knickerbockers and a tweed jacket with an Eton cottar and a thin black tie. He is heavily built, rather stout, with fine blue eyes and thick lips. I feel I have seen him before.

'What is it?'

'I have come about your advertisement, the one you put in the paper. You know. About the owner of –'

'Oh . . . come in.'

'I go in through a door opened only just wide enough to allow my passage. The hall inside is quite empty; my feet creak on the bare boards. The wallpaper is peeling off the walls. There is a smell of dust and mildew, and also some more unpleasant smell.

'Come in here,' says the boy. He leads the way into the old drawing-room which I remember from visits as a tiny child. This is empty of ordinary furniture, but the sad daylight falling through the wide bow windows shows a camera, some screens, a couple of fancy chairs and a decorative stage as background. Bending over the camera is Mr Wylde. I remember now he has taken my photograph last year. I wore my new grey suit. But Mr Wylde does not move or look round; he is crouched over his camera like a waxwork, and it is as if we do not exist in the same world.

'In here,' says the boy, and he leads me through into the conservatory which backs on to the drawing-room.

I see that there have been big changes here. Instead of the little formal garden beyond with the lily pond there is a huge pool, feet deep, constantly swirling as if being stirred from within by great fish. Although it is open to the sky it is an even darker sky than the one I have left in Dickinson Road, and the air is so cold that it strikes to one's bones. There are people sitting round, feet almost to the edge of the pool; but it is too dark to see their faces. I see only their boots: big men's elastic-sided boots, women's button boots, clogs, elegant shoes, jodhpurs, wellingtons, slippers, mules.

I look at the boy beside me. I say: 'Where have I seen you before?'

He smiled with his teeth. 'I'm your brother.'

'Oh no, you're not!' I said. 'My brother's years older than you.'

'Not *that* brother,' he says. 'I'm the other brother. The one that died in the womb.'

The light is very poor, but I can see that he is still smiling. It is a poor joke, whatever it is meant to be. A nasty joke. I wonder what a womb is and do not like to ask. A man comes up.

'Is this the boy?'

'Yes, Great-grandpa. And he's brought the fish. He claims –'

'Never mind what he claims. Bring him over to the other side.'

I cannot see the man's face. It is as if it is all wrapped up in dark. But he is wearing carpet slippers which scuff as he moves; and he has a gold signet ring on one hand, and carries in the same hand gold pince-nez swinging by a thin cord. There is a smell of snuff as he moves. Sometimes the sense of smell burrows deepest into the unknown, and as I follow him a memory stirs within me, some natal memory, as a beast stirs in a deep sleep.

We follow him to the other side. Here it is different; lighter but with the foggy light of impermanence. I can still see no faces, but only legs and boots. Sometimes one moves as a foot is crossed over. The boots are more bizarre here, of types I have never seen before, some with coloured heels, some laced to the knee. One hears also the faint whisper of voices, like the breeze among palm leaves.

'Cast in your fish,' says this man.

I look down at the jar I have been carrying all this time, and see that the cover, soaked with water, has broken away and my trout is swimming round and round with great agitation, as if struggling to be free from this confined space.

'Why?' I say. 'Why throw it in there? I may never see it again.'

'You'll never see it again,' whispers the boy at my side, 'but you'll have the knowledge. You'll no longer be on an island.'

'What knowledge?'

'You'll be one of us,' says this man. 'Cast in your fish.'

I stare up through the hazy light. I can see nothing of their faces, except the boy's, and I am afraid. It is a fear that moves in my backbone like the beginnings of dysentery. But, having come here, the irrevocable step has already been taken. This my soul apprehends without the courage to ask why.

The water is stirring all the time, and every now and then it breaks up as fishes come to the surface; but what is exposed is so smooth and pale that it might be drowned faces surfacing and plunging.

A hand grips my arm. It is the boy who claims to be my brother. But it is not a boy's hand, it is a claw.

'Cast in. You have always been one of us.'

I pull the last pieces of paper from the top of the jar and then hold the jar over the pool. A silence falls. I had not known before that there was noise, but now I know there is silence. I turn the jar over, the water falls with a great splash, and seconds after, my beautiful fish, as if now struggling to remain with me, slithers out of the jar and falls into the water with a plop.

From everyone, from all the people round me, there comes a great 'Ah!' Then I look again into the pool, hoping to catch a glimpse of the fish, and a white thing surges to the surface just where the trout has fallen in, and the white thing is my own face.

I sway a little, feeling faint, knowing now that there is a change in me, that in some way now I can never go back. A hand takes my arm again, but it is the old man with the pince-nez. His grasp, unlike the boy's, is friendly, joking. 'There's a ba-ba. There's a fine boy. There's a lovely fellow.' He might be humouring a tiny baby instead of a boy of nine. I feel him trying to settle the gold pince-nez on my nose.

I neither repulse him nor aid him, feeling just then too sick to care. As he puts the pince-nez on the bridge of my nose, lights, prisms, flash to my brain, colours, reflections, noise, glimpses of scenes, of faces come and go. It is always difficult to put even simple rimmed spectacles on another person's face. At last I put a hand up and steady them.

And then quite suddenly, the darkness and the haze about the pool disappear and I can see every detail of the scene.

I slip back, half faltering, half running, out of the green door, across the pebble-crunching path, out of the paint-peeled wooden gate, across Dickinson Road in the half dark, a tram croaking and screeching towards me. Somewhere I have left the jar too, and run, scarf flapping, thick hair spreading over eyes, cap in pocket, alongside the tall convent wall of Scarsdale Road.

While I have been inside, the frost has come down like thin icing sugar on branch and brick and flag, and the pools in the dented road are glazing over like the eyes of a man dying.

My watch has stopped, and I do not know the time, but from the bustle of people it seems likely that it is nearly five. If so my mother will be up and I shall be questioned about going out when I have been ill. Not that this will be any problem; she believes what I tell her without doubting that I am telling the truth.

I do not know all that I will soon know, but my mind is adult and withdrawn. It is able to look on the thin, pale, tow-headed, breathless, running boy as if it were apart from him and could judge him impersonally. It is able to see the semidetached house with the gas lights twinkling in front room and kitchen as if with new eyes, as if never seen before.

I slip in.

My mother is down and has had tea and is in the drawing-room practising scales on the piano. My father is not yet home. Scales are one of the things my mother plays supremely well. She has put on weight recently and her curly brown hair is losing its colour and turning grey.

'Why,' she says, stopping playing, 'wherever have you been?'

I make up a simple but plausible story. I have always had a talent for making up simple plausible stories, and as I have said, she has always accepted these without question. Not that she does not know of the existence of lies, but she has taught me they are wrong and she does not believe me capable of such wrong.

Sometimes I believe she does not think the *world* capable of wrong. She is an innocent, as I shall never be again. They live on an island of innocents, my father and mother, products of our age and a class which has protected itself from the physical world, which knows evil only at second hand and as an abstract concept ever to be defeated by good, which believes in the perfectibility of man, which believes right is greater than might, which knows that God is in his heaven even if by no means everything is right with the world. Theirs is not complacency, for they are too modest for that, it is a gentle, ignorant loving-kindness that I can only envy without participation. At nine years old I am escaped from them and at one with my earlier ancestors and my descendants. This island, their island, will be borne away by their death, perhaps never to recur.

And the third largest trout swims everlastingly out to sea.

Gibb

He'd been lucky, right from the start, you had to admit that. No convenient fog, which everybody said was the only chance; not even darkness; he'd just slipped away from the working party in full daylight and made off unnoticed for the trees on the other side of the valley. Then there'd been the lucky bicycle; he'd gone down that rough track like a lunatic, pedalling for dear life and hoping he wouldn't strike a stone. Before the warders had blown he was out on the main road and cycling briskly along, and you might have thought he was a curate out sick visiting if it hadn't been for the awkward question of clothes.

Two motorists had stared at him coming the other way, and he'd jumped off the bicycle at the foot of the long hill and run beside the river until he came to the house. There again it was touch and go, but he went up to a side window and broke it and climbed in. In the third bedroom he found a suit and a cap. He grabbed them and was out again before anyone saw him. He spent the rest of the daylight in the wood on the slope of the other hill. Lying there, there was plenty of time to take in the smells of damp earth and young leaves and lichen and the roots of trees; they were a real tonic after two years inside; but they didn't feed him. When darkness came it was a long and hungry tramp, making so far as he could south-east by the stars. He struck the hilly and deserted road through Holne Chase and walked for a while with the River Dart bubbling alongside. He slid through Ashburton when the first dyes of dawn were blueing the east. As he went by a blackbird piped a noisy alarm – not at him but at a tabby cat weaving in and out of the fading shadows on the other side of the road.

After that it was bird song all the way. A city man, Leslie Gibb hadn't realized before what a row they all made, and he innocently supposed that this went on the year round and was not limited to a month or so. By now hunger gripped like the beginning of cramp, but he would make no move to steal food. The last the police would have heard of him was a broken window and a stolen suit near Dartmeet. If he stole food he would be drawing an arrow on a map.

Full dawn saw him through Bicklington. He thumbed at one or two truck drivers but none of them stopped. There was sure to be a road check, and he kept a look-out at each village. He wished his suit fitted better: he was strung uncomfortably high.

There was the fussy, waspish sound of a motor behind him, and he raised his hand hopefully as he turned. It was a private car and to his surprise it stopped. Driver and car were antiques, the driver sixty-five or more, in a bowler hat and a worn blue suit, with a wing collar made for a bigger man.

'Want a lift for a few miles? I'm only going as far as Sidmouth.'

'Thanks. Thanks very much.'

Gibb ran round the car and got in. It palpitated breathlessly for a few seconds, then the old man shoved in the gear with a sound like a small boy rattling an iron stick over railings. They jerked into motion.

'Lovely morning, isn't it! Lovely morning,' said the old man. 'Makes you feel good to be out and about!'

'You're dead right, it does,' said Gibb, relaxing on the lumpy seat with relief. Oh, to get off his feet!

'Going far?'

'Well, yes ... London, sort of.'

'Well, well, very enterprising to be off so early. I personally like to be up early, y'know. Always have done, ever since I was a lad.'

'Yes,' Gibb agreed. 'I like to get up early too.'

The old man crashed the gears at the foot of a hill, and they ground up it at a fast walking pace. The engine roared and quivered madly as if it was going to take off and leave them behind. A bright, red-faced perky old man with sharp features, and a way of thrusting his thin neck out like a bird. Like an elderly Rhode Island Red, just about ready for the cooking pot.

'I'm going to see my sister at Sidmouth!' shouted the old man. 'Always go every month! You a Londoner?'

'Yes.' They got to the top of the hill and rattled down the other side. Gibb glanced at his driver. One of the inquisitive type.

'Been working down here?'

'Yes,' Gibb said swiftly, sidelong. 'Been on a dock job at Plymouth, I have, see, but yesterday I hear my little girl's been knocked down! Car come on the pavement behind her. Just coming home from school, she was, poor kid. Pushed her into a lamp-post. Broke two ribs, they say. Couldn't sleep when I heard. Terrible, isn't it?'

'Terrible,' said the old man, clucking his tongue. 'I'm *very* sorry for you. Very sorry indeed. Have you heard how she is?'

'Not since. I set off this morning, soon as it was light.'

'Motor-cars,' said the old man. 'The bane of life today. Ought to be prohibited. Will in another generation or two.'

'Yes,' said Gibb, ready to agree to anything. 'I shouldn't wonder if you're right.'

They hummed recklessly through another village. Two policemen were there talking to a motorist. Gibb braced himself but they got past.

'But wouldn't it have been better,' said the old man, 'to have gone by train? It's little more than four hours by rail.'

Gibb licked his lips. There was a lovely spanner in the cubby-hole of the car. 'Well, y'see, I was laid off three weeks ago. Laid off, I was. I've stayed on expecting another job, see, but you know how money goes, especially sending it home as well. I just hadn't got the cash.'

The old man clucked sympathetically and to Gibb's relief began to talk of his own life. He was a retired schoolmaster – 'just a village school, you understand.' Gibb heard all about school meals – which made his stomach turn over – and the education act and the effect of inflation on pensions.

Presently they began to approach Exeter. 'Tell me where you would like to be put down.'

'Well, if it's all the same to you, maybe I'll come part way to Sidmouth.'

'That'll take you well out of your way.'

'Sometimes you stand a better chance of picking up a lift on one of these side roads. I reckon.'

'As you please.' For the first time the old man's rinsed-out blue eyes rested on his companion with a hint of doubt. Silence fell.

They branched off beyond the River Exe. The countryside was in full bloom; apples and cherries waved their blossoms wantonly in the breeze. Past a road junction, in a quiet part of the road, Gibb said: 'This'll do.'

'My dear young man, you're right off your proper direction here. However, if that is what you want, so be it.' He brought the car to a grunting stop.

'Now you can get out.'

The old man looked startled. 'What d'you mean?'

Gibb picked up the heavy spanner. 'I mean I want your car. That's plain enough, isn't it? Out . . .'

The old man licked his lips. A vein corded in his neck. 'What are you going to do?'

'I'll not cosh you if you play the game, but one shout or move and I'll lay you out. Got that?'

They climbed out of the car. No one was about. Gibb opened a gate and led the way into an apple orchard. In the middle of it they might have been in a Japanese flower world. Every time they moved a shower of scented petals floated over them.

'Against that tree. Sit down. I want your braces, to take the places of my strings, see, because I want my string to tie you up.'

The 'string' was rope he'd stolen with the suit. The old man said: 'For twenty-eight years I have been offering lifts to people on the road. This is the first time . . .'

'Well, there has to be a first time for everything, hasn't there. Didn't they say about me on the radio last night? I bet they did. Les Gibb, serving a three-year stretch for robbery with violence. Chanced it, last night –'

'With violence.'

'Yes, with violence. I'd as soon cosh you as not, see. What's that?' Gibb raised his head.

'What?'

'That cuckoo noise. That's not a real cuckoo, is it?'

'Yes, of course.'

'First time I ever heard one. They don't live where I live.'

'Be careful,' said the old man nervously. 'My circulation is poor. If you tie my wrists too tight ...'

'O.K. I won't kill you, at least not if you behave.' Gibb stood up and stared at his victim. 'You'll do, I think. You know you remind me of my old schoolmaster. He didn't like me much. Used to call me "Gibb by name and glib by nature".'

'I can understand that,' said the other bitterly. 'You certainly took me in with your lies.'

'Well, maybe it's easier if you're brought up right, like you was. I wasn't, see. My old man used to beat the daylights out of me. It makes you a bit glib, that does ... Just try it some time; you got to think of an excuse quick or get a bash on the earhole. It *makes* you glib ... Afraid I'll have to gag you.'

Protesting like a drowning swimmer, the old man had his scarf tied over his mouth. It wouldn't last long, but it would muffle him for a while. Gibb thumbed through the schoolmaster's wallet. He took the driving licence and four pound notes.

'Sorry about this,' he said. 'So long. Someone'll find you sooner or later, and it's a nice sunny day for a picnic.'

He went back to the car, got in and drove off. He kept to the main A.35, cut out Sidmouth but didn't avoid Lyme Regis, and the old car nearly died climbing the great hill out of the town. He held up a long stream of traffic, and felt himself like a carnival queen at the head of a procession. At the top he drew into a gate to let them all past, and mopped his brow. Not a thing worked on the car except the engine; he couldn't see what speed he was doing, what petrol he had got, whether he had oil or water. He was light-headed for lack of food, but somehow he'd overcome the first pangs and he decided to press on while the going was good. Neatly noon now, and the sun beat down. He tried to lower one of the windows, but after struggling for a time the door came open and nearly caught on a passing post. After that he was content to sweat and swelter.

At last it was Dorchester 3 miles. All depended how long before the old schoolmaster was found. Risk it. Down the long straight main street, which was crowded with traffic. A policeman held him up, and when he was waved on he stalled his engine. Watched with mild contempt but without suspicion, he pulled the starter a half dozen times before the engine fired. Then with sweat crawling all over him like a nest of worms, he jerked ahead.

Out of the town, take the left fork for Salisbury. A toss-up but you followed your hunch. In Salisbury he'd have to stop, buy something to eat and drink. Couldn't go on no longer. His throat was parched, his tongue swollen. But he never reached Salisbury. He turned a corner and saw, at first not realizing. It was the sort of queue you get at a frontier post, except that it only seemed for cars going his way. Then he saw police.

He was within twenty yards of the last car in the line. Between himself and the last car was an overgrown lane: he turned almost on two wheels into it, jolted and lurched over deep ruts and then nearly into a ditch. Down it, rattling and wobbling; there was a stream at the bottom and a ford. Through with a sound like tearing linen; water whooshed at either side of him, and he took the hill like a racer. But the old car, forced too hard, had had a coronary. Half-way up it coughed and missed and began to die. He was just able to steer it under the shade of a tree before it breathed its last.

Out double quick. Not sure if the police had seen him but there was no time to stop and find out. He jumped a gate, ran round the edge of a field of green oats, looked hastily back, and, seeing no one but a farm worker who gazed at him with vacuous interest from the seat of a tractor, began to walk away more slowly, keeping the sun on his back.

He walked for an hour. It was a dream walk, half a nightmare. He was in a land of stately trees planted here and there on wide green fields with all the gifted irrelevance of the 18th century. Birds darted across his path, cows stopped their chewing to watch him pass, a foal kicked its heels and galloped away. All his life a city dweller, he had never seen anything like it before. In his weak condition it all seemed too perfect to be real, an Elysian field in which he walked standing still while invisible scene-shifters moved the monuments of green beauty unsteadily past him.

A cottage by the road. His knees were giving way under him. He went up and knocked on the door. A middle-aged woman with grey eyes opened it.

'Could you – let me have – a glass of water?'

She looked at him suspiciously, hesitated, and then he folded up on the doorstep.

He didn't remember getting inside the house but he supposed afterwards she must have helped him. She had given him water and then a weak whisky; he could feel it seeping into his veins like raw new blood.

She sat quietly with folded hands on the other side of the kitchen while he told her he'd been walking all morning and had lost his way and hadn't realized it was so hot, etc., etc. The kitchen was as clean and neat as she was, not a hair out of place; he was in luck because there didn't seem to be a man. And she wasn't wearing a wedding ring. You could always manage a woman on her own. He got up, making a pretence of going, but quickly sat down again, putting on what he thought was a rather good act of feeling faint and saying that as a matter of fact he hadn't bothered with breakfast and had she by any chance a bite to eat in the house to help him on his way? He'd gladly pay for it, he really would.

Gibb had a way with him; people somehow always fell for his easy talk, and the woman said: 'I have some cold meat – a few cold potatoes. You're welcome to them if you want them.'

'Thanks. Thanks very much. I wouldn't ask but I'm not long out of hospital. You get proper out of condition, lying up like that, no exercise.'

'I'm sorry,' she said, bringing him a plate of beef that made him hardly able to think straight for the sight of it. 'You are convalescent?'

'Well, in a manner of speaking, yes. I'm up and down, you know. It's from the war, y'see. Long time ago, but it keeps on giving me a bit of trouble.'

She looked at him quickly, with her steady grey eyes. 'It *is* a long time ago. I shouldn't have thought you were old enough.'

'I'm forty-four. I was *just* old enough. Worse luck.' He laughed. 'Time goes, don't it.'

'Yes,' she agreed soberly. 'Time goes.'

He ate the food, trying not to wolf it. Every moment he felt better, but he didn't hide from himself the job it would be getting to London if the cop had reported the stolen car in Dorchester. Once or twice she went out of the kitchen but was soon back and kept passing into a small scullery where he heard her moving pans about.

He said: 'This somebody's park round here?'

'No. Why?'

'I thought it looked like a park, all those trees, like.'

She smiled for the first time. 'No. It's just – farm land. You're English, aren't you?' She was quite easy on the eye when her face lit up.

'Oh, yes. But I've not seen much country, not like this. Been round London docks most of my life.'

'I see.' She had unobtrusively cut him more bread.

'D'you have a farm?' he asked.

'No. Oh no. I – Live in this cottage.'

'All by yourself?'

'Yes.' He saw that after she spoke she regretted it. So she wasn't too comfortable about aim, eh? She added: 'My fiancé was killed in the war.'

'You don't say.' He wiped his mouth. 'That was bad. Real bad. So we got a sort of bond, haven't we?' '

'What do you mean?'

'Well, look what the war done for me. Where was he killed – where was your fiancé killed?'

'Arnhem.'

He said easily: 'Why, that's where *my* number came up! What a chance! Isn't that something. It's a small world!'

'Yes, it's a small world.' She picked up his plate and carried it out. He eyed her retreating figure.

When she came back she said abruptly: 'Have you been in hospital in this district?'

'Well, no, not in this district, as you might say. I'm just staying near by. How far are we from Salisbury?'

'Eighteen miles.'

'Phew! Where's your nearest town?'

'We are four miles from Shaftesbury.'

'I reckon I'll make for there and get a bus back to Dorchester. I reckon that's better than going home the way I came.'

'Were you in a parachute regiment?' she asked.

'What?' He lifted his head and stared. 'Why, yes. Funny you should guess that. Funny, I'd say. Did your – was your fiancé in airborne?'

'Yes. They all were, weren't they?'

'Yes, of course they was, I suppose. Funny, I don't remember much. I got mine pretty soon, you know. Knocked right out.'

By the window, with her back to the sunlight, she still watched him. 'Would you like to borrow a bicycle?'

He stared into the sun. 'What, me borrow a bike? You got one? How could I let you have it back?'

'Leave it at the Old Bell. They can bring it back when they come visiting the next farm.'

'That's – well, it's generous ... And me a stranger! You might never see your bike again,'

'It isn't mine. It belonged to my fiancé ... No doubt he would be glad if I lent it to someone – wounded in the same battle.'

He was uncomfortable. Sharp enough in his own way, he sensed irony in her voice. But he couldn't lose by saying yes. 'Thanks. Thanks very much. A friend in need is a friend indeed, that's what they say, isn't it?'

'Yes, that's what they say.'

He offered to pay for the food. He offered to give her something for the loan of the old bicycle she wheeled out of a shed. But she refused both. Her arm half raised to shade her eyes from the sun, she quietly accepted his thanks and his handshake and watched him get on the bike and after a preliminary wobble go off down the lane.

She watched him until he was out of sight over the brow of the hill. She'd heard all about him on the one o'clock news, but she was quite alone and did not feel like being brutally tied up and left in an orchard the way some old Devonshire schoolmaster had been.

Even now she did not rush to telephone, even though she hated him bitterly for trying to ingratiate himself by lying about his part in the war. She could not bear fox hunting – however many chickens the fox might have stolen, however sly and slippery he might be.

Gibb was feeling a different man, and if only his shoes didn't hurt ... That was why he kept the bicycle. He kept the bicycle and bought a map of the district in Shaftesbury and took a road north towards Warminster and then turned right for Wylye. But after a few miles he saw another road block ahead, and he dumped the bike in a hedge and began to cut across the fields. It took him two hours to do four miles and he had gone off course again. A bus came marked Devizes and stopped to let off an old market woman. On impulse he took her place. He was making no progress, but it might shake him free of the police cordon. The bus was full and he was glad of the crowd around him. He understood people so much better than he understood nature.

At Devizes he saw another bus marked Newbury and climbed on that. If he could make this part of the journey he reckoned he had a chance. Once the bus had started he began to feel sleepy. Two or three times he dozed and sat up with a start, dunking that prison officers were standing all round him.

By the time they were through Marlborough the sun was on the slant and from here you could see across miles of open countryside with hundreds of great trees standing alone like monoliths. Not for the first time today, things stirred in the underworld of Gibb's consciousness. Maybe after a time it would be dull; but you wouldn't *feel* the same, living in a place like this, you *couldn't feel* the same.

Imagine being born here instead of among the tall trees of the London warehouses.

There were police at the bus stop at Newbury, but he had got out the stop before. He came quietly through the town, slouched past the bus station. There was a bus temptingly marked Reading but it wasn't worth the risk.

Seventeen miles from Newbury to Reading, and after two he began to lift his thumb, still determined to make London tonight. He was hungry again. A lorry picked him up but it was only going four miles and soon he was out on the road again. His feet were killing him. The sun was low, and the high hedges threw half the road in shadow. Fifty miles more. So near and yet so –

A long black saloon drew up with a slither of tyres. 'Want a lift?'

A big youngish middle-aged man with a clipped moustache as narrow as an eyebrow, a cap dead straight over his eyes, and a mate-in-three-moves suit. 'Going far?'

'Well, London. That's where I'm hoping to get.'

'Can do you as far as Twickenham, if that's any good.' Cuban cheroot smoke drifted across.

'Thanks. Thanks a lot.'

They accelerated away with a well-bred whine. The needle dickered up to sixty-five, to seventy. Cor, what luck. 'Smashing car,' Gibb ventured.

'Yes, sure. New last week. Just running her in. She'll do well over the ton. Pretty good animal all round.'

'Aren't you supposed to run a new car in slow, like?'

'She's all right. And the firm buys me a new one every year.'

They swirled round a corner at seventy. At a 30 sign, the man slowed to 50. It wouldn't be much joy if they were stopped for speeding.

Gibb breathed again as they slid through Reading. He thought he was pretty well safe now. The man cut south to avoid Slough and went on talking about the blondes in his life. Abruptly he said: 'And what are you doing on the road? You don't look like an ordinary biker?'

Gibb thought quickly. You chose your piece for your listener. 'I – er – no. I been working in Bristol. Bristol docks, you know.'

'Ah. Going home for a few days?'

'Yes. Bit of family trouble.'

'Ah. Family trouble. What I don't know about family trouble you could write on a visiting card.'

Darkness was falling as they drove through Egham.

'Wife or girl-friend?' said the man.

'Eh? Oh – er – wife.'

'What's wrong?'

'Gone off with another man, she has.'

Gibb thought that would appeal to his companion. It did.

'Too bad. Wish mine would.'

'You wish yours would what?' said Gibb.

'Go off with another man. Instead of sitting at home waiting for me.'

'It all depends how you look at it, don't it,' said Gibb cautiously.

The man offered him a cigarette, which he took. It would keep the hunger away. 'What are you going to do?'

Gibb's cigarette was lit from a blowing thing pulled out of the dashboard. He tried to sound thoughtful. 'Me? I don't know. Depends if I can find her, see.'

'Know the man?'

'Ye-es. Old flame of hers. Name of Chertsey.'

'That's odd,' said the driver. 'We just passed a signpost saying *Chertsey 3 miles*. Think he's there?'

'Ha, ha,' said Gibb, sweating. 'That's funny, that is. No, I reckon he wouldn't be there.'

'You're not pulling my leg?'

'No. No, of course I'm not.'

'Maybe you're well out of it,' said the other, dragging his cap a half inch more over his eyes. 'Women always try to tie you down. Even blondes – you only have to know 'em a fortnight and they start getting their hooks in.' He made a racing change and overtook a Bentley which was proceeding at a comfortable sixty.

After that silence fell, and to Gibb's relief his friend did not speak again until they were in Twickenham.

It was easy from there. You said goodbye to the type and watched his numerous tail-lights disappear; you walked along the main street looking at the shops and the people, thankful you were back in your own surroundings and that darkness had brought you safety. You had a snack meal at a café and then you got on a red double-decker – two years since you had seen a red double-decker; and you dozed all the way into central London. Then you changed to another bus and dozed again while you bobbed and swayed out to Shadwell.

The windows of the bus were open, and it was a different smell out here. A smell of weed and water and tar somehow crept through all the ordinary city smells of an early summer night. It might be no beauty spot, not like all he had seen today, but it was home.

After he got off the bus he walked right past the warehouse they had broken into. Everything had gone wrong from the start, that night. Then Alf had panicked and slugged the night-watchman. You could never tell how a man would be in an emergency, not until the emergency came. Alf had been the biggest mistake of his life.

Across the Highway and up towards Cable Street. Now it meant going slow again. They'd be on the watch for him round his old haunts. They'd keep a sharp watch round the Basin, expecting he might try to stow away on one of the ships. He stopped at a stall and bought one or two things, then went up the narrow street beyond like a cat slinking towards its own back yard.

Half-way along the street he turned down an entry, picking his way among the broken milk bottles and the cans. A dustbin gave him a convenient lift over a wall. About him the shabby houses were lighted, but a little mist had drifted off the river and was smearing the sharp outlines; a baby was crying; somewhere a man and a woman were having a flaming row.

On the roof of a wash-house he slid off his shoes, moved along the ridge; then he began to climb a drainpipe with his feet pressing into the angle of the wall.

The window was lighted. He tapped but there was no answer. He got his hand under the sash and shoved it up. It made a screech, and by the time he was in the kitchen an old woman had opened the door opposite and made a dried-up noise exactly like the opening window.

'Les!'

' 'Lo, Beat, you not expecting me?'

She took a hand away from her mouth to shut the door behind her. It cut out the music from a radio. 'Well . . .'

'Mean to say you hadn't heard?'

' 'Course I 'ad, but . . . I didn't know if you'd *try* . . . I didn't think you'd dare try. I thought they'd be sure to catch you before you got 'ere.'

'I'd like to see 'em. Where is she – here or . . .?'

'Sal? She's 'ere. They sent 'er 'ome this morning.'

'What's she like? Is she bad?'

'They say she'll be O.K. It was a lucky escape. I near died . . . Now *careful*, don't give 'er a shock. Let me go first.'

In the next room a girl of ten was in bed listening to the radio. She had a bandage round her head. 'Dad!' she screamed.

'Now take it easy. Take it easy. What you been up to, you little monkey, then – getting into this sort of mess. Cor, how you've grown!'

She tried to put her arms round his neck, but grimaced and lay back on the pillows and let him kiss her.

'I'm bristly,' he said. 'Haven't had time to clean up. Been travelling, y'know.'

'I said Dad'd come, didn't I? I did, didn't I! I said you'd come, Dad . . . I said he'd come. How did you? . . . Have they –'

'Never mind about that, then. What about you? Tell me about it.'

'It was a van,' said Beat from the doorway. 'Come round a corner and skidded. Crazy fool driving. Crushed 'er against a lamp-post. They thought she was badly 'urt.'

'She *looks* hurt,' said Les, peering sourly at his daughter's thin face.

'She's got two ribs broke. But nothing else, they says. I says they should have kept 'er in 'ospital another day, but they says she's O.K. to come 'ome.'

'I'm glad they did,' said Gibb, 'else maybe I wouldn't have seen her.'

'But you're going to stay now, aren't you, Dad?' Sally said. 'I heard about you on the radio! They gave it every news! Can't you stay now you've come? It's been so long . . .'

'I got you a present,' said Gibb, taking out the thing he had bought at the stall. Then he looked at the length of the figure in the bed. 'But I reckon I made a mistake. I . . .'

He handed her the doll he had bought, and while she exclaimed over it he looked across at Beat, who was still in the doorway. 'You don't notice time passing where I been. Honest to God, you don't. Least, not in the same way. You don't realize Sal's getting too old for dolls. It'll be fancy hair-do's and high heels before you know where you are.'

'Lay off it. Sal's never too old for dolls, are you, Sal?'

'It's fabulous,' said Sally. 'It's fabulous.'

'Think you can risk it 'ere tonight?' asked Beat. 'They won't think you'll be 'ere yet.'

'I don't know. I'd like to, but . . .'

There was a photo on a table by the bed. It was the old newspaper cutting framed: 'Max and Maureen, Melody with a Smile'. His wife. She hadn't changed much. And Max with that smile. He'd knock it right off his bloody face if he got the chance. Gibb slapped the photo over on its glass and stood up.

'I want a word with you, Beat.'

He followed her into the kitchen and shut the door and stood with his back to it, looking at the old woman.

Beat said: 'She's coming back, Les. I had a wire this morning. She should be 'ere tomorrow.'

'So she went off with him after all.'

'What d'you mean, went off with 'im? Who told you that?'

'I got a letter.'

'Who from?'

'It wasn't signed.'

'Ah . . .' The old woman wiped the back of her hand across her mouth. 'Don't it make you *sick* – always somebody ready to make trouble.'

'It isn't them that's made trouble,' he said between his teeth.

'It's Maureen, the bitch. I knew all these years she was dying to go back to her act – and him. Well, now she's gone – left Sally, left me. I suppose she couldn't do without a man.'

'Les, you ought to be ashamed of yourself! She 'asn't *left* you. She only left Sal temporary. You know how Max was always plaguing 'er to go back. Well they got this offer of a three-week tour in Scotland. Good money. She thought she'd do it – earn a bit extra. She took 'er 'oliday and the Dock Board give 'er a week extra. That's all.'

'*All*! And three weeks with Max!'

'Man, don't you know 'e's *married*! His *wife's* with them.'

Gibb slowly rubbed his hand up and down the bristles on his chin. He glared at Beat and then rubbed the other side of his chin.

'You can't 'ave fairer than that,' said Beat.

Gibb looked round the room. Two more pictures of ships from calendars on the wall. The clock had stopped and the minute hand was broken. The tin where he used to keep his cigarettes was still on the shelf. It all smelt the same.

'Why the hell didn't she *write* me?'

'Les, you know what she's *like*. She says, I *must* write to Les, and then she don't. She gets out paper – often I've seen 'er – and she writes three lines and then she sits biting the end of 'er pen. There she sits, and she says, I can't think what to *say*. You ought to know what she's like by now.'

Gibb rubbed his nose for a change. 'Maybe yes and maybe no. But it sounds different in that place and she *ought* to've written.'

'Yes, of course, she ought, but –'

There was a knock on the door. Gibb's attitude, which had been slowly easing, tensed up again. He jerked his thumb at the old woman and slid quickly into the other bedroom, which was in darkness. Beat went to the door.

A plainclothes man with two policemen behind him. 'Good evening, Miss Royal, we've come for Leslie Gibb. I have a warrant here, and all ways out of the house are guarded.'

'Why, I don't know what you're talking about! The idea. Forcing your way in! *Reelly* . . .' Protesting, Beat was pushed aside. In a few seconds the men were in both rooms. Gibb stood by the open window of one, looking down at the policeman in the area below.

'Well, Gibb . . .'

'Looks like a fair cop, don't it.'

' 'Fraid so. I hope you're going to come quietly.'

'You don't want a rough house?'

'You know it'll do you no good.'

'I'll come quiet on one condition.'

'What's that?'

'Give me half an hour with the nipper. It's a long way to come – just for nothing at all.'

The plainclothes man hesitated. 'You're a slippery customer.'

'Not all that slippery.'

'I'll have to sit beside you.'

'O.K. It's a deal.'

Watched carefully, Gibb went past them and was followed closely into the next room. Just inside he stopped.

'Well, stone the crows, look at that!'

Sally was asleep. The radio still going, she lay with her bandaged head half off the pillow and with her new doll clutched in one hand.

'Looks as if you won't need your half hour,' said the plainclothes man.

'Now give me a break! Think I don't get pleasure just looking at her like that? What d'you think!'

'O.K. If you feel that way.'

The other two policemen went back into the kitchen and the plainclothes man sat on a chair near the window while Gibb stood by the bed for a bit. Then he pressed up the pillow cautiously so that she was lying straight. He held her plait in his fingers for a minute or so. 'Hair like her mother's,' he said. 'Not a bit like mine.'

The plainclothes man offered him a cigarette; Gibb nodded his thanks and accepted a light. 'You got kids?'

'Yes, two.'

Gibb sat on the chair and looked at his daughter.

'Hope she don't want it cut off.'

'What?'

'Her hair. Kids these days . . .'

The plainclothes man tapped his cigarette.

'She's not like me at all really,' said Gibb. 'I've got coarse hair. Always had – even as a kid.'

'Yes?'

'Yes. I expect she'll be like her mother when she grows up.'

Time passed.

The music on the radio faded and the midnight summary began. At that moment there were voices outside in the kitchen and hurried footsteps and the door was flung open by a dark woman of about thirty-five. Her glance took everything

Gibb got up.

'Well, Maureen.'

'Les! . . . I didn't expect *you*! . . . I been in the train all day!' She came up to the bed. 'Is she all right?'

'Seems like it!'

'God, what a fright! . . . I nearly *died*!' She scowled at her daughter carefully for a few seconds as if making sure no one was deceiving her. 'It's – she's just asleep? That's all? Just asleep?'

'Yes.'

She turned to Gibb. 'Les, you *fool*! You *are* a flaming fool! This'll mean longer for you when you get back . . .'

'Maybe.'

They hesitated, and then he kissed her.

The radio voice said: 'Search is continuing for Leslie Gibb who escaped from Dartmoor at 5 p.m. yesterday. Gibb, an ex-paratrooper wounded at Arnhem, is serving a three-year sentence for robbery with violence . . .'

At The Chalet Lartrec

I was looking out for a village. Almost any sort of village would have done, because things had been difficult for the last hour.

The snow had started just as I reached the top of the pass. They'd told me in Pontresina that the road was still clear, and I'd found it so: a few piled heaps of white here and there like dirty linen waiting to be collected, but nothing new at all. Right at the summit by the now-empty hospice I stopped the car to let the engine cool in the icy wind and strolled about to ease my stiff leg; but I didn't stay long. The clouds were lowering all around like elephants' bellies, and it was lonely up there, more than a mile high, with nothing human or alive anywhere, the great peaks half hidden and the first fall of winter long overdue.

So I climbed in and the engine fired at the fourth push, and as I turned the car round the first corner the flakes of snow began to drift absent-mindedly about in the wind.

It's a nasty road at the best of times. You go down and down but never seem to get any lower, round dozens of acute hairpin bends and through echoing tunnels with faint relics of daylight at the far end; and every time your tyres slither on the loose surface you look down thousands of feet into the dark pine-wooded valleys wreathed in cloud. It's like some medieval artist's vision of judgment; and of course if you slither too far the vision becomes an immediate fact.

In a mile or two it was snowing hard, and the car had no chains. It was nearly five o'clock – the climb having taken so much longer because of that plug – and very soon it would be quite dark. The snow was fine and soft, and for a bit the strong wind blew it off the centre of the road, piling it in drifts in the unexpected corners. I'd hoped to make Tirano and find a hotel there – it looked no distance on the map – but today it just wasn't going to work out. I couldn't remember whether there was anything at all before Tirano except the frontier post. It might be better to try to spend the night in the car than to skid to the edge of a precipice and then ... whoo!

The screenwipers were making heavy going of it, and I had to stop and get out to clean them. The snow was soft in my face, like walking into a flight of cold wet moths, and the wind was howling away in the distance across the valley. Somewhere nearer at hand just for a moment I caught the musical note of a cow-bell, but there was no other traveller, no other human being anywhere. They might all have gone long ago to some more civilized land.

With the dark I had to stop again and again, because the screen was freezing over and it was easy to miss the turns of the road. I could see the paragraphs in the papers: 'The victim of a sudden storm in the Bernina Alps was Major Frederick Vane, aged 33, a British officer attached to UNESCO, who unwisely attempted to cross from Switzerland into Italy by the Bernina Pass, which is normally closed to vehicular traffic in October. His car ...'

And then I turned one more contorted bend and the headlights showed up a few farm huts and the narrow cobbled street of a village.

It was a welcome sight. There was no one about, and the wind whistled through the slit between the houses like an errand boy with bad teeth.

Almost at the end of the street I braked in time to avoid a man with a handcart. After the lonely drive, I felt warmed towards him as towards an old friend. But the feeling wasn't returned because he didn't like standing in the draught and didn't feel warmed at all. However, after a minute or two our conversation attracted attention even on that bleak night. Two other figures appeared, anxious to help. Yes, they said, it was as Angelo Luciano stated: nothing here and doubts about Bagnolo, the next village, fifteen kilometres on. Beyond that was the frontier and then Tirano, but ...

Then quite suddenly, as an afterthought, someone mentioned the

Chalet Lartrec, and at once they were all agreed it might be worth trying at the Chalet Lartrec, which was off this road and only about a kilometre distant. The season being over, they said, Monsieur Lartrec would have closed down his house, but it was just possible he would make an exception in a case like this.

By now my screen had frozen over completely, so I scraped it into a state of semi-transparency and thanked them and drove on, reflecting how often people forgot the important thing until nearly too late.

At the stone marked 10, I turned as directed down a narrow track barely wide enough for a car. I knew that somewhere not far away the valley fell into further cloudy depths. Two gateposts showed up and beyond that a light. I left the car in the semi-shelter of three waving pines and picked a way across snow-filled frozen ruts towards the light, carrying my smallest suitcase.

The chalet was a three-storeyed place, painted in green, and all the shutters were up except at the window that showed the light.

I knocked on the door and waited.

There was no reply. I knocked again, picturing the unknown Lartrec crouching ill-temperedly over his log fire. Just then there was the screech of bolts and I stood back a step.

Light came out and I saw a woman.

'Er – Monsieur Lartrec?' I said.

She was staring at me. Perhaps she was surprised at seeing a stranger.

'You wish to see my husband?' she said in French.

I explained. While I was speaking the wind was shaking the door in her hand, and it blew little infiltrations of snow into the hall. She was quite young, with a lot of dark hair and deep-set black eyes.

When I had finished she said: 'I regret, monsieur. We cannot put you up. We have no bed, no food. We are closed for the winter.'

I pointed to the snow. 'It is five or six inches already. All I need is shelter until daybreak.'

'We are closed, monsieur. It is not possible.'

'But I have no chains! I don't think I could even get my car to the main road again!'

She hesitated. 'I will see my husband.'

She shut the door tight, leaving me on the step, stamping my feet and thinking bitter thoughts. I reflected that French was not her first language any more than it was mine. She was probably Swiss-Italian, or her mother tongue was perhaps that odd Romance dialect that a few Swiss still speak. Then the door came open and this time a tall man stood there. He peered out at me as if I were a typhoid-carrier.

Wearily I explained it all again, and again came the same refusal. But by now I was getting bloody-minded and was not to be moved from his doorstep. Did he, I asked him, expect me to freeze to death in the car?

Suddenly he gave way. 'Oh, very well. I see that it is bad for you. We must do what we can.'

I followed him in, just holding my tongue; and it was fortunate that I did because, once they'd capitulated, they seemed willing to put a good face on it. I felt stiff and uncomfortable, willing to lie on a board somewhere and no thanks to them; but M. Lartrec showed me into a pleasant enough bedroom in which the central heating pipes were going full blast, and I gratefully thawed out and presently was called down to a meal of pasta, stewed steak, cheese and grapes, with a half litre of new and raw Chianti. So I began to feel a whole lot better towards them and to life in general.

Lartrec was not above thirty-five, distinguished-looking in an angular way, brutally thin, with great bony shoulders that he would shrug nervously as if his shirt were chafing him. Mme Lartrec was probably a bit younger, good-looking in her way, with finely shaped hands that had been roughened and reddened with work. She might, I thought, have been ill, for the fine olive skin that usually goes with such looks was over-sallow. Their only servant was a slow-witted boy with hair of a length that he did not know was fashionable, who followed his mistress – in person or with his gaze – wherever she went. Of Lartrec he seemed afraid.

For a few minutes after supper I sat in the large bare hall with my feet on the only square of carpet and tried to read last week's *Die Weltwoche*. But German has never been my strong point, and for the most part I listened to the lament of the wind and wondered if the roads would be quite blocked in the morning. To spend a night here was one thing, but I was due back in Rome on Monday.

The fingers of the thatched-barn cuckoo clock in the corner climbed up to nine, and when it had hiccupped I rose to go to bed. I wandered round the room staring at the pictures, an impressionistic view of Lake Maggiore, three impossible snow scenes, a photograph of a fat young man with beady eyes; then I went through the dining-room to the kitchen door and tapped.

The door was flung open and Lartrec looked at me.

'Yes?'

Behind him shining pans, my unwashed dishes, skis in a corner, a big stove, the tear-stained face of his wife.

'I thought I'd just tell you I'm going to bed.'

'Certainly, monsieur. Everything is to your liking?'

'Indeed yes. I'm most grateful for the food and the shelter.'

'You can find your way to your room? No, no, I'll show you.'

I insisted this wasn't necessary, but he took absolutely no notice and I followed him upstairs. In the bedroom he seemed reluctant to go, and we made a few forced remarks. There was no ease between us, but he still stood by the door, tall and gaunt, like an unfrocked priest.

'You are Swiss?' I said, feeling sure he was not.

His blue eyes flickered as he shook his head

After a pause I said: 'If I could have my breakfast at eight . . .?'

'But of course.'

'Anything will do. Anything you have: honey or an egg or even just a pot of coffee.'

'Of course.'

'I hope the roads won't be completely blocked.'

'It seldom happens with the first fall . . . You must think it strange, monsieur, that my wife – that you should see my wife in tears.'

'I'm married myself.'

He stiffened. 'It is not at all what you think. It is not domestic.'

I said I was pleased to know it, and waited for him to go.

'You are in part responsible for this tonight.'

I stared at him. 'Sorry. I assure you I'll not stay here a minute longer than I can help.'

'No, no. It is not just your coming, it is your coming tonight of all nights that gave her a shock. It is exactly the anniversary of something which happened twelve months ago. The anniversary to the day and to the hour.' He weighed me up. 'You are from England?'

'Yes.'

'I thought so from your accent. I have never been to England but I have often wished to go.'

There was a pause. We didn't seem to be getting very far. 'Cigarette?' I said.

'In England you suffered from two wars, but not in the same ways. In Hungary . . .' He stopped.

Light dawned. The high cheek-bones, the blue eyes, the rather metallic voice. 'You are Hungarian?'

'Yes,' he said half reluctantly.

'I spent a few days in Budapest once. A beautiful city.'

He gave that nervous twitch to his shoulders. 'My native town is Szeged . . . that conveys nothing to you?'

'I'm afraid not. Where is it?'

'A hundred and ninety kilometres south of Budapest. The second city of the republic. It is where the revolution of 1956 began.'

'The rev . . .' I stopped. 'Oh . . . *that* one. Were you there?'

'I was one of the leaders of the student movement.'

Neither of us spoke for a bit. 'Cigarette?' I said again, interested now.

He came back into the room and took one. I lit it for him, and his face, nodding his thanks, came out of the smoke, rapt and painful.

'Did you get away?' I asked sympathetically.

'No . . .'

'What happened?'

'I was transported to Russia. I was there – in Siberia – eight years.'

I studied his face. I have seen these men before. They are of all nationalities, but once you have seen the signs in one man you recognize them in others.

'You revolted against the Communists?'

He drew on his cigarette with hollowed cheeks. 'I think you have to clear your mind, monsieur, of some misconceptions, like most westerners. When the war ended in Europe I was eleven. After that *everyone* in Hungary was Communist. There was no alternative. What we were revolting against in 1956 was not Communism as such, but the iron hand of *Soviet* Communism as exercised through Rakosi, the secretary of the Party. We did not want everything at once, but just the *beginnings* of freedom, such as Yugoslavia enjoyed; and Mr Nagy, our prime minister, had undertaken to set on foot some of those liberal forms, including free elections. All this was set at nought by the sudden arrival of Russian forces in Budapest and the deposing of Nagy. It was against this, and against the pressure of a foreign power occupying our territory, that we organized the first demonstrations.'

He stopped and frowned at his cigarette, moved to tap the ash into the plastic ashtray on the dressing-table.

'Is your wife Hungarian?' I asked.

'My wife? Yes. Why?'

'It was a natural inference. Did she escape, then?'

'In 1956 Maria was not my wife. In 1956 I was twenty-two. In our childhood she and I had been sweethearts; but while I was at the university we drifted apart and she had just at this time married Julius Zigani. She was nineteen then and he was twenty-five, the oldest of our group. He came of an old Magyar family and had a little money of his own ... She was not happy with him.'

The room was warm and I loosened my tie. Outside the wind howled like a bereaved dog.

'She was not happy with him, monsieur. I knew later that all the time she had loved me.'

'The demonstrations? ...' I prompted after a minute.

'We students were an idealistic lot, dreaming of new freedoms, and *reasonable* freedoms . . . But we were also practical. Each week secret pamphlets were written and distributed. Much preparatory work was done. Of course our group was only one of many. In our group there was Maurus Kozma, who was our leader, and Emeric Erdy – and Julius Zigani, Maria's husband. Those first demonstrations . . . I cannot tell you how full they were of high spirits and of hope. After the first day in Szeged we drove in trucks to Budapest to join the students and the factory workers there. Then of course the trouble.'

'Trouble?'

'Well, it led, as I suppose one could have expected, to clashes with the A.V.H., our own abominable secret police, whom we hated even more than the Russians. Next morning Russian tanks moved in to support them and opened fire on us. But by now we had ample small weapons, for much of our army had joined us. It was a noble struggle . . .'

'Yes . . .'

'An exhilarating struggle. Half Budapest was laid waste; but we got our way – or thought we had got our way – and the revolt died down. Mr Nagy was brought back. Our efforts and sacrifices, it seemed, were not to be in vain. But you know how the Russians always work. You know the rest.' He sighed. 'Three days later armoured divisions of Soviet troops moved into the city. Thousands were bloodily murdered, the legal government was overthrown and a puppet government was set up in its place. Mr Nagy could only take refuge in a foreign embassy. From there he was decoyed out by a lying promise of safe conduct. As soon as he was out he was seized by the Russians and sent to imprisonment and execution. This was perhaps the shabbiest thing of all. Then mass executions and deportations of the other leaders of the revolt took place. I went into hiding with Kozma and Erdy. Julius Zigani and Maria were somewhere in the city but we lost touch with them. Many tried to leave the country, some with success, but at that time we had not given up. To leave one's country is to leave one's hope . . .'

He stopped then and moved slowly to the window to peer out.

There was something furtive in his movements, as if years of exile had left their mark.

'But in the end?' I said.

'In the end we were caught. Someone had informed on us. Kozma was shot. Erdy and I were deported. Erdy died in exile. I lived to come back.'

'To Hungary?'

'Not to Hungary. But to look for Julius Zigani.'

'Why?'

'It was he who betrayed us. The Russians told us. They told us he had bought his freedom by selling his friends. Not only did he betray us but six others also. Maria did not know, though she tells me now she once suspected and then dismissed the suspicion as too evil to be true. They left Hungary and settled in Switzerland. Zigani had been able to bring out a little money and he bought this chalet and opened it to summer guests.'

'You – found them?'

His shadow gave a jerk on the wall as he twitched his shoulders. 'It was twelve months ago. You understand. The tracing does not matter. He had changed his name but that does not matter either. In the afternoon I came to this chalet just as it was going dark. I was not sure even then, not at all sure. I came up to it but I did not knock on the door as you knocked on the door. Instead I crept round to the kitchen and looked in at the window. They were *there*, in the newly lit lamplight, Maria putting food on his plate, and Zigani bending greedily to eat it. She seemed scarcely changed, but he had put on some more weight. He was always as fat as a pig, with small eyes, old eyes, and short lashless lids.'

I was suddenly reminded of the photograph of the fat man in the hall. Lartrec had paused. Until now I had been too interested to care, but at this moment it occurred to me that I did not want to hear any more.

'Don't you think you've told me enough?'

He said: 'I went round to the front then and knocked. The boy came, the rather simple boy. I pushed past him and went into the kitchen, shutting the boy out. They looked at me as if frozen where they sat. Something had been spilled on the stove and was hissing. I said to Zigani: "There are nine of us here, Julius, not just one. Nine of us, all of that one group. Maurus and Stephen, who were shot, and Erdy and Victor who died in captivity, and Leo who was killed by the hounds . . ." I went on to the end, and all the time he sat there with a stain of egg on the corner of his mouth. When I'd finished I looked at Maria and said: "Did you know that this man –" And then I heard him move. He'd jumped – so quick for a fat man – to a drawer and I went after him to the oven. As he turned with a revolver I hit him across the head with the iron poker.'

Lartrec dropped his smouldering cigarette in the ashtray. Whatever I said now, he was going on to the end.

'He was dead within five minutes. I felt no sorrow and no sense of guilt. It was what I had come for, what I had intended to do for so long. But we had to face the outcome. We were no longer in a country at war where such things pass unheeded. It seemed that the only possible way would be to flee while there was still time. Italy, or more probably France, might give us asylum. France has accepted and absorbed so many refugees in trouble, and Maria and I could begin a new life there. But it was Maria, yes Maria, who suggested another way. No one knew of my presence in the neighbourhood. If I were to carry the body to the bottom of the cellar steps and leave it in the appropriate position, it might well appear that he had fallen and caught his head on the iron stairs. The boy was devoted to Maria and would say anything she told him. Suppose I went away again as I had come, there was no one in the house strong enough to inflict such a blow. And he was a heavy man and the fall down the steps would be great. There was danger, of course, but the other way there was also danger – to admit the crime, as it were, and to run away. Maria had Swiss citizenship. The Swiss police are persistent. It could be that they would trace Maria and apply for her extradition. The way she suggested – if it worked – neither she nor I would be hunted. In a few months, after it had all blown over, I could come to the district and meet Maria and marry her with no fear of suspicion. Those were the alternatives, monsieur. What would you have done?'

Lartrec's cigarette was still sending up a spiral of smoke as straight as a smoke signal. I found I was sweating. It wasn't just the heat of the room.

'You really want my opinion?'

'Of course.'

'Well, it won't help much, will it, at this stage; you made your choice: but I think on the whole you were lucky to get away with it. And you won't get away with it much longer if you start telling the story to perfect strangers.'

'You are the first and the last. It was something . . . it came out. I can rely on your discretion?'

'Yes.' Travelling over Europe today in spite of its new prosperity, one comes constantly upon the old sickly scars. 'Is your boy – the slow one – is he a Catholic?'

'Yes.'

'Then I think I should have been afraid of your wife's scheme for two reasons. I should have been afraid of the boy telling what he knew in confession. And I should have been afraid that the Swiss police, who as you say are persistent, might have found something in Zigani's injuries inconsistent with the theory of a fall. On the whole I should have preferred the risk of an escape to France where I imagine you would find others from your country who would give you shelter. But I wish you hadn't told me this.'

'And the killing,' persisted Lartrec, leaning forward. 'As an Englishman, would you have done different?'

'I don't suppose so . . . No. Probably not.'

'Thank you.'

There was silence for a while.

'I too am a Catholic,' he said. 'The instinct of confession dies hard. But in one way, in the *right* way, this can never come out. Perhaps it is my excuse for troubling you. That and your arriving so unexpectedly – on the anniversary. Your coming tonight – we could not get over that.'

I thought of some men I had seen in a hospital in Austria. 'I shouldn't let your conscience get too active,' I said. 'Traitors – traitors only deserve what they get. But I think you have made a mistake in continuing to live here. In this house you'll never be quite free.'

Faintly from downstairs came the sound of the cuckoo clock announcing ten. It seemed to bring him back to his duties as a host. He smiled a little, coldly, courteously.

'What time would monsieur wish to be knocked in the morning?'

I was a long time dropping off. My leg was aching, and whichever way I moved it it wouldn't stop. And I thought all the time of Lartrec's story. Presently I got up and bolted the door ...

I woke at seven and the wind had dropped. I was almost afraid to open the shutters, but relief, the storm was over. There had been a fair fall of snow but not enough. The roads would be passable. I wondered if Mark would still be in Milan. I thought again of Latrec's story and wondered if he would refer to it again. Probably he would be bitterly repenting the confidences of the night. I should be glad to be on my way. It is not pleasant to be guest to a murderer whose safety now rests on your silence.

I'd not ordered breakfast until eight, but I washed and shaved in lukewarm water and stuffed my things into my bag. It was now getting on for eight, and I thought I'd go out and inspect the car. I could hear someone chopping wood, but that was the only movement so far.

It is always a little depressing to be the only person in a guest-house, and the place looked shabby in the morning light. The first thing I saw in the hall were my other two bags. It was thoughtful of Lartrec to have brought them in.

The shutters were to in the dining-room, and the hall was untidy and cold. I opened the front door and stepped out. The sun was bright now but hazy like an opaque electric bulb, and I made for the three pines, the crisp snow crunching. When I got to them I stopped. The car was no longer there.

I looked round, rejecting unpleasant thoughts. The wind had been so strong that it had blown away the track marks, and I thought perhaps Lartrec had moved the car into one of the sheds for protection. Still he should have told me.

I went back.

'Lartrec!' I called in the hall.

'. . . trec,' came the echo upstairs.

'Lartrec!' I called in the dining-room.

They were probably all at the back. Someone was chopping wood again.

I went into the kitchen. The remains of supper were on the table. It was not chopping but knocking. It came from the larder. I pulled back the bolt.

The boy stared at me stupidly. His hair was a damp twisted mat on his forehead. He burst into tears and began to gabble.

I took him and shook him.

'Where is your mistress, boy?'

He stared at me in fright, blinking as if he had just come out of deep water.

'Gone, signer.'

'Gone? Gone where?'

'I do not know, signer.'

'And Monsieur Lartrec? Has he gone too?'

'No, signer, he is still here.'

'Then take me to him.'

'No, signor. I am afraid.'

'Don't be a fool. I'll not let him hurt you.'

The tears running down to his chin, the boy faltered across to another door, which I opened. There were steps leading down and a smell of old wine. He tried to run then, but I stopped him and lit a lamp and pushed him down the steps before me.

It was a long flight, and half-way down the boy clung to the side and wouldn't move at all. I peered past him and saw something lying at the bottom. I went down and pulled at a tweed-clad shoulder. A stranger, yet it was a familiar face: a fat man with small staring eyes and blood dried on his forehead.

I stepped back and nearly upset the lamp. The boy hadn't moved.

'This – this is not Monsieur Lartrec!' I said.

'Yes, signor, this is Monsieur Lartrec.'

There was silence in the cellar.

'But,' I said, 'this . . . all this . . . happened twelve months ago.'

'No, signer,' said the boy. 'Last evening. Before you came.'

Then, I suppose, the strength came back to his limbs, and with the echoes shaking among the wine vats he went swarming up the steps, and through the empty house out into the winter sunlight beyond.

Vive Le Roi

The King was going: everyone knew that. The only question was when. The physicians said it might be a week yet; but William and Henry, watching each other across the sick bed, thought, what if he dies without sharing out, what if he sinks into a coma and slips away and nothing settled?

Twice they'd tried to get round to the subject, but they couldn't press too hard because the lion still lived and had a growl on him they recognized.

He'd repented of his errors on Sunday, repented like a stout sulky boy, with all his monks and his priests nodding their tonsured heads and whispering yes, yes, in unctuous sibilant approval; he'd agreed to the release of all those high-up people who had grown sallow in grim castles for more than twenty years.

But it had been grudging, a reluctant giving in to Christian impulses that came to him from outside. In many ways he was a pious God-fearing man but he'd never taken kindly to suggestions from other people. This morning for a while he was nearly his old self, sitting up for a few minutes, snapping at his chief prelates and barons, ordering up the barber to trim his moustache, sucking at a bowl of soup and watching the zealous attentions of his followers out of those small stern bloodshot eyes which for sixty years had done him well. He'd judged men with them, assessing which were his enemies and which his friends, deciding if he could cheat this one with promises or lure that one with gold. And he'd made few mistakes. It didn't pay to make mistakes.

Clear-sighted, people thought him. Well, he was clear-sighted enough to know this hint of recovery wasn't going to last; the lump in his side was no better, and he knew all his greatness, all his money, all his lands, couldn't save him now by so much as a day.

It was a pity, he thought, a crying cursing pity how he'd come to this state, for he was vigorous enough in other ways and might have lasted another ten years. Cousin Philip, might he rot, had been the cause of it all. It was that cheap joke that had started it. Yes, he was fat, sizable round the stomach like many a lusty man in his late prime. And because he'd been ill and forced to keep his bed a week or two Philip of France had cracked the joke. He'd said that the King was a long time lying-in and no doubt there'd be a fine churching when he was delivered. Venom carries quickly on the tongue, and when the King heard it he went purple up to the ears and swore by the birth of God that he'd be churched in Philip's own cathedral. Philip's cathedral not being as yet in reach, he had fallen on Mantes to begin and had burnt and butchered until nothing was left except ashes and the spread-eagled corpses of the people who had lived there. It was not pretty but it was his way: it had always been his way. You couldn't expect a change at his time of life. But this time, just once, things hadn't gone right. Riding up to see for himself, as he always did, he had put his horse on to hot cinders and been thrown, So this rupture and slow mortification.

And on the whole he judged better than his surgeons how much time was left. That morning he thought a fortnight more and perhaps with an effort he'd see his sixtieth birthday, but in the night he had a terrible dream and woke in sweat knowing the worst. He said nothing to Peter the monk, nor anything to Gilbert the bishop who had stayed up to pray at his bedside and fallen asleep there. But next morning early he sent word that they were all to come.

They crowded into his chamber, the priests and the nobles, pushing each other, as they thought unnoticed, and edging for position about the bed. Then he sent for his two sons.

They came quickly enough. They'd not been out of arrow-shot for a week and they came solicitously, anxiously, submissively, saving their sharp looks for each other. The King stared at them, and then he glanced up at the rest. Already, he thought, while the breath's still in the body, they stand in little groups, one against another. What when my hand has gone, will it all be as before?

'Yes. Father?' said Henry. 'I hope you're no worse? Give us that assurance, I pray you.'

The King said: 'I'm one day nearer death,' and raised his voice. 'This is my last will. Hear you all.'

Instant silence fell, the whispering and scuffling died in a second, noise seemed to run away from the bed and escape at the door like wind from a balloon. The King knew the expectancy but did not hurry himself. He looked again at his two sons, at their bent heads beside the bed, at once separated and united by the bed. Was it the only link? The two youngest of four: Richard caught by a stag, its horn had come out of his back; Robert – Robert Short Legs – ill-disciplined, rowdy, rebellious, chivalrous, lazy Robert, curse him, absent as usual.

'To my eldest son Robert,' he said, 'though he's borne arms against me and has been unfilial to the end, I leave this Duchy of Normandy. It fulfils a promise long made.'

He stopped, and one of the apothecaries gave him a sip of cordial. No one spoke, though glances went about, minds quick to think how the succession would affect them.

'My kingdom,' he went on. 'My kingdom I give to no one, though I'll leave it to him who can hold it, as I held it, with my sword. If God wills, I think that that one should be William, who has campaigned with me and served me well and on the whole been dutiful to me all his life.'

His son took a deep slow breath and raised his close-cropped, wide-browed head, his truculent, sourly swelling face. Enough – it was enough. He could hold it as his father had done, and if blood ran on the floor it should not be his. His eyes met those of Henry, clashed a moment and then turned towards the old man. The King was lying back with closed eyes, a trickle of moisture at the corner of his mouth. The virtue had gone out of him.

'And what,' said Henry, his voice cracking a little, 'and what do you leave to me, Father?'

The King irritably waved away the apothecary. With a grunt he turned on his side.

'Five thousand pounds weight of silver, my son, which you can get from my treasury when I'm dead.'

Henry swallowed noisily. 'A splendid gift, sire. But what shall I do with silver if I've neither lands nor a home.'

'You can keep your soul in patience,' said the King. 'You're by twelve years the youngest and your time will come.'

Again the eyes of the brothers met. Your time will come, Henry, thought William; but take care how you step or your time will come too soon. My time will come, thought Henry staring, when I am old and feeble; but strong men can take time by the hand.

He was off again, the tired old man, ordering that money and jewellery should be given to his half-dozen daughters, directing that this burnt abbey should be rebuilt, that church or monastery more richly endowed. He'd always been generous to God, since God had been generous to him. The monk at his side scratched it all down as he spoke. In the back of the room now were groups who clustered and whispered, having heard what they wanted to hear. It was hot in the room. It was going to be a hot day, and the flies were already troublesome. From somewhere outside came the flat musical echo of a goat bell.

At last it was over, and clergy and laity trooped out into the September sun. The two brothers walked together down the cloisters, their heavy spurred boots clinking on the ancient stone. They might not have been full brothers for they were unalike – children of the King's different moods, of his different lives, separated widely in time and circumstances: the tall handsome purposeful boy and the squat rufous-faced cynical seasoned veteran. They might have found common ground in the unfair benefits given to Robert if the greater issue had not divided them for ever.

So they came to the gates of the monastery unspeaking, and spurred off in opposite directions without a backward glance, William to take his kingdom and shut up again the men his father had just set free, Henry to weigh out his silver pound by pound.

The King had waited for them to come back; he had thought

any minute they would be back; and it was the fall of night before he realized he must die alone. For he dies more lonely who is a king with all his servants and courtiers than a beggar with a son beside him.

All that night, though they thought him asleep, his mind was active and alert, turning this way and that – like a cat in a cage sensing it will soon be dropped in the river. Sometimes he thought of his life and was content. He'd seen much, done much, come far. Coming so young to the high estate seized by his wicked and fratricidal father, he'd shown what he was made of, his ruthless ability and military genius, right from the beginning. Whatever he had taken he held, and if there was opposition or revolt he met it with the sword. Where he ruled, the law – his law – prevailed. He'd been a good father – domineering perhaps, for you couldn't get out of the way of ruling; he'd been a faithful and a loving husband – and that was something with all those smooth-skinned pale-haired English women about; and – when the itch for revenge didn't clash with piety – he'd been a religious and a temperate man.

All things to stand with him at the Judgment Seat: he'd much to be thankful for. But now and then in the darkness old scenes, old faces floated through the night. The lying, the broken promises, the bad faith, the cruelties and the massacres; these would be with him too. In particular he thought of the slaughter following the Northumbrian affair. They'd deserved revenge and he'd planned revenge; that Christmas Day eighteen years ago he'd sat in York and planned it all. Perhaps it wasn't the right day for thinking such thoughts, but his mind then, full of its own vigour, had worked in its own way. You did what you pleased and built an abbey or said a Te Deum afterwards. So he'd sent out his troops to butcher every man, woman, child and beast for sixty miles round, and so well had they done it that even now after all this time the country was desolate and waste and barren, a dead land uninhabited by man.

Just after that, he remembered, he'd taken that nightmare march across the Pennines to Chester, and the winter and the countryside seemed against him. He'd chosen to walk with his tired and grumbling men, leading them back out of blind gulches hidden in deep snow, across gale-swept moorlands and through semi-frozen streams, cheering them and encouraging them while all the time inside his anger grew again, demanding new appeasement.

Generalship, numbers or luck, he'd always been on the winning side wherever he'd been, losing his horse, the man beside him, crossing the broken bridge just before it collapsed, beaten only once in personal fight and then, rolling in the dust, finding his life spared because Robert Short Legs recognized the voice of his father.

Well, it was all over now. Tonight for the last time the ghostly battles could be re-fought, the pitched battles and sieges, grey in the morning mist. The tramp of marching men, long lost, long forgotten except by their leader who lay now in the dark, stirring the ashes of his memory for the last faint glow ...

There was a light drizzle next morning and day was late. More than usual had stayed with him through the night because some had caught him in the right mood last evening and wheedled concessions out of him, and hope was a powerful spur to devotion in the others.

As light grew they put out the guttering torches, and Hugh, Bishop of St Albans, opened the lattice window a few inches to let in the smell of the boxworm and the warm damp earth. A few birds cheeped and chattered in the herb garden. Then the monastery bell began to ring.

The King stirred and opened his eyes as from a deep sleep, and at once the watchers moved and yawned and stretched and gathered round, and the dozing servants were shaken or kicked. Montfort the physician took up a spoon and stirred the broth on the fire.

The King said: 'What's that bell?'

'The monastery bell ringing for prime, sire.'

'What day is it?' he asked.

'The ninth of September, sire.'

He closed his eyes. 'Holy Mary, Mother of God, receive my soul.'

They waited for more, dutifully, unexcitedly, knowing his long habit of praying to begin the day. But he didn't speak, only lay there, apparently considering his words. Montfort came forward with the broth and held it ready, close by. So it was he who first saw the change. He stared and put down the broth. Then he leaned and looked at the King, looked hard with puckered brows and tightened lips, then he slowly straightened up and crossed himself.

'The King is dead.'

The light was growing, a grey ashy autumn light, not the warm butter-yellow sunshine of yesterday. No one spoke. They were so used to the iron authority that they couldn't believe it gone, and waited for a harsh contradiction from the great figure on the bed. But they looked uneasily, sidelong, doubting, and saw that somehow the great figure had shrunken.

It was a shock to them all. They'd been expecting something, but not this sudden leaving, this desertion, this abdication of power. They didn't know how to meet it.

The hush was broken by Peter the monk who began to mutter his prayers in a harsh voice, and one by one, almost shamefaced, the others joined in. But already something was spreading among them, a slow contagion of alarm. It was not death they disliked so much as the consequences of death – this death. Only a few had legacies to gather like William and Henry, but all had property to hold and protect. Until five minutes ago it had been safe, sheltered by the unseen ramparts of the King's law. Now, in a few seconds, there was no law; it had flickered out in the wind. No one knew it yet; no one except the men about the bed.

Bishop Hugh, seeing Sir Henry de Tyes slip out on the heels of two others, thought of his own properties, warm and comfortable and fat and unguarded, and sidled round, still praying, nearer and nearer to the door. Montfort, about to compose and lay out the body, turned his narrow head to see several men pushing a noisy way out. What of my house in Rouen and Godric at the spinning-wheel and the cattle and the horses?

It was as if they had found the marks of plague on his body, as if the purple blotches had come suddenly to his face and hands; split, one split in the collective mind and the white milk of reason, of restraint is gone. Fear became panic and the flight a rout. They fled from his body, from the room, the abbey, this way and that, to tell their friends, to wake their relations, to shout the news in the camp outside as they galloped home.

Except for the servants two monks only were left, one fat and plethoric, the other with nervous veined hands and thin-skinned tonsured head. They stared at each other across the body. They stared and lifted their heads and listened. Then without a signal they stopped their prayers and turned and gathered up their cloaks and fled.

There were five of the servants in the room with the body of their master. They had watched in silence and now waited in uneasy silence for the priests or the doctors to come back. Some surely would think better of their flight. Five minutes, ten minutes.

John Ozbern was the King's personal armourer; he'd fought and campaigned beside him ever since Gerberoy; a lean scarred man, with a face so dark that it seemed permanently in shadow. He uncrossed his legs and moved away from the wall where he'd been propping himself; he moved across the room; he stared down at the silent man on the bed. He wasn't awed by death; he'd seen too much of it; it was the only certain thing in life; why treat it with respect?

'Be he really gone?' A young tall sandy-haired man had come up behind him.

'Dead as meat,' said Ozbern. 'Dead as his father and my father and all the rest of 'em. Dead as dust. Dead as rock. See, he can't hurt you now.' He lifted one of the King's hands and the young man took a step back in fright. Ozbern examined the hand of his master, then pulled two splendid rings off the fingers and slipped them into his jerkin.

'Here,' said the young man, who had not been too frightened to see this. 'They be not yours by no right. Put 'em back.'

'They're mine by the same right as they were his,' said Ozbern. 'Where d'you think he got 'em? D'you think they growed on his fingers like warts?'

They were all there now, all five of them, hesitant, frightened but greedy. To rob the body of the King; that meant death and thankful if it was quick. But who was to see? Who was to tell? Not the King.

'And these. And these.' Ozbern jerked a jewelled crucifix from round the dead man's neck and pulled a fine diamond off the other hand. 'If you've the fancy you would like 'em instead of me, just see if you can take 'em.'

They glanced sidelong at Ozbern, at each other, at the door, at the silent figure on the bed. Someone made a half move and the last rampart gave way. One snatched a leather belt with coins in, another a fine doublet and a gold dagger. Two together seized a silver cup and quarrelled over it, dropping it on the floor and rushing to snatch it again.

The tall young man, late on the move, found the best taken and clutched at the purple silk coverlet of the bed. While he was rolling this into a bundle two soldiers, brought by the noise, looked in. There was a moment's pause as they entered, and Ozbern drew his dagger. But they too stared at the corpse and found their allegiance gone. One moved through the servants up to the bed and after a second glance at the King pulled the rich cloak from under his shoulders. The other, snatching at the sheets, tumbled the body on to the floor where it lay in sprawling protest among the rushes and the trampling feet. The servants seized the last of the plate, quarrelling over the linen and the robes.

But they didn't waste time, knowing that some law, if not this man's law, might return. One by one they pushed their way out, and, when there was no more to take, the last tramping foot echoed away down the stone corridor outside and the King was alone.

Hours passed and the rain stopped and a watery sun broke through, falling through the lattice upon an outstretched hand. The broth, Montfort's broth, bubbled on the fire and as the fire died its bubbling died, while in neighbouring Rouen Montfort guarded his house and his mistress and his horses and his cattle from the rioting mobs that paraded the streets. There was no reason or sense in it, but the hand, the lawmaker's hand was gone. All men, as the news came, barred their doors and hid their money and saw to their swords and knives.

In the abbey bee garden the bees were on the move; the sun had warmed them to a lethargic honey-laden activity; they droned in and out of the late flowers and bumped lazily against the lattice panes of the silent room. Tierce bell sounded, and at last a soft footstep came down the passage and halted at the open door. It was the monk with the thin veined hands. He peered nervously into the room and at first thought the King's body had gone. Then he took another step and saw it lying half naked on the floor of the ransacked room. He turned on his heel and fled.

But this time he came back with others following him, and then someone found William the archbishop praying in his cell, and William came and told them to lift the body back on the bed, to compose the limbs decently and bring fresh linen. Then they formed a silent shamefaced procession and carried the body into the chapel before the high altar and began masses at once for his soul.

They'd bury him at St Stephen's, they decided, the abbey he'd founded himself; it seemed suitable and right; it was sixty-odd miles, but they could make up a sizable procession. It would cost money, but someone would pay; the King had relatives, three sons, daughters, cousins, old friends. Some sort of show was only fitting for so great a man. The sons were not here, true enough, not even Robert who must come soon to claim his inheritance, not even Henry who had disappeared somewhere with his retinue, five thousand pounds of silver and all. The cousins? No, they had vanished. And the bodyguard? And the servants? They couldn't be found. Even gold plate belonging to the monastery had gone.

Fortunately just at the last a man called Herlouin turned up. He had a small estate nearby and a good reputation. He didn't know the King well, but he seemed willing to organize the thing and pay out what was needed.

The monks said they were glad of his help. In the meantime they sent some of their number to inquire for the King's relatives, but no one came, and three days after his death the King made his last journey with strangers at his side.

They were expecting him at the town and had prepared. A procession with the Lord Abbot at its head met him outside the walls and turned and led the way in. Townspeople lined the streets and mixed with the monks and clergy who followed the bier. They stood and watched him pass and thought: Well, he's come for the last time; it's right that he should lie here where his wife is; he had his faults but there were worse; if they'd murdered him as they tried, as they murdered three of his guardians when he was still a boy, the others would have been much worse; and the old ones shook their heads and thought of Robert his father, Robert the Devil they called him, who'd been much worse, and the years of banditry that followed before this one put it all down; this one at least had been more like one of them; his mother's father had been a tanner, the peasant streak was strong in him; he was a great man.

There is always something about a funeral.

So they crowded into the abbey church, and stood and knelt dumbly and many wept, though they couldn't have told exactly what they were weeping for except, vaguely, for the mortality of all men. After the mass the Bishop of Evreux preached a moving sermon, while more people than ever crowded into the church and crushed about the bier and some thought they would suffocate.

'Oh, my children,' said the bishop, 'here lies your duke and your king. A great and a good man. A nobleman with all the knightly virtues of chivalry. A prince of Christendom. But in this present life no man can live without sin, no, whether he be king or commoner; so I ask you for the love of Christ that you intercede with God Almighty on behalf of our deceased prince; and, as you hope for your own forgiveness, that you forgive him if in anything he has offended against you.'

They thought that was the end, and crossed themselves and bowed to take the blessing. But someone else began talking, close beside the bishop, and they looked up to see a tall haggard man standing between the bishop and the bier. He was speaking in a clear shrill voice.

'This place,' he said, 'this place where you propose to lay this man was once the yard belonging to my father's house. Over there – ' he pointed – 'were the stables, and here was the walled garden where as a boy I used to play. That man you pray for seized all this land, without any excuse in law, because he was all-powerful and no one could question him. But now he's gone I publicly lay claim to the land that was stolen from me, and in God's name I forbid that his body, the body of the spoiler and thief, should be laid to rest in the ground he stole.'

They waited with open mourns, gaping and pushing and staring. No one knew what to expect, and if the King's kinsmen had been there the man would have been cut down. But only churchmen were present, and the tall man was untouched. He stood there, an obstruction to all the dignity of the ceremony, a grim uncompromising bar to the last solemn obsequies; he must be dealt with somehow, by reason or by violence.

The bishop said in a quiet voice:

'Is this man speaking the truth?'

A priest standing by the bier turned and said:

'He is Ascelin son of Arthur, my Lord. The King despoiled him. I know that to be true. It was his land the King gave to found this Abbey of St Stephen.'

The Lord Abbot had come up beside the bishop and they whispered together. The Lord Abbot was furious, his white, ascetic face flushed and blotchy; this man had committed sacrilege by his interference in a holy place.

The bishop said: 'You are Ascelin son of Arthur whose land this was?'

'Whose land this is, my Lord, for it was unlawfully taken from me.'

'You would claim this soil which has been consecrated and given to God?'

'God is the defender of right and cannot surely condone injustice.'

The abbot was about to make an angry reply, but the bishop put a hand on his arm.

'Supposing your case to be a good one, my son, you'll agree that we cannot tear down this church and restore your home and your garden. What then would you have us do?'

'At least turn this man out. Scatter his bones where you please but don't bury him here.'

'You see the grave,' said the bishop. 'It's dug and the coffin is waiting to be lowered, the corpse blessed and embalmed. It is late to turn back now. Let us buy from you the seven feet of earth in which this man shall rest. Then justice will be done and he can lie in peace.'

For the first time the tall haggard man hesitated. A glint came into his eye. 'What do you offer me for it?'

The bishop turned to the man at his side.

'Forty shillings,' snapped the Lord Abbot.

'It's worth eighty,' said the thin man.

The abbot glanced angrily at the gaping mob.

'Fifty shillings and have done with it.'

'It's worth eighty,' repeated Ascelin. 'Land changed hands near here not a month since. Apart from the value of the house and stables. I'll take seventy as a concession.'

The priests whispered together again. The Lord Abbot was now for violence.

The bishop said: 'The abbot will pay you sixty shillings for the grave. It is not an unreasonable price. Come, my son, I think that is fair.'

'And for the rest? I'll take sixty shillings now if the rest is compensated for at the same price.'

'How much of this have you fair claim to?'

'About half.'

'For the rest proportionately then,' said the bishop, taking it on himself. 'Go with this monk and he will give you the first payment at once.'

'You agree to that, my Lord?' said Ascelin to the abbot.

'I agree to that!'

'Very well. It has been agreed before all these people. Be it so.' Ascelin turned and followed the monk.

When his tall bony head and shoulders had disappeared at the chancel door Bishop Gilbert made a hasty sign to the Lord Abbot and they resumed the service.

But the emotional temperature had fallen, and in so falling the reverence and the sorrow had slipped away. Men stirred and murmured together. The close confinement, the heat, the smell, were too much, and many were already pushing out of the church into the street where they could talk and argue in greater ease.

The bishop lifted up his fine voice. 'Oh, Almighty God, we beseech thee to receive the body and soul of this thy faithful servant, William, sixth Duke of Normandy, first Norman King of England. Grant him rest, mercy at the Throne of Judgment and the eternal glory of salvation through the intercession of Christ thine only son. Amen.'

As the coffin was lowered into its grave the great bell began to toll. It disturbed the pigeons in the tower and they rose in a flock, like handfuls of paper thrown with the wind, fluttering noisily into the hazy sky above the town and above the thick congealed smoke of the burning houses, above the thin snake of the river and the flat rich Norman plains. They turned in a great circle against the land and the sky. Far in the north the sea glinted and glimmered in the afternoon sun.

As the bell finished tolling, the last of the people streamed out of the church and the pigeons began to settle into the tower again.

The Cornish Farm

We were looking for a farm.

It seems to me that a great many people have this ambition at some time in their lives, especially in years of tribulation. Their yeoman ancestry comes out; they want to own a few acres and see things grow.

Many no doubt give up after a while. But I was lucky enough to find one.

It was Philippa who suggested we should try the West Country. She'd a fancy for the milder side of England and had a few relatives scattered about who might help. I began in Wiltshire and worked my way zig-zag in a series of knight's moves farther and farther west, gathering disillusionment.

I'm no stickler for absolute cleanliness and order, but it depressed me to discover the squalor in which so many people live. Or perhaps it is only people who want to sell their houses who live that way. It also depressed me to discover the wickedness of estate agents. After a time one gets tired of being shown into the 'well-equipped' kitchen to find it dominated by an enormous stove installed about the year of Gladstone's wedding and smoking from every crack; then, coughing heartily and with eyes smarting, to be led through a broken glass door into the 'conservatory' which in fact is a lean-to shed with a little stove of its own where all the real cooking is done and ventilation is by way of a sloping tin funnel. No more desirable is the 'desirable residence' which turns out to be a paper-thin bungalow divided from the cowsheds by an hour-glass pool of liquid manure, while the sacks of chicken meal are piled in the lavatory and double carpeting in the hall fails to hide the dry rot.

And these, mind you, properties for which large sums of hard-earned money are asked, sums requiring sober visits to grey-faced bank managers, and swearing one's life away, and the long yoke of mortgaging. When I reached Cornwall I was nearly giving up, because there was no farther to go unless one jumped into the sea.

And then a word over a glass of beer in a local pub sent me across country to the south coast looking for a farm called Pencarrion.

I found it, empty and for sale.

This wasn't the sort of place I'd been looking for either. The farmhouse was really an old Elizabethan house come down in the world. In parts 'come down' were the operative words. One room had a sycamore growing out of the roof. And there was no market town near. But it had 40 acres of pasture and 9 of woodland, some fruit trees in the ruins of a walled garden and a short drive bordered with blue hydrangeas. In the skirts of the woodland was the chimney of an old tin-mine. The place had been empty about a year, but a neighbouring farmer had used the land, so it came near to being in the 'good heart' that one reads so much about in the advertisements.

The price was not unreasonable for these days, I mean not more than would have bought a country estate and a mansion twenty years ago. But it was a third less than most of the other ruins I had been inspecting, so I sent a soberly worded telegram to Philippa. When she came it took her exactly seven minutes to make up her mind, which was three minutes less than I had reckoned on. Only once, just before the contracts were exchanged, she said to the local solicitor who was acting for both parties:

'I hope there's no snag that we don't know about – a plague of rats, for instance, or too much arsenic In the subsoil . . .'

It's quite unusual these days to see false teeth as regular as piano keys – they're going out at last – but he gave us a good view of his.

'Nothing to our knowledge, madam. It was the big house of the district at one time, and the old men seldom made mistakes where they built their homes.'

Well, we moved in. There *was* nothing wrong, except what neglect and weather had done. It was probably the collapsed north end of the house that had scared away buyers, but in fact we solved that pretty quickly. Two bricklayers in a matter of weeks sealed off the end and we were left with half a house that was quite reasonably weatherproof and cosy. We took on two local men, one called Bray and one called Aukett, and we got down to the hard business of making a living.

At first the district was strange. There are parts of Cornwall which are still foreign to the Anglo-Saxon. It took time to get used to the antiquity of the house itself. I used to look round sometimes and speculate that the masons who had laid these stones had perhaps been doing so while Anne Boleyn was an up-and-coming young deb at the court of Henry. Men living then might have remembered Bosworth Field. It was difficult to realize. I would have liked to find out more about the Pencarrions who had first settled here and who for three centuries had been masters of the district, but Philippa said no.

'Let's take it as it stands,' she said. 'It has no memories for us. Why should we try to create them?'

Sound enough advice, probably. But as it happened it was she who made the first real discovery about the people who had lived here.

No one had touched the apple trees in the semi-walled garden for about five years, and before the leaves had fallen I was at them with saw and pruning knife and creosote, not because I believed this occupation would ease our financial stress but for pure love of aesthetic form. Nothing looks worse than an apple tree gone to overgrowth, nothing better than one pruned back to its fruiting spurs.

It was while I was at this scarecrow occupation, balanced in a ridiculous posture fifteen feet in the air while sawdust blew in my eyes and the branches whipped and jabbed, that I saw right across the farmyard to where Philippa was in earnest conversation with Aukett. The conversation roused my curiosity because it went on so long.

Over supper that night I asked her about it. She seemed to want to put me off, and then when I wouldn't be, she said:

'What was the name of the last owner here?'

'Tredinnick.'

'And before that?'

'Boduel, I think.'

'That's it. Boduel. Aukett was telling me about Boduel. He went raving mad.'

I said: 'He must have banged his head once too often on that lavatory door.'

'No, seriously. This was about seven years ago. They'd only been living here about 2 years at the time. Boduel was a Cornishman, Aukett says, who'd made a lot of money in London and came to retire here. He came down with his wife from London, and they brought a couple of servants with them.' Philippa looked round the room. 'It was Boduel who renovated the place.'

'He did *what*?'

'Well, apparently he did quite a lot. It was even more of a ruin when he bought it. You were saying to me yesterday that *somebody'd* spent money on it before us ...'

'Yes, I know ... It's certainly been patched up.'

'Apparently Boduel came down here and bought this house mainly to please his wife – and then about eighteen months after they got settled in she left him. She just took a suitcase and some personal jewellery with her. Aukett says the village were pretty sure she'd run away with another man – a poet who'd been living round here – but Boduel wouldn't give anything away. He took it very hard and put it out that she was expected back at any time. But she never came, and after a bit he began to speculate on the Stock Exchange and lost his money. So one night he tried to hang himself. He tried to hang himself in our bedroom, Aukett says.'

'A bit of local colour. These old chaps are great on the personal touch.'

'Anyway, he was cut down in time, but afterwards he was examined by doctors and certified insane. After he was taken away the Tredinnicks got the place for a song; but they were all great drinkers and let the house go completely to pot.'

That ended the conversation, and we began to look through a tractor catalogue. But when we went up to bed that night she said:

'I wonder which beam he used.'

Philippa isn't in the least a neurotic girl, and the Boduel story dropped between us like a stone and left no apparent trace. Anyway there was too much to do. When you take over a place that's been neglected, the pressure builds up to do everything at once. The land had to take precedence because while you can board up a window or knock in a few extra slates at any time, nature's like a damned obstinate old man who won't be hurried. If you miss one season you've got to wait twelve months until the chance comes round again. I sighed for thirty men and three bulldozers.

So we were too busy to think about anything else. All the same I'm glad she was away in December when the rest happened.

Aukett and Bray and the woman who did for us lived in the hamlet of Pencarrion at the foot of the hill, so while Philippa was visiting her mother I slept in the house alone, and rather liked it. I always like being in a house alone. I think one somehow gets to know it better, and I wasn't troubled by a fear of meeting ten generations of dead Pencarrions on the stairs, or even waking one morning and hearing the creak of a rope.

But I did wake and hear something one morning nevertheless.

It was the fifth night I'd been alone, and for the two previous days a gale had been striding across the land, birch-brooming the hills and the valleys with angry rain. For two days chimneys had boomed, windows had rattled, everything that could bang had banged, everything that could leak had leaked, cobbles oozed liquid mud, mats wriggled like snakes, and there had been no peace in the world.

Usually I wake about six-thirty, and when I woke this morning I knew we had been left behind at last by the storm. It was very quiet, a quiet such as one only gets in the country, and in the winter when the birds are still. Although the room was dark, you could see the pale oblongs of the windows with their pear-shaped architraves. If allowed, Pencarrion was very free from creaks and other noises. The early Tudors knew how to build.

And, just as I was thinking that, I heard a very distinct creak in one corner of the room. It was in the alcove beyond the windows and therefore in the greatest darkness. In this alcove was an easy chair and a table with some books.

The creaking stopped, but I lay there listening for some time, not quite so sure of myself as usual. It's surprising how quickly confidence ebbs away when the untoward seems about to happen.

Well, dawn was breaking and the light began to grow. It was infinitely silent. My breathing grew longer again. There would be a lot of work to do today, making up two days of lost time. Philippa was returning tomorrow and would be bringing . . .

Just for final reassurance I pulled the bedclothes quietly down so that I could stare into the corner. It was still shadowy there, but now something was coming into view.

The first thing I was certain of was a hand with a gold signet ring. Then the light seemed to catch on a shoe. Farther back and higher up you could just see a faint oval blur.

When I had swallowed back about a pound of gut, I sat up in bed with a jerk.

'*Who's there?*'

No reply. In the distance now a faint wind moved like an echo of yesterday.

'Who's there? What the hell d'you mean coming into my room?'

A man's voice said: 'I might ask you the same question.'

In spite of what my eyes could see, the fact that somebody actually answered shocked me still further.

I was sitting stark upright in bed now. I couldn't move any farther. My muscles were in a sort of cramp.

'But then,' the voice said, 'I suppose you're the present owner.'

It was going to be a bright morning, and light was coming quickly. The man sat with his legs crossed. In his right hand he was holding something below the level of the table.

'What d'you want?' I croaked, and stopped. My throat was constricted as if someone were holding it.

He said: 'As a matter of fact I'd forgotten all about anyone else being here. But we won't dispute the ownership. My name's Frank Boduel. Does that mean anything to you? Ah, I see it does.'

He was about fifty-five, bald, with intent watchful eyes, and a few days unshaven. His clothes were curiously old-fashioned without conforming to a period. His loose tie was not unlike a stock. His buckle shoes were either a hundred years old or in the height of fashion.

He said: 'I bought this house once but never really had a chance of enjoying it. Last night when – when I was able to free myself I came back. Can you blame me?'

The shock wave was at last receding and leaving the hard pebbles of anger behind. I made a move to get out of bed, and for the first time he stirred. He lifted his right hand. In it was a butcher's knife.

'Since I've been certified insane by all sorts of doctors I must claim the advantages of the complaint. Lie down.'

I lay down. I needed the rest. It wasn't a nice position. No one would be coming to the house yet.

He said: 'You seem to have made a thorough mess of the garden. What *did* you do with the ash tree?'

After he had repeated the question, I realized he required an answer. 'I cut it down.'

'I *planted* that. Good God, you vandals from up country don't realize how hard it is to grow trees in this country with the winds that blow. And that depressed-looking little hedge. Whatever is it?'

'Which hedge?'

'The one by the gate.'

'Pittasporum.'

He grunted. 'You'll not rear it. All this salt in the air.'

There was silence.

'I won't try to persuade you I'm not insane,' he said, and gave a brief dry laugh. 'The word means nothing anyway. One is persecuted for taking an unpopular view, that's all. So were the saints.'

I said: 'Why were you persecuted?' If he would go on talking long enough Aukett would come.

'Ah, you must know all the ordinary details. I'm sure I'm still talked of in the district.'

'I've been here only a few months. I don't go to the village.'

'Are you married?'

'Yes. But my wife's away.'

He smiled slightly and put down the knife. 'Are you sure she'll return?'

I tried to think of a way of continuing. 'Yours did not?'

'Ah, so I see you have heard.'

'The barest details.'

He was looking up at the beams of the ceiling with an intent stare.

'It's an intensely unpleasant death, being strangled by a rope,' he said. 'I suffered it and then they brought me round. It wasn't fair. She was the last of the Pencarrions. I suppose you know that. She persuaded me to buy this place. It had been out of her family for a century and she wanted it back. Sometimes I have thought she wanted the house more than she wanted me. When we got here she tried hard to persuade me to change my name to Pencarrion. I wouldn't ... She was a beautiful woman. Dark hair, milk skin, features like a doe. I was fascinated by her. The last of the Pencarrions! My father was a postman.'

I dragged up the eiderdown and pulled it round my shoulders. He watched my movements carefully.

'But I wouldn't change my name. What utter damned nonsense all this pride of name is, this glorifying of ancestry! The Fitz-something-this and the De-something-that go back only as far as the name of the humblest labourer. We come out of the stewpot together, and when we're done we go back in. Annabel wouldn't see that. She took pride in the most ridiculous things. Shade of her ancestors! They'd been a lawless lot; but by the time it came to my wife the Pencarrion blood was running thin.'

Boduel got up restlessly with the knife in his hand and walked to the window. 'You've been pruning the apple trees, I see.'

'Yes.'

'I could never get the things to fruit. Good blossom, and then the wind would come.' He felt the edge of the knife with his thumb. 'Are you quite alone here?'

'What happened?' I asked.

'What happened where?'

'Between you and your wife.'

'Oh ... We quarrelled from the start. She'd a sort of weak stubbornness, a thin pale obstinacy more durable than any anger. I'm not a vicious man. I'm not a brutal man. I was an ordinary human being asking for human companionship and affection. But the only interest she showed in anything or anyone was an intellectual one. No; a sham intellectual one, for intellect isn't separate from life, is it? She'd a mind with blinkers on, fastidious, selective, afraid of the mud.' He went slowly back and sat down again. 'Of course perhaps I wasn't entirely without blame. Have you ever heard of the Gorsedd?'

'How did you get in?' I asked. 'All the doors were locked, weren't they?'

He considered me. 'The Gorsedd is a Cornish thing in which they elect Bards and parade about in white robes like Druids. Utter damned nonsense. I'm as Cornish as can be, but this dressing up, this trying to revive something that never was, it makes me sick! Annabel got involved in it. Last descendant of one of the oldest families. It suited her perfectly – all the make-believe. She lived on make-believe. And after a while she took up with a Cornish poet called Trelowarren. He wrote poetry in the Cornish language! Can you match that! As if there aren't enough languages in the world without trying to revive one that never was any good anyhow and never had any literature of its own. Could anything be more futile? I used to laugh at her, deride her. I used to say, could anything be more futile, Annabel. She didn't like that at all!'

It was almost full light now. His clothes were in a bad way and there was thick mud on his shoes. He looked as if he had been out in yesterday's gale.

'D'you get on with your wife?' he demanded suddenly.

'Yes.'

'No doubt you make allowances sometimes. I tried hard to. I tried to believe we could go on as we were. I knew other men envied me. But it wasn't any good. In the end things went too far. This poet, this Trelowarren fellow, left the district. He made his *living* out of insurance or something, and his firm sent him to South Africa. Of course they'd been very friendly for some months before he left. By chance I found one of his letters. It was full of sympathy for her, with ridiculous quotations from his own poems, a sort of metaphysical love-making; and *pressing* her to leave me and join him. Then I intercepted one of her letters to him and found it a distortion of my every act, representing herself as martyred purity, talking about the sacredness of Celtic culture ... and – *promising*, making a pledge to leave me and join him as soon as it could be conveniently arranged, while I was away. Have I struck you as mentally deranged up to now?'

'No.'

'No indeed. But maybe this shows that I am after all – because I didn't let her go.'

'You – didn't let her go?'

'No, I didn't let her go. Instead I stormed up to our bedroom – this bedroom – with her letter in my hand – and *there* she was standing in front of the mirror in her white Gorsedd robes admiring herself! Over there it was. The long mirror was against that wall. I – I waved the letter at her and told her what I thought of her, and for once she lost her temper too and called me all the names her high mind could remember. She said she supposed I was used to opening letters since my father was a postman and no doubt had done it before me. It went on and on and on, and a great bitterness welled up in me. I took her by the neck and shook her. It was not unpleasant. I often think that damned Gorsedd robe was partly to blame.'

Boduel paused and sighed through his large yellow teeth.

'Are you cold?' he asked.

'No,' I said carefully.

'I was cold,' he said, 'when I'd done it. Just for a little while I was cold. D'you remember that Browning poem of the man who strangles his mistress and then sits all night holding her head against his? What utter damned nonsense. You can't love a corpse. You can't even hate it. There's only one thing you want to do and that's get rid of it. It was midnight when I'd finished and the servants slept out. You know the old tin mine in the orchard?'

'Yes.' My mind was racing ahead of his story.

'It goes down thirteen hundred feet and links with all the disused workings in the vicinity. It's been flooded for sixty years. I carried her downstairs and through the orchard dressed just as she was in her Druid's gown. There was no moon. Many times I've dropped things down that shaft. And some of them have made more noise than she did. Then I went back to the house, packed her suitcase and threw it after her. That was a gesture that pleased me somehow. Then I came back and unlocked the front door and went to bed.'

Boduel got up restlessly again. 'I don't like your furniture,' he said. 'I had some Sheraton antiques in here; and a four-poster bed with a figured canopy. God, that dressing-table!'

'We did our best,' I said humbly, 'with what we could afford.'

'I suppose things are different these days. But tell me, is every murderer a madman? If not, why am I? The thing worked well enough. She had stolen out in the night – and I was broken-hearted. I told people she was away for a holiday, but I let the vicar know in confidence that she had left me for Trelowarren, and that way it got about. The whole thing was quite clever, I thought, because even if anyone had suspected the truth there could have been no proof of it. To do that they would have had to spend £200,000 draining the mines. Even with the present price of tin you can't afford to lay that much out.'

He went across to the window, and peered out again. The light glinted on knife edge, signet ring, tie-pin, bald head. Then he went to the door and opened it an inch and listened. A man's voice could be heard downstairs.

'That's only one of my farm hands,' I said nervously. 'He'll do you no harm.'

He smiled sadly. 'I came back to see what it was like. Living in that other place I used to *wish* myself back here. I used to dream about it. But there's no *real* life for me here. Things have moved on. They always do. I'm a stranger now, an intruder. Besides . . . they'd look for me here in the end.'

'What are you going to do?'

'In a way I suppose she's won, the bitch. So it would be appropriate if I joined her. I've always wondered what it must feel like to go straight down an air adit.'

'Don't be a fool!'

'These rugs,' he said. 'They're terrible. You should go to Wherry's of Plymouth. They import direct. Mention my name, if you like.' He stood half in the door brooding. 'But they'll have *forgotten*. Everything is forgotten in a few years. That's why I'd like you to remember me and what I've told you. Nobody else knows the truth. I did want someone to know.'

He was gone.

In the December daylight I found myself staring at my own cold face in the glass. It was drawn and older than I remembered it last night. Then the front door slammed. I dug my feet into slippers, snatched a coat from the wardrobe, ran downstairs and out. Round the corner Aukett was standing gaping.

'That man, sur, he's just been in your 'ous. He looked like –'

'Stop him!' I shouted.

I ran through the walled garden with the remnants of ungathered prunings cracking under my feet. I could hear the tramp of Aukett close behind. At the broken gate I stopped. Boduel was already on the wall beside the mine, his stocky figure like a pin-man against the bright morning sky. Beside him was the ruined finger of the mine chimney.

I shouted to him and ran on, but he jumped down the other side. I got to the wall and pulled myself over. He was already on the rim of the low wall round the air shaft. I shouted again.

He saw me and lifted an ironical hand in which the butcher's knife still gleamed. Then as I started forward again he jumped.

From where I was I couldn't hear much, but as I reached the wall the echoes of his fall were still coming up the shaft.

They recovered his body. A difficult, job, but fortunately it was lodged about three hundred feet down on some timbers across the farther drop. The woman's body wasn't found.

I wired Philippa to stay away until the inquest was over. It was an unpleasant business altogether.

Thinking it over in the weeks that followed I wondered, as he clearly wondered, with what degree of greater ingenuity a supposedly sane man could have acted, always supposing the sane man had wished to dispose of his wife. The course he had followed – once embarked on – had the merit of simplicity, spontaneity and tidiness. The stumbling-block in so many crimes is, of course, just that disposal of the body. Get rid of it and even the utmost suspicions and the cleverest detectives are likely to stumble and fail.

That Boduel had made one mistake – in spite of his claim – did not become apparent until months afterwards, until well into the following summer. Philippa, who just never will allow things to rest, eventually located his wife, now living as Mrs Trelowarren in South Africa, where she had fled with a man who in his spare time still writes Celtic poetry.

The Wigwam

Business was bad when the young man came in. There'd been two customers all morning and there was nobody in either of the chairs. The young man sat in one of them and Bristow came across and met the other's eyes in the big mirror.

'Haircut?'

'Not a cut. Hardly even a trim. But there's one or two ragged edges. See here. And this. Then I'll have a shampoo.'

Bristow tucked in the none-too-clean sheet round the young man's neck and fitted a strand of cotton wool between his neck and his collar. He began to snip, but warily, because the young man's dark hair was the length that a girl's used to be at the time when Bristow learned his trade. Bristow was forty-nine, a stocky rather stolid man who had none of the superficial chatter that successful barbers are supposed to have.

So there was not much talk for a time, except about the way the young man wanted his hair done, and when that was finished it stopped altogether during the shampoo. Bristow rubbed the hair dry with a couple of small towels and then began to comb it out.

'Thanks,' said the young man, whose name was Morgan, 'I'll do that myself.' Bristow stepped back resentfully and watched him.

'Stranger round here?' It was the best he could do in small-talk.

'Yeah. Never been in Crowchester before. Pretty quiet, aren't you?'

'Yes, quiet.'

'I suppose it's the time of day.'

'No, it's quiet most times.'

'Town seems pretty busy.'

'Town may be. This is the wrong trade.'

The young man was carefully and skilfully parting his hair, a hand and a comb flicking the heavy, still-damp hair into place, patting it and pressing it so that the natural slight wave was encouraged and moulded.

'You know how to do that,' said Bristow grudgingly.

'Yeah?' The young man was examining his reflection.

'Like something on it?'

They discussed sprays and pomades for a minute or two. The young man chose a spray. After the mist had died down and he had used his comb again he said: 'Ought to know how to do this. It's my trade too.'

'What is?'

'Hairdressing. Or one of 'em. I've been out of it for a couple of years.'

'Where did you work?'

'Brighton.'

Bristow shook out the sheet. 'You got out the right time.'

'Oh, I don't know. What makes you say that?'

'All these . . .' Bristow hesitated in time to avoid insulting young men who grew their hair long. 'Fashion. Nobody has their hair cut any more.'

'Maybe not. Or not in the same way. Chap I worked for in Brighton seems to be doing all right still.'

'Yes?'

'What made you leave, then?'

'I got a better job. Or thought it was.'

'And wasn't it?'

'It was for a year or so. Then it folded. Some ways I'm sorry I left Brighton.'

'Why don't you go back?'

'Someone else has my job. You're right on that. They're not taking on any *more* assistants.'

'I sacked mine six months gone.'

Morgan looked speculatively out of the window. 'There's plenty of people about. Like I said. In a country town like this, fair buzzing with life . . .'

'I can tell you the truth,' said Bristow, shaking the sheet again. 'And the truth is I'm thinking of giving up myself.'

'Many others in the town?'

'There's Cowland's at the other end. That's all. But it don't *pay*. My rates've doubled in four years. You don't get it *back*. I tell you, when I moved here fifteen years ago there was queues on Fridays and Saturdays. No young fellow in those days thought he was properly turned out until he'd had a short-back and sides. Now you're damn lucky if they come in for a trim-up twice a year. More often than not they do it at home!'

Morgan said: 'How much you going to charge me for that?'

'Forty pence.'

'Forty! Isn't that something!'

'Well, it was a trim *and* a shampoo,' Bristow said belligerently.

'Forty! It's too *cheap*.'

Bristow stared and then shrugged and dug for a cigarette in his pocket. 'Your fancy Brighton shop can maybe get away with it, but you try asking more here.'

'Have you tried?'

'What? Well, no. But I know from what folk say. That's what Cowland's charge, and if I put my prices up, the few customers I've got would go up the hill.'

Morgan stood up and went for his coat, put it on, passed a fifty piece. 'That's O.K.'

'Thanks.'

The young man had a green velvet jacket and tight corduroy slacks and yellow sandals. He stood in the centre of the shop with his hands in his pockets staring about him.

'Cigarette?' said Bristow.

'No, I don't. What's the population of Crowchester?'

'About 30,000.'

'And plenty of villages around?'

'Yes, I suppose. They come in here market days looking like a lot of damned gypsies.'

'And two barbers. Look . . .'

Bristow lit up and waited but the other didn't speak. 'What were you going to say?'

'I was going to say did you want a partner?'

Bristow threw the match through the open shop door. 'You out of your senses?'

'No. Not that I know. What lease have you got of this place?'

'Oh. it's not a lease. It's the wife's. Her father owned a bit of property and this was her share. But it's only a lock-up. We're thinking of selling it for what it'll fetch.'

'What about taking me as a partner instead? I'll take no pay but we'll halve the profits.'

'Profits! You're out of your mind, man!'

'Well, it depends how you run it, don't it. It all depends how you run it. I'd like to get back into the trade. Maybe we could talk it over sometime . . .'

'Talk! There's nothing to talk about! I shall count myself bloody lucky if I'm still in business by this Christmas!'

The dark young man in the green velvet jacket sat down in one of the empty chairs and swivelled it round. He looked speculatively up at the ceiling.

'The trouble with you, Mr Brais – what's your name – Mr Bristow, is you're out of date. Nothing else. Sorry to say so, but it's true. You got to move with the times. Know what I should do if I was your partner here? Know what I should do?'

Bristow looked at his watch and then decided to humour his customer. 'No. You tell me then.'

'Well, first of all, I'd divide this off so that instead of being one shop it was two compartments, like. And I'd put you in the first and I'd put me in the second. First, though – first I'd change the name of the shop. It wouldn't be *Bristow, Gent's Hairdresser*, with a pole outside. For crying out loud, a pole! I'd call it *The Wig-Wam*, or some such name. *Men's Hair Stylist*. And I'd change the window altogether. Look at it now! It's a dead loss. You'd be better *without* a window. All you got now is a skating rink for flies! I'd change it all, put a sort of backcloth in so that people couldn't see into the shop. Then I'd dress the window with pictures of pop stars.

143

Not the very way-out ones but the ones with good hair styling – the sort of hair you'd like yourself.'

Bristow spat into one of the wash bowls, then turned a tap to rinse it away.

'You can shampoo O.K.,' said Morgan thoughtfully.

'Well, thanks.'

'No, I mean it. You're O.K. with that. You want some better shampoos, that's all. So it'd be like this, see. A fellow comes in for the treatment. So he comes in to me first, and I advise him on a style, and I give him a trim-up or whatever I think he needs. Then he comes out to you for a shampoo. Then he comes back to me and I give him a styling. Presto, he goes away a new man!'

'Pop stars,' said Bristow. 'They make me vomit.'

Morgan swung his chair. 'You can think what you like but you've got to live with the times. Remember in the dark ages when you started it was the girls who used to cut pictures out of mags and say, I want my hair like – well, whoever it was in those days: Dietrich, Crawford, Garbo. Nowadays it's the man's turn. The women do it still but it's the men who're the new peacocks. Give 'em your sort of treatment: 25p. for a hair cut, short back and sides, and you *will* be out of business by Christmas. Give 'em everything women have – the works – charge 'em £2 a time, and Bob's your uncle!'

Bristow let out a slow breath. 'Well, d'you know, just for a minute I was fool enough to get interested. I thought, maybe the lad's got something. But now I know you're barmy. Maybe you could get away with that sort of price in one of your fancy seaside towns like Brighton, but they'd drop dead before they paid that in Crowchester! Or anything like it! Try some other sucker, lad.'

'The trouble,' said the young man, 'the trouble is you don't ever *think* of the way times has changed. When you began nobody under twenty-five had any money. Now they're the big spenders. You think they won't pay £2 for a special hair style? Who buys all the discs of pop music? I ask you. Young chaps think nothing of paying two or three pounds for a long play. They all have their own transistors. Look at the shops now. Maybe you've not got a

144

Carnaby Street or a King's Road in Crowchester, but I'll bet there's some shops cashing in. Three pounds, four pounds for a shirt or a pair of slacks. What d'you think these cost? These I'm wearing? You wouldn't get the whole outfit for twenty-five quid. Think if I wear things like this I'm going to be content with forty pence spent on my head? It doesn't make *sense*. Think it over. It doesn't make sense either way up.'

Bristow stubbed out the end of his cigarette and dropped it in the waste bucket. The shop was still empty. Outside a traffic warden was moving on a car that had tried to stop.

'There's a place up the road,' he said. 'Dailey's. Used to be a draper's. Now they've gone all mod. Might be selling stuff for a carnival. How they get rid of it . . .'

'But they do, I reckon.'

'They do, you reckon. Now you answer me one question, will you? Why've you come to me?'

'Why? I didn't *come* to you. I was passing through, visiting a lad I know; he's got a garage, wanted me to go in with him but I said no. Cars aren't my line. Messy. Why mess up your hands? They're O.K. to drive. I drive a little Mini. But that's all. Hairdressing, that's what I like. And I'd a few hours to kill, so I thought I'd do a bit of prospecting, casing the joint, see what Crowchester's got in the way of classy establishments. So I dropped in on yours.'

Their eyes met. Bristow's showed doubt and a vague suspicion; Morgan's a cheerful irony.

'No, it don't make sense,' said the older man suddenly, shaking his head.

'O.K., O.K. I only asked. It was just a thought, as you might say. Scrub it.' Morgan rose from his chair and began to comb his hair through again. It was nearly dry now and showed its fine texture.

'What's your proposition?' said Bristow.

'I've told you. Anyway you're not interested. Go broke in comfort, and good luck.'

'Oh, I'm *interested*, if this isn't a have-on. But you can't just come in here one morning and make a proposal after being here half an hour, a proposal that'd mean a – a complete change in everything. Sinking more money in the shop when I'm nearly on my uppers anyhow – taking a partner I've never seen till this morning.'

'Well, I'm like that, see. Make up my mind quick –'

'And unmake it just as quick?'

'Yeh, I see, that's a point . . . You mean you couldn't do this on your own, and I might run you into the cost of it and then get browned with it all and fade. Yeh. Well, we'd have to get it in writing somehow. Articles of partnership or something. One of these writ-scratchers would know.'

Bristow was not a quick thinker, and it worried him to have this proposition thrust at him until he had had plenty of time to look at it all round. The young chap was likeable enough so far as it went, and for all his free and easy manner he gave you a feeling that underneath he was business-like and all there. You could see he would be a success with customers because he had all that pleasant small talk that Bristow lacked. But it would lead to – Hell, it might lead to *anything*: a quick bankruptcy where before you might count on being able to get out in time.

'What'll you do,' he said, 'if I say no?'

'Get my car off of the car park and push on as far as Norwich. I've a cousin there, and he said to look him up if I was ever in these parts.'

'And if I say yes?'

'Oh . . . stay the night at some pub so that we can talk it over after this place is shut. Even if we don't go so far as a lawyer, we'd have to have things fairly cut and dried.'

Bristow chewed his bottom lip. 'Well, it . . . You could do that anyhow, couldn't you. See if it came to anything.'

'Yeh, I could. If you're interested. A day won't matter either way.'

'I tell you what. This is a lock-up, I told you. I got a bungalow down Parkers Lane, by the river. I'd like you to meet the wife, see what she thinks about it. Come to supper tonight. Seven o'clock we usually eat. Come at half six.'

Morgan patted the back of a swivel chair as if inviting a child to sit down. 'O.K.,' he said. 'I'll do that. See you then.'

Bristow's wife was fifteen years younger than her husband. He had married late, a shop girl who worked in the dress department of Fortescue's, and she still worked there ten years after. Peggy was a good-looking blonde, a bit colourless, with not much more than a tendency to overweight. This she watched carefully, and she never corrected the natural pallor of her face because she thought this made her look slimmer and more delicate. She and Walter did not have much in common, and even had different groups of friends, but it was a marriage that worked as well as most. He claimed his rights twice a month, and with this she appeared to be content. Only sometimes when she went into the lounge bar of one of the local roadhouses with a couple of her girl-friends did she become shrill and bawdy.

When Ken Morgan arrived for supper Bristow had told her of his coming but not why, and when she heard the proposition she was cautiously in favour of it. Eighteen years in business had given her a good sense of the practical, and for her it was not whether the idea was good – she could *see* it was good – but what it would cost.

She behaved correctly and in a lady-like fashion to young Morgan, putting on the manner that she used when dealing with one of her better-class customers. He was cool, casual, alternately persuasive and indifferent. After supper they got down to detail.

Six weeks later, after the shop had been closed for alterations for a month, the new men's hair-styling salon, called *The Wig-Wam*, opened its doors to Crowchester's inquisitive male youth. Very much as Morgan had first outlined it, the shop front had been changed, though without big structural alteration, so that against a black, silver-starred back-drop, a number of studio portraits of the more handsome and couth of the pop stars was arranged, and between them a half-dozen wigs on stands with names under them:

Page Boy, *Cavalier*, *Roundhead*, *Plantagenet*, *Brummel*, and *Aztec*. Below the name was another card which read: *Styled by Morgan*.

Inside, the shop had been divided into two parts and reequipped so that everything was of the most modem: basins, chairs, hair-dryers, waiting seats, mirrors. The bank, after some reluctance, had agreed to an increase in Bristow's overdraft. Peggy Bristow, caught up by sudden enthusiasm, had advanced £500 out of her own savings.

Crowchester's young males came in, most out of plain curiosity, many of them, after being charged £2 for less than an hour's treatment, never to return. Even those who did not begrudge the cost returned at long intervals. But In Crowchester and its surrounding villages and countryside there was a surprisingly large number of young men, and word of the salon got about. It grew to be rather the thing to try it once: young men joked with each other about it and compared heads.

It was a hard first six months. Most of the old clients, such as they were, took themselves off grumpily up the hill to Cowland's. A few customers, considering themselves overcharged, refused to pay, and over these Morgan took a soft line – very different from what Bristow wanted to do. 'Let 'em go,' said Morgan. 'It's all advertisement.'

The style that first caught on was *Page Boy*. This was a bit of a surprise to Morgan himself because he'd thought it a bad name. But it happened that Lennie Heath was in a TV show in Norwich and chanced to come over and stopped in the shop and had a styling. After that seventy per cent of the young men who came in wanted a *Page Boy*. The salon became known farther afield: some said there wasn't another like it in East Anglia.

Bristow on the whole adapted himself well. He couldn't work up a really good manner, and this was a drawback; but he could shampoo really well and he learned to do a modified trim for clients who didn't want the whole treatment, Morgan was nice to everyone but he was never servile, and he never gave the impression of being effeminate. This was important. You went there for modem treatment for a man and you received it from a man – no nonsense about that.

Morgan took a little flat in the High Street. It was down a narrow alley and had a back door looking on to the river. This was ill-lit and was convenient for getting out of and into unobserved. Twice a week Peggy Bristow visited him there.

THREE

There had to be someone else in it, of course, and that was Carol Martin; because on these evenings Peggy was supposed to be out with her. It had been Carol Martin who had been drinking with her in the White Lion that evening when Ken Morgan had first come in and got talking with them. That had been the evening before the day when Morgan wandered into Bristow's shop. Peggy could see she was big time with him just meeting that one evening; but even so she never imagined he was what he was or that he would have the sauce to go into Walter's shop and con him into taking him in partnership.

Since then they had been on a slippery slope; but all things considered they both behaved with great discretion. It paid them to. If Bristow found out, the partnership would end on the spot. And this was to nobody's advantage. The money Peggy had invested, and the Bank's money, would be lost, for Walter hadn't a hope of continuing without Morgan. And then love affair would be lost. It was a sensual passionate affair that took Peggy's breath away, and was something that he appeared to feel deeply too; but there had been no talk of going away together. It was an experience such as she had never had before, lust, indulgence and exhaustion following each other as surely as dawn, noon and dusk. She looked no further than the next meeting. To run away with and marry a man seven years younger than yourself was not on the cards – particularly when he did not ask you. Besides, his job now was here in Crowchester.

At the end of six months Ken Morgan was almost as much of a mystery to her as he had been on the day they met. Although he had a fund of small talk, he spoke scarcely ever about himself, and when asked usually turned the point away. He'd been on the loose, as he put it, ever since he was seventeen, had been apprenticed to a London hairdresser and then gone to Brighton for a spell. These last two years he had been doing something else, but he was reticent as to what that something else was. She sometimes wondered if he'd been in prison – yet he didn't look the sort: he was too easy: you don't serve even a short sentence and come out looking as easy as he did. And he wasn't a natural law-breaker, she was sure. He always disliked it if his car wasn't on a meter or on a regular car park; he was almost finicky about PAYE returns; he had no use for sit-down strikes or student demonstrations. It was two sides to a mystifying character. But she was mad about him. When Walter brought him home to supper, as he did once a month when they were working out what his percentage of the takings was, her mouth went so dry she could hardly speak, and her flesh crept and quickened so that she was afraid Walter would notice something peculiar about her.

Unfortunately Crowchester is not quite grown out of the small town mentality, and, although Walter noticed nothing, Carol Martin went out with other women who asked where Peggy was, and the lies Carol told weren't always the most convincing, and so tales began to get around. They reached Bristow.

One night he said to Peggy: 'You got another man?'

Her heart changed gear. 'What ever do you mean?'

'You're not out with Carol Martin when you say you are. You go off on your own. She goes with the rest of the click. You're not there.'

'I'm not *always* there,' she said. 'I get *fed up* of them. Sometimes I go to the flicks. Why not? It's my own money. It's my own life.'

'That why you not let me get near you for the last five months? Going to the flicks? That satisfy you?'

'Oh ... That ... I've just grown fed up of it. We've been married ten years. It depends how you're made, doesn't it? Some folk go on, and some drop off. It's not *everything*.'

'You mean you've grown tired of me.'

'Not specially ... But like I say – it's ten years.'

'And who's the fancy man?'

'Leave off. You don't know what you're talking about.'

'Is he somebody I know?'

'I didn't say there was *anybody*! You're *dreaming*!'

'He'll be dreaming if I ever catch him.'

She stopped short, one hand on elbow, the other holding a cigarette. 'Look, Walter, be your age –'

'Oh, so *that's* it! Why, you –'

'Oh. I didn't mean *that*. You're O.K. that way. It's an *expression*, for heaven's sake, be your age. Grow up. It's the 'seventies. Marriage vows don't mean so much these days –'

'You dirty bitch, you –'

'I'm *not*!' She came up to him, arms folded, stared him out. 'You're fifteen years older man I am. I was twenty-four when I married you. You were thirty-nine. Can you tell me *one* minute in ten years when you've caught me looking at another man?'

'Not caught you, no –'

'Nor have I never! Never! Not until now –'

'Ah, so you admit it!'

'Admit! What d'you want me to admit? I've a friendship –'

'*Friendship*! That's a name for it! That's a new one –'

'If you don't like it, divorce me! Except that you've got no evidence! Nor never will! I've had a man friend take me to the movies once or twice. Think you can get a divorce for that? Eh? Just try it on!'

'Who is it?'

'Fellow I met in the pub. You don't know him. He comes from Norwich. Only here about twice a month on business. So you don't need to worry.'

'One of these reps, I suppose.'

'I tell you you don't need to *worry*!'

'Married?'

'Yes, as a matter of fact. What's that got to do with it?'

'Wife know?'

'That's his problem.'

'And you're my problem, eh?'

'I'm not anybody's problem, Walter. I live my own life. You've never bothered to ask what I did when I was *with* Carol. Think she's a saint? Why should you bother what I do when I'm *not* with her? I'm grown up. I take care of myself!'

FOUR

When she told Morgan he said: 'So we'll have to watch our step. It wouldn't do to break things up just now.'

'Oh, I know. It's a good job you've got this back entrance. It's easy. I go into the Waggoner for a gin and tonic, then I go to the Ladies, slip out through the outside door and down the alley. It's easy.'

'Think he's likely to follow you?'

'Never. You know what he's like after a day's work – has his supper and then sits in front of the telly. Doesn't matter what's on, he just sits there.'

'Jealousy might stir him up.'

'Even jealousy wouldn't get him into the Ladies.'

Morgan didn't laugh as she thought he would. 'It's other people then. We'd best lay off next week.'

'Why?'

'Full moon.'

'You getting tired of me, Ken?'

'Oh, yeh. Does it look like it?'

'Well, I just wondered.'

He was staring past her reflectively, through the cigarette smoke. 'We're just marking time now – breaking even. Another couple months it'll be coming about right. That's why we got to be wary now.'

'Anybody'd think,' she said stormily, 'that you'd gone into partnership with Walter because you wanted to, and net because you fancied me!'

'Oh, come off it, Peggy. I'd never've gone *near* the shop if it hadn't been for you. But I don't want a round of bloodletting now: you out on your ear, my job gone, and him losing the rest of his money? It stands to reason.'

'Yes,' she agreed, but without warmth. 'It stands to reason, doesn't it.'

So another two months passed. The *Page Boy* hair style grew more than ever prevalent among the young men of Crowchester, and with Christmas the corner was turned: the salon began to show a profit. In spite of protestations on both sides the love-affair cooled. It was his fault, and they both knew it.

Soon after Christmas a girl was assaulted in Crowmoor Woods. This was really a piece of open common land between Aston Ford and Crowchester, with clumps of trees and bushes and a few well-worn tracks across it. The main road between town and village took a four-mile curve; to walk across or cycle across the common was a little under two. The girl had been pushed off her bike and almost stripped of her clothes before she could get away. It was a dark night and she could not describe the man, except to say that he was of medium build, wore a grey mask and had long hair.

Later in January there was another attack. This time although the girl got away in the end she was badly bruised and spent a couple of days in hospital. The description of the man was the same.

Morgan's prophecy about the shop came true. After the rush of Christmas January saw no tailing off. They instituted a system of appointments. Morgan called them dates: it was a less formal word, and more manly. So men came from neighbouring towns and villages. Bristow engaged a boy assistant, an apprentice who was learning the trade and was able to do the odd jobs. The shop was too small to take more than three of them, and anyway Morgan was against it: with this sort of work it was the personal touch or nothing.

Unfortunately as trade boomed the relationship between the principals worsened. Bristow had nothing against Morgan and they worked well together, but his natural lack of small talk had degenerated into moroseness. Peggy still visited Morgan but now only about once a week, and then sometimes they would quarrel instead of making love. The most difficult evenings were the month ends when the profits were worked out after supper in the bungalow by the river. Walter was on speaking terms with Peggy but not much more; and the feeling between Peggy and Morgan was often so charged one way or the other that it was hard for them to have ordinary conversation.

Morgan had made few other friends in the town. On Sundays he went off in his Mini and was rarely seen. Peggy charged him with having a woman somewhere else, but this he denied with his usual ease of manner. It was this ease of manner which had first so entranced her and now so infuriated her. She was still in love with him but now there was an abrasion working between them. And the abrasive element was his growing indifference.

One Monday morning in the middle of February two policemen called at the salon. They came at nine, when the shop opened, and only the two hairdressers and the apprentice were there. The first 'date' was for nine-thirty. The two policemen introduced themselves as Detective Sergeant Taylor and Detective Constable Spinner. A woman had been attacked and raped the night before on the common land known as Crowmoor Woods.

'Oh, so he's made it at last,' said Morgan lightly.

The two policemen looked at him sharply. 'What d'you mean by that?' asked Detective Sergeant Taylor.

'What do I mean by what?'

'What you've just said.'

'Well, I suppose it's the same man who did the other attacks, isn't it? Both other times the girls got away. So I said he'd made it, didn't I?'

'Maybe. That's as maybe. We just wanted to ask a few questions, if you please.'

Bristow stared. 'What are we supposed to have done?'

'Nothing yourselves but . . . the victim's description of her attacker is just the same as the other ones: masked, middling build, with long hair. And they all described the hair style just the same. It's a style like that wig in the window, a style like yours, Mr Morgan. It's got a name, hasn't it?'

'Oh, *Page Boy*. Yes. That's the name I gave it. *Page Boy*. D'you mean this man –'

'This girl, the victim, knows the style and she knew the name

154

of it. *Page Boy* was what *she* said too. And yours is the only shop that trims hair, that sets men's hair that way. This shop,' Detective Sergeant Taylor glanced round; 'it's not like an ordinary barber's at all, is it. So it occurred to us you would know the names of your customers who – adopt this hair style.'

Morgan whistled and glanced at Bristow. 'That's a tall order, Sergeant. Unfortunately it's our most popular style. There must be forty or fifty men styled this way –'

'And you'd have the names?'

'Some of them. There's one coming in this morning: Ellis – Tom Ellis – from the garage. But he's a big tall chap. We're kept pretty busy, see, so people make dates. Where's our book, Walter?'

Bristow frowned and went to the rear of the shop. 'We've *some* names,' he said. He came back with the appointments book. 'You're the one who knows the styles, Ken.'

'Well, we'll take the names you have, if you please,' said Taylor. 'If you'd go through the book with us, Mr Morgan.'

But in spite of all the efforts of the police no arrests were made. It got about, the fact that the wanted man had a *Page Boy* cut, and this style rapidly went out of fashion in the salon. The nearest to it was *Aztec*, and Morgan spent some profitable hours converting one style into the other: this was easy because it meant cutting the hair instead of waiting for it to grow longer as would have been the case with *Cavalier*.

One evening in March Morgan had it out with Peggy. 'It won't do,' he said. 'Honest, it's too chancey with the light nights. It wasn't dark tonight, not properly dark, till eight.'

'I can come at nine. Trouble is you don't want me, do you?'

'That's not it. It's the risk . . .'

'Remember the risks we took to begin?'

'Yeh, I know. It's funny, that. You *take* risks at the start of something, like you don't realize how big they are. Then the longer you take them the bigger they look.'

'More to lose and not so much to gain, eh?'

'No, not just *that*. But we've been at it all winter, and Walter knows you go off somewhere. It's a miracle we've kept it quiet so long.'

'Well, it's just as you please. I'm not one to push myself where I'm not wanted.'

Morgan thoughtfully eyed Peggy's taut back. 'I didn't say *altogether*. We'll *make* times.'

'What times?'

'We'll fix some. But they'll have to be special ones. And maybe not here.'

'Then where?' she flared. 'Crowmoor Woods?'

He grinned. 'I don't fancy myself at that. There's too much around that's easy, to try to get it the hard way.'

'You insulting bastard –'

'Now, Peggy, ease off. Ease off, I say. Your think-box isn't working, so I'm trying to think for us both. You got any relations?'

'Well, what d'you think? Think I grew on a tree?'

'All right, all right. Well, I was wondering if maybe when the weather gets warmer you couldn't get off for a day and visit your Aunt Elsie or someone. Maybe we could join up one Sunday.'

'You mean that, Ken?'

'Yeh. But it would have to be well away from here. London maybe. We'll make a plan next month when the spring comes.'

'O.K.,' she said. 'O.K. I'll go along with that. If you really mean it.'

He was looking at himself in the mirror. 'I think maybe *I* need a change of hair style. I was dreaming up something a bit different the other night. I think I'll call it *Pharaoh*, More off the face.'

'Who's going to do it for you?' she said mockingly, 'Like me to try?'

But over this he was unsmiling. 'There's a pal in London. I might nip down one Sunday and persuade him to do it out of hours.'

FIVE

But his hair stayed the same. Peggy thought he was maybe too busy with his out-of-town woman. She had gradually drifted back to her evenings with Carol Martin, but Walter did not ask and she did not tell him. She made giggling excuses about the light nights to Carol and did not care whether she was believed or not. The shop prospered. Bristow bought a new Mini in place of his old Ford. Morgan bought a new Mini in place of his old Mini. Part of the bank overdraft was repaid. Morgan and Peggy made an arrangement that she should go and see her sister in Oxford during a week-end in early April, and that he should join her in London. It never came off.

On the Tuesday before, Morgan went as usual to supper at the Bristows' bungalow in Parkers Lane. Peggy wasn't much of a cook and nine-tenths of her food came out of tins, but tonight she had made a stew and then they had a trifle and cheese. Morgan had bought a bottle of wine, but his tongue was the only one it appeared to unlock. He chattered away cheerfully all through the meal, taking no heed of Bristow's silences. He thought they ought to sell more in the shop the way London hairdressers did. Of course it wasn't just razor blades and hair cream like they did at present. He meant the better after-shaves, skin-tonics, hair dyes and a few masculine scents.

'It's only what every gent used in the 18th century,' he said. 'It won't be long before men take to make-up either. It's all part of dress.'

Bristow looked at his partner's frilled purple shirt. 'We're not going to be able to tell one sex from the other soon.'

'Oh yes we will. You bet we will! But not by one sex being *duller* than the other. *That's* the mistake. It isn't true, you know, and the lads are realizing it isn't true.'

'When I was your age,' Bristow began brooding, 'we were still on rations after the end of the war. Too glad to get food to worry about all this –'

There was a ring at the doorbell, and Peggy got up from the table and went. She came back with a peculiar expression on her face.

'It's the police.'

Detective Sergeant Taylor and Detective Constable Spinner were shown in.

Taylor said: 'Afraid we're interrupting your supper.'

'Well, sit down,' said Morgan, taking on the duties of host. 'Get you a drink?'

'No, thank you. We came to ask you a few more questions.'

'Questions?' said Peggy startled. 'What about? The shop's all right, isn't it?'

'Yes, Mrs Bristow, the shop's all right. But we called in once before asking a few questions. Perhaps you weren't told.'

'Told? Told what? I wasn't told anything. What's wrong?'

'These girls that were attacked in Crowmoor Woods,' said Morgan. 'The man that did it had a long hair style. The police were inquiring for names at our shop of customers who had the *Page Boy* style, that's all. That's all, isn't it, Sergeant? Any joy, yet?'

'Another girl was attacked on Sunday,' said Taylor.

'Oh?' said Morgan. 'Didn't know that. It wasn't in the papers, was it?'

'No, we were able to keep it quiet.'

'Did he get her this time or did she get away?'

'This girl – this young woman – put up more of a struggle and was able to give us a better description. We've kept it quiet while we made inquiries. We've visited nearly everyone with this style of long hair in Crowchester.'

'Ah,' said Morgan. 'And now you've come to me, eh?'

'That's right, Mr Morgan, in a manner of speaking.'

'I was away all Sunday. Didn't get back to Crowchester until after midnight. So it can't have been me.'

'This time we don't need to bother about alibis. This girl – they had a real fight – she says she scratched the man all down one arm, elbow to wrist, she says. So this time it's more a question of finding a man with scratch marks.'

'I see,' said Morgan thoughtfully. 'And who've you been to? It must have meant quite a lot of calls, all those lads with long hair.'

'Yes, it has.'

'And you haven't found him yet?'

'Not yet.'

Morgan glanced at Peggy and then at the policemen. 'So what you want –'

'If you'd mind taking off your coat, Mr Morgan, and rolling up your sleeves.'

Morgan sighed and shrugged. 'Oh, well, if you feel like that. But I think it's a bit thick. I mean me, trying to attack girls ...'

He took off his coat, slowly took out his enormous cuff-links and as slowly rolled up the purple big-cuffed sleeves of his shirt. His arms were rather thin and pale but there were no scratches on them.

'Satisfied?'

Taylor stepped back. 'Yes, thank you.'

'So now maybe we can get on with our supper, eh?'

'Of course.'

'I think you might have come at a better time, anyway.'

'We're making an intensive search. I'm afraid it's not always possible to pick on times.'

'Well, I wish you luck,' said Morgan. 'It beats me why they do these things. I mean, it isn't as if women were *hard* to get –'

'Oh, Mr Bristow,' said Sergeant Taylor, as Bristow was about to go back to the table.

'Yes?'

'While we're here, might we just look at your forearms? It's just a question of checking up.'

'I've not got long hair.'

'No, we know. It's just trying to see all possibilities. Just checking up.'

'What are you *talking* about?' said Peggy. '*Look* at his hair – it's going thin on the top! You must be crazy!'

'We have to try to check every possibility, Mrs Bristow. Now, sir, if you wouldn't mind ...'

Bristow had gone very white and he made no move at all. Sergeant Taylor gently took his coat sleeve. Bristow pulled away but Taylor followed him. Bristow was wearing a short-sleeved shirt and the coat slid easily up. All the way down his forearm were long red scratches.

There was a gasp from Peggy. Bristow stood there swaying.

'Well!' said Morgan. 'Stone the crows! I thought that wig in the window looked a bit messed up on Monday!'

Bristow put his hands to his face and sat down in the nearest chair.

'We shall have to ask you to come with us to the station,' said Taylor.

'Why, what's he *done*?' shouted Peggy. 'What are you *saying* he's done? What's he done?'

'Well, Mrs Bristow, I think we have to work that out, don't we?'

'Now, now, Peggy, take it easy,' said Morgan. 'I reckon there's been some mistake. It'll all be cleared up in no time.'

'I must ask you to come to the station,' said Taylor to Bristow. 'You can make a statement then.'

'It's ridiculous!' said Peggy. 'Downright ridiculous. Where did you get those scratches, Walter? Where'd you *get* them?'

Bristow made no move. Then he slowly withdrew his hands from his face and stood up. Without anybody speaking he went slowly to the door and, with Sergeant Taylor beside him, went out. He did not once look back.

Constable Spinner said: 'Would you like to come along, Mrs Bristow?'

'I'll bring her in my car,' said Morgan. 'You go ahead. I've got my car outside.'

Spinner went out and Peggy and Morgan stood there in silence listening to the shutting of the front door, the whirr of a self-starter and then the drone of a car pulling away.

'Stone the crows,' said Morgan again. 'I'd never've believed it of him! Poor old Walter! D'you want to go down, Peggy? D'you want to go down to the station. It'll look better. I'd never've believed it of him.'

He put his hand on her shoulder but she drew sharply away. 'Don't *touch* me!'

'Why, what's wrong with me? I wasn't in it!'

She was glaring at him. 'I'll go down, but not with you. Not ever again with you. I'll go in our own car! And you can clear out!'

'What d'you mean? Don't take it out on me! What've I done?'

'It's *our* fault! D'you know that? *Our* fault! *Our* fault! *Our* fault! *Our* fault! Get out of here and out of the shop tomorrow! Get out of this town! I never want to see you again!'

He stared at her, and realized that at least she couldn't be reasoned with tonight. He picked up his jacket and put it on, ran a hand through his hair and went to the front door, which she was holding open.

'I suppose you realize that —'

'Get out!' she shouted at him. 'Get out! Get out!'

The Old Boys

Kendrick hadn't been near his old school for upwards of fifteen years, but an appointment in the town and an hour or so to spare before the next train out gave him the chance to walk up and look around.

When he turned in at the gates he expected to see the place swarming with boys, and it took a minute or two to work out the date and to realize that the school had broken up probably yesterday or the day before. You get out of the habit of remembering. There were only two figures in sight and they were gardeners mowing the headmaster's lawn; and there was a solitary lop-eared dog chasing the pigeons around Newcome's Tower.

But it didn't matter much; perhaps it was for the best, Kendrick thought, as he walked in past the porter's lodge and the chapel. Alone like this, without today's hefty youths milling all round, it was easier to think back to what it had been like long ago.

New Field, for instance, where the First XI cricket was played; there didn't seem a blade of grass different. He remembered the one time he'd made a decent score: forty-seven against Stanmore – then that fool Smithfield had called him for a short run. The only occasion he'd ever been near fifty. The number of times he'd raced round the edge of this field, too, nearly late for locking up – there was fire and brimstone if you ran *across* it.

Up there was the window of his last study-dormitory. When it was hot in the evening you could just squeeze yourself out on that tiny balcony and be full in the sun. The setting sun struck fire from the window today; he wondered who inhabited that room now, whether the iron bed still had one leg shorter than the other three so that you had to wedge it so as not to rock in your sleep. And

Sellers Quad; the dismal parades there as a new boy; the Stinks Lab on the other side.

The formative years, they were supposed to be. Well, well, he didn't know whether they'd formed him much. He'd gone along, free-wheeling most of the time, just getting by, enjoying himself on the whole; but he'd had a lot more fun since. It was piffle to talk about.

The bright shafts of sunlight were casting long shadows between the sham Gothic arches, and it looked to him as he was about to turn away that there was someone standing at the corner of Small Quad. He veered over that way and saw there was.

The odd thing was that the figure had something quite familiar about it, but he scoffed at himself for thinking so. After all these years you didn't suddenly bump into a man who'd ... Well, it certainly wasn't one of the boys, anyway. A master probably. Out of the sun it was easier to see.

Rather a big chap in a long dark overcoat and a green felt hat, with a pipe in the corner of his mouth. It seemed nearly like two lifetimes since those days, and as he got closer Kendrick still told himself he was wildly mistaken. Yet why do some men grow up and broaden and go grey and still look exactly unmistakably the same as they do at eighteen? Perhaps it's not so much that they grow middle-aged as that they have been middle-aged all the time. Clamp was such a one. He ...

The man in the dark coat finished stubbing a finger into his pipe and moved off; his figure disappeared suddenly in the shadow of the cloister and might never have been there. Kendrick frowned. Then he saw it again.

'Clamp,' he called. 'I say, Clamp!'

The figure stopped and turned. It took its pipe out of its mouth and stared.

'It *is* Clamp!' Kendrick exclaimed as he came up. 'Well, my saints, what a chance!'

Clamp narrowed his eyes. 'I'm sorry, I don't think I know you, sir ...' He hesitated. 'Or it can't be ... is it Kendrick?'

'Right first time,' Kendrick laughed, and they shook hands.

Clamp's hand was cold and clammy and had no grip at all. He had begun to smile but the smile had withered on his face.

Kendrick said: 'I don't know what the chances are against this happening! What on earth brings you here this afternoon of all afternoons? I haven't seen you since I left school, and I've only been back here twice in all these years!'

'It's not perhaps such a coincidence,' Clamp said stiffly. 'I come quite often. I live only a mile or two away. Perhaps you didn't know that, what?'

'I certainly didn't. I live in London. I'm carrying on my father's firm – estate agency, you know – and had to come down here about the Compton estate which we're handling ... And you? You're fatter, of course, but I'd know you anywhere. You haven't really changed.'

They began to walk together along the cloister and then out of Small Quad and beside the Second XV football pitch. Kendrick had not been a close friend of Clamp at school – a rather intense, humourless type – but after the creeping melancholy of his own company he was delighted to find someone of his own year to talk to. He ignored Clamp's cold manner and tight-drawn mouth and chatted on about Staggers their housemaster who had died ten years ago, about Mortimer who had done so well in oil, about Press and Harris who had been killed in an accident and Valentine who had made the England rugger team and now was apparently in some dead-end job in Hove.

The sun had gone and the twilight was shorter than usual because of the heavy clouds blowing up from the west. Clamp, Kendrick thought, might have been a bit middle-aged at eighteen; it was equally true that at forty-six he didn't seem to have lost his schoolboy words and mannerisms. He was behaving now like a sulky boy. Or perhaps it was more than that. His knuckles were quite white where they gripped his pipe.

'Is something the matter, Clamp? Have I said something out of place?'

Clamp stopped. 'Mean to say you don't remember?'

'Remember? What?'

'The last days of our last term, Kendrick. Before we both left the old school for good.'

Kendrick stared. 'Not a thing. Should I?'

'Mean to say you don't remember about Veronica Fry?'

Kendrick's greying eyebrows came together in a frown. 'Veronica Fry? I remember the name . . . But of course! She was that glamorous town piece we were both taking out that last term!'

'She was the chemist's daughter,' said Clamp coldly.

'Dear little Veronica. How that brings back memories!' Kendrick sighed. 'Well, well. Oh, yes, of course, we had words about her, didn't we.'

'We did. You called me a tin-pot Romeo and a dirty skunk!'

'Did I?' Kendrick chuckled. 'I say, that was going it a bit, wasn't it? Tell me about her, I remember the row but forget the exact details.'

'You said I was behaving badly towards her by not inviting her to that Breaking-up Concert on the Wednesday. You said I'd been making up to her all term and was then just going to walk out of her life. You said I must be ashamed of her and, just to prove *you* were not, you were going to invite her to the concert yourself!'

'Ah, yes. Go on, go on. I remember I read you a bit of a lecture, didn't I.'

'If calling me a dirty skunk can be called a lecture. Don't you remember the rest?'

'No.'

'I said: "All right, if you think I'm a dirty skunk, we'll meet tomorrow morning, behind the chapel, and I'll teach you which of us is the skunk!" '

'Yes, I do remember now. Funny to look back . . .'

Clamp's story had indeed brought back many memories. Discipline had been fairly lax under Staggers just before he retired, and as prefects that last term or so they'd been able to do much as they liked. Of course it had all been painfully innocent and very respectable. 'Taking out a town girl' hardly described the meetings in a bun shop, the stolen half-hours on the river, the rivalries and pairings that took place at the School Dance which was given every

December in the Town Hall But at the time it had all been breathless and dashing.

'And what happened?' Kendrick said.

'When?'

'About our fight behind the chapel?'

'You never turned up.'

Kendrick roared with laughter. 'Of *course*! I remember now! Did you ask Veronica to the concert after all?'

'Yes.'

'I didn't go. I suppose it was a bit of a trick, old man, really. You see, I never had the least intention of asking her to the concert, or anywhere else – not because I was ashamed to, or thought you were, but because I'd found another girl and wanted to take her to the flicks instead. Veronica was dead set on going to the concert, and I was afraid I'd be let in for taking her if I didn't goad you into smart action. It was obvious you were getting a bit tired of her, too, and I had to make you keener again. Well, there's nothing like a little rivalry ... I find it in my profession constantly; two people after the same house, as it were; it makes all the difference. I wonder you didn't tumble to it because if I'd *really* wanted to take her I shouldn't have lectured you on doing the straight thing!'

'And the next morning?'

'I remember did set my alarm for six. I was quite willing to punch your nose if you wanted me to. But lying in bed I thought, what price glory! I'm going to have another hour in bed. And I did!'

'You never turned up!'

They had crossed beside the cricket pitch and now stood in the shadow of the school chapel. Clamp stopped. 'You never turned up,' he said again.

'Well, there was another reason. This other girl I'd dated – I *wish* I could remember her name – Mary something, was it? – she'd quite caught my fancy, and I was meeting her again that last afternoon before I caught the train home. And I thought: what a fool I'll look turning up for my appointment with a black eye and a swollen nose. I was rather vain about my looks in those days!'

Clamp wrenched his arm free. 'You never turned up and you never explained; I never saw you again from that day to this. That's what *I* call the act of an absolute rotter – a dirty skunk, in fact!'

'Oh, come off it, man,' Kendrick exclaimed, irritated himself now. 'Keep the thing in proportion. It all happened *twenty-eight* years ago. That's more than a quarter of a century. I'm prepared to admit that you've a marvellous memory but –'

'My memory's quite a normal one. It shows what a shallow cad you are that you should have forgotten all about it!'

They had come to a stop again in the shadow of the trees. Kendrick shrugged his shoulders. 'Well, really, if that's the way you feel I think it's time you went to see a psychiatrist. I'm really sorry for you. I never heard a man talk such damned rot in my life, and I'll wish you good afternoon.'

'Wait!' Clamp caught his arm as he turned. 'It may be a quarter of a century since I issued that challenge but it still stands! And you've insulted me afresh over and over again this afternoon. Here we are, in just the spot behind the chapel, where we agreed to meet. Now put up your hands!'

Kendrick stared at the other in incredulous astonishment. It was now dusk. There was no one about, and the gardeners if they were still working were right round the other side of the school.

'I'll do nothing of the sort. Take your hands off me, you silly man!'

Clamp's answer was to release him and give him a hearty painful thump on the ear. Kendrick saw red. He swung round-arm with his fist and caught Clamp on the side of the jaw. Clamp hit him in the eye.

They closed, two middle-aged portly men, out of temper and out of condition. They grappled like elderly dinosaurs, broke apart, came together again; then they fell into the bushes with an enormous thump and flurry and crackle of leaves.

In half a minute the years had rolled away; Clamp had Kendrick by the arm and was trying to twist it; but Kendrick heaved Clamp off him and fell on him as he tried to rise. Stertorously they rolled over.

Then as they struggled another figure appeared from round the corner of the chapel. Although the school had broken up yesterday the Head had not yet discarded his gown.

They both saw him at the same moment. They both stopped fighting. Then Clamp muttered '*cave!*'

They both scrambled up to go. The Head had not seen them yet but he was coming in their direction. Kendrick moved to duck towards the chapel alley, but Clamp caught his arm. 'No, that way's blocked! Follow me.'

Clutching battered hats, they crawled panting through the shrubbery towards a five-foot brick wall.

'Who's that!' said a voice behind them. 'Who's there?'

'Quick, this leads into Goodwin's Lane,' Clamp whispered. 'Then we're safe enough . . .'

He tried to lead the way but the wall was too much for him. His brown suède shoes scrabbled ineffectually at the mortar.

'Here, let me.' Kendrick knelt down and gave Clamp a hoist. Clamp arrived at the top of the wall, balancing precariously like Humpty-Dumpty; he lent a hand, and with its help Kendrick joined him. A black chasm yawned.

'It's a bit farther this side,' Clamp panted.

But the Head was pushing his way through the shrubbery. They jumped, landed on all fours in muddy earth. Clamp managed to get up first. Again he gave Kendrick a hand, and then they both made off like thieves towards the lights at the end of the lane.

After a minute Kendrick said: 'I don't think he was near enough to recognize us.'

'Not you, certainly,' gasped Clamp. 'But I've met him two or three times. It would be damned undignified to be caught out like that!'

As Kendrick remembered this lane it led to another which ran beside a stream into the little town; but when they came out he stared about in surprise. A town street brightly lighted; the stream had disappeared; modern villas lined the road, and then shops.

'It's a bit different since our time, Kendrick,' Clamp said. 'The school's practically surrounded these days.'

They stood there regaining their breath and brushing themselves down. Kendrick's ear felt too big for his face, and Clamp's nose had been bleeding. After a minute Clamp hesitantly raised a hand and began to brush down the back of Kendrick's coat. They were thick with dirt and leaves.

'What time's your train, Kendrick?'

'Six-forty. If I turn left here it'll lead to the station, won't it?'

'Yes. I'm coming that way, too.'

They walked off together in silence. Clamp dabbed his nose. He grunted and hesitated once or twice and then said: 'Don't know what got into me just now, Kendrick. Seeing you after all this time, it just bubbled up. And the way you treated it, as if it was a joke.'

'Well,' said Kendrick, his good humour never far away, 'I must say I didn't come back expecting anything like this!'

They walked down the street into the town.

'I remember this part now,' Kendrick said. 'That's the old bookshop, isn't it. And the place where they sold those hot buns.'

'They were first-class, weren't they.'

'Yes, Clamp, it all comes back.'

'Remember what a row there was that time Johnson was caught smoking in the White Hart?'

'Good Lord, yes.'

Clamp brushed a last bit of moss from his lapel. 'Maybe you've time for a cup of tea, Kendrick? What time does your train go? Oh, yes, you've told me. Well, there's half an hour yet.'

They had stopped outside a tea-shop.

'Well, I really should be getting along.' All this horseplay had touched up the rheumatism in Kendrick's shoulder. 'I can get something at the station.'

'Nonsense; I owe you that, at least. I've got to go in here and a cup of tea will do us both good. Come along, my dear fellow. I insist.'

Kendrick hesitated and then gave way. At the door of the shop they each waited for the other. 'No,' said Clamp heartily. 'You first, Kendrick; you're my senior by three months.'

They went in. The shop was crowded, but Clamp led the way

clumsily but unerringly to a corner table at which sat a plump, grey-haired lady.

'Darling,' he said nervously, 'sorry I'm late. I bumped into an old school-friend of mine up there. Name of Henry Kendrick. Wonder if you'll remember him. Kendrick, may I introduce you to my wife. Perhaps you'll remember her better under her maiden name of Veronica Fry.'

I Had Known Sam Taylor For Years

I had known Sam Taylor for years but never closely, for we really had nothing whatever in common. As a member of my club, he was often in and out, and we spoke sometimes; but really we belonged to different sets. D'you know. He was a journalist, partly free-lance, and therefore led a precarious life, sometimes in the money, when he spent lavishly and drank himself stupid, more often on the verge of being broke, when he wasn't above touching his friends. Hail-fellow-well-met. I never actually disliked him because he was too unimportant to rouse any strong feeling either way, and at his best he was boisterously witty. He played snooker well, usually with a long cigar wobbling between his yellow teeth; and I do not play at all. He couldn't stand bridge and this is my great recreation. By profession I am a solicitor, and I am known in the art world.

So. Until one day I was at lunch, concentrating on a particularly succulent fillet steak, which had followed a *sole veronique*, which had followed a smoked trout, when the scrape of a chair beside me and the careless slumping manner in which the newcomer sat down gave me an inkling that Sam Taylor had come to take a place at the table.

He was about forty-eight at the time but looked considerably older. He was a rickety figure of a man, very dark, with hair streaked across to hide a bald patch, a thin red face, handsome twinkling black eyes and a thin bulbous nose which a friend once compared – not unjustly – to the end of a garden thermometer.

'Oh, Wilfred, just the laddie I wanted to see.' That was the way he talked. What sort of Queen's English he wrote I never attempted to imagine.

I chewed for a moment, savouring the flavours, before answering.

His tone, the extra friendliness, suggested that he might want to ask for a loan, but even he would not essay it at the luncheon table. And anyway he knew better from past experience than to ask me.

'Well, you see me,' I said, 'so your day is made.'

'Very well expressed.' He chuckled and studied the menu. 'Very well expressed. And it could be true. Depends all on your goodwill, Wilfred. I know you're a generous character. Wouldn't refuse a friend. I'll have a ham omelette and chip potatoes and some peas, Alice, dear.'

I winced at his free and easy manner with the waitress and at the nature of his order – what *was* the good of pressing for improved catering standards for the club when there were people like him about – and my depression deepened when the wine waitress came and he asked for a large whisky and soda.

'I have been known to refuse even an enemy,' I said.

'Ah, well, it's that hard legal side, that big legal brain at work. That's not what I want of you, Wilfred, dear boy. It's another sort of favour altogether. And I come to you because you're the best man we've got in the Hanover Club – on art and furniture and things that fetch money these days in the salerooms.'

I sipped my Chambolle Musigny and said nothing. I wondered if this were a cunning attempt to please me, for I am only an amateur in the world of the big salerooms, and we had two or three professionals in the club. Nevertheless, I *am* well informed, and enjoy nothing better than to use my knowledge, and he knew it.

His whisky came and he took a gulp. 'You know I've never owned anything worth a tinker's cuss: I live in a modern flat on my tod, and when the cash comes in it's the basic necessities of life that claim it. But an old aunt has just rattled off in Hendon and left me a house full of stuff. I don't think there's anything much there, but you never know these days, and I wouldn't want to make a bloomer and let something good slip through my fingers,'

I finished my steak and asked for the Stilton. 'What have you done about it?'

'Well, I've had the local people in, and they've itemized and listed everything. I've got the inventory in my pocket if you'd like to see it.'

'No, thank you.'

'They say it's pretty well all poor stuff and had best go to the local salerooms. They think it will fetch about six or seven hundred pounds in *total*. But there's one thing here.' He fished a sheaf of paper out of his pocket. 'They say: "Two French watercolours of the Seine by Walter Parr, dated and signed 1912. Could be valuable and suggest expert valuation." D'you know him, Wilfred?'

'No . . . I know a painter called *Carr*, but I don't believe he ever left England. At least, one has never seen . . .'

He began to tuck into his omelette. 'What I wondered, laddie, was whether you'd care to come up and have a decco at these pictures for yourself?'

The Stilton came, and this gave me an opportunity to consider the matter while I dug into it. There was absolutely no reason why I should give this shambling man the free benefit of my wide experience, and the obvious response was a curt refusal. But I always greatly enjoy looking around old houses and old furniture. It has always been my hope that one of these days I shall make a real discovery, something that will startle the world and profit myself; but so far it has never occurred. Once in my early days as a collector I had bought a fine tea set of Coalport china with 1754 stamped on the bottom of each piece, and bought it cheap, only to discover that the 1754 stamp proved it had been made after 1880. Once in a shop in York I had unearthed a Cox watercolour which fetched in the auction rooms six times what I gave. Once I had found a Charles II pewter mug in an old cottage in Kent. But these and a half dozen other minor successes and failures only whetted the appetite for more.

'You can get a man from Sotheby's,' I said. 'They'll send a man up with pleasure.'

'I never trust these people. Before you –'

'They're just as trustworthy as I am, and they know far more about it.'

'Well, why don't you come and have a decco first? It's only a taxi ride.'

'I'm a busy man. I have very little free time.'

'Oh, come off it, Wilfred. You're always in the salerooms. I'd trust you to go over this stuff and pick out anything valuable before I would any of these pros.'

'Flattery will do nothing for you,' I said. And in fact I was not at all flattered by his obvious wish to obtain my advice. It was too transparent altogether. Yet he *was* a member of my club, and he *was* the sort of rash, slapdash fool to let something good slip through his fingers for the sake of making sure. And Walter *Parr*? One had never heard of the man. These local valuers were noted for their carelessness. But if it were *Carr*, would that be much of a find? I doubted if Sotheby's would even be interested . . .

'What else is there in the house?' I said.

'A *lot* of furniture. Some rugs. A few more pictures. It's a shambles, laddie. The old girl was eighty, and I doubt if she had had a good turn out for fifty years.'

He gobbled through his lunch, so that we finished together. Downstairs he bought me a vintage port and showed me the inventory. One could tell *nothing* from it.

When I handed it back to him he said: 'Doing anything this afternoon?'

I stared at him. 'My dear fellow, I am not a free-lance like you!'

'Well, I only thought. It would take no time in a taxi. Buzz up and buzz back. Actually, I promised these people a reply in the morning. They want to take the lot off my hands.'

It happened that though I was expected back at my office I had no appointments, except one that I wished to avoid. I had intended to be 'not in' when my client called – since I knew he came only laden with trivial time-wasting complaints. It might be more effective if I were really out, called away on important business. I stared at Taylor, who just then was exchanging foolish badinage with another member who came to lean over his chair. When they had finished he turned and grinned at me and dropped a half-inch of ash from his cigar on to my shoe.

'How about it, Wilfred? Be a sport?'

'An hour,' I said. 'At the most I can spare one hour.'

TWO

In the event it took far longer, as I suppose I should have anticipated. But indeed all my reckonings were confounded right at the outset by Sam Taylor's behaviour.

He flagged down a taxi outside the club, muttered something to the driver and we both climbed in. I am a man of considerable size, and taxis these days are not so accommodating as they were. We jerked casually through a dozen traffic lights, Taylor expatiating unnecessarily on my good fellowship; and then suddenly the cab stopped on the corner of a street and Taylor opened the door.

'Are we there?' I said. 'You told me –'

'No, but I thought it a *bonne idée* if we stopped *en route*. Can't do this sort of thing unless one does it *en prince*.'

I started to protest, but he was pulling me to get out, and I saw that we were at a public house half-way up Tottenham Court Road. We could not have been moving five minutes, and I was very irritable at being led into a public bar, where Sam ordered himself a double whisky and prevailed on me to take a brandy.

I accepted it in injured silence and thought about my wife while Sam joked with the barmaid and consumed his whisky in two swallows and ordered another one and drank that before I had properly inhaled the fumes of the brandy. I suspected that he did not take drink for the pleasure of drinking but merely for its ultimate effect on him.

Eventually we returned to the waiting taxi and were off again. When we started Taylor insisted on telling me some rambling story of his journalistic life, and I regretted more than ever the foolish impulse which had persuaded me to come. Suddenly the taxi stopped again, and with sinking heart I saw another public house offering its synthetic welcome. To my protests Sam returned that 'they' would soon be closed, and it was essential to lay in a good foundation before the desert of the afternoon began. So in we went again and the pattern was precisely repeated: he taking two double whiskies to my one brandy.

I am not familiar with all the licensing hours of north London, but it fell out, by what means I do not know, that we found three more public houses open, proceeding in a series of erratic moves, until we reached Hendon. My friend Sam had a singular ability to take drink without apparent effect; but I must confess that on coming out of the last public house we both stumbled over a step that was not there.

And so at last the quarry we had all this time been seeking. A tall semi-detached, built, I would have thought, about the turn of the century, and grey with dirt and time. Sam took a little while to find the key, and afterwards a little while to find the keyhole, and then we were into a grey ill-lit blue-tiled hall.

It was worse than I thought, worse than I had ever expected. There are few periods in furniture when some good things are not made; no periods in art, however enervated, when some good pictures are not painted. It is like claret in the off years. But of course one has to allow for the perverse ingenuity of the purchaser. All the stuff in this house had been bought, I would have thought, between 1912 and 1918, and for the most part it had clearly been bought for its ornateness and its cheapness. It was gimcrack: bamboo and deal and fumed oak and plywood. The one or two really solid pieces were monstrous in their size and ugliness. As for the paintings, they were all dark brooding landscapes of Highland cattle, painted by nonentities, or indifferent etchings of some semi-classical subject, spotted with mildew and badly framed. I quickly concluded that Sam Taylor's aunt must have had many affinities with Sam Taylor.

We trudged, somewhat stertorously, up all three flights of stairs and solemnly trudged down again.

'These two pictures,' I said, breathing my displeasure. 'Watercolours of the Seine. Where would those be?'

'Ah,' he said, 'they're locked away! I was leaving those until the end! Here! In here! I'll show you!'

He went into the dining-room and unlocked a cupboard and drew out two pictures wrapped in brown paper. I unwrapped them and stared. They were *exactly* as described, watercolours of Paris bridges across the Seine, signed Walter Parr and dated. And just as clearly Walter Parr was some amateur, perhaps a cousin of the purchaser, who had set up his easel and made two facsimiles of the scene without a trace of talent or even the amateur originality of the primitives. The pictures were worth the value of the frames and nothing more.

I looked up and shook my head at Sam's thin red face, which was irritatingly close to mine. I stood up to get away from his alcoholic breath.

'Worthless. There's *nothing* in the house at all. You'll be lucky to get the estimate that these people made. Nothing! Absolutely nothing.'

He looked woebegone and slightly tearful, but perhaps it was only the whisky coming out.

'There's these prints,' he said. 'Aren't they any good, laddie?'

'*Nothing's* any good. I am afraid your aunt was the wrong sort of buyer. We had better leave now. I must get back to my office.' Although to tell the truth the five brandies I had willy-nilly taken scarcely disposed me for work.

I pulled over the stack of prints he indicated in the corner and took out a small painting about the size of a piece of quarto paper, badly framed in green velvet and gilt, and was going to thrust it back when some quality in it took my attention and I carried it nearer the light.

It was an oil painting – not, I thought, a very good one – and it showed a woman in panniers and a white bonnet taking a step in a dance in company with a wigged gentleman in knee-breeches and a sort of frock-coat. It was just the kind of artificial composition that some run-of-the mill Victorian or Edwardian artist would choose to make up when he lacked the inspiration or talent to do anything original. Find a couple of models and put them in fancy dress. Or perhaps not even bother with models: copy the dresses from some book on 18th century manners.

But at least it was an oil painting different from all the Highland cows and the lowering sunsets; and in spite of the stiff postures of the two people, the brush strokes were firm and the colours well chosen.

I said: 'Do you mind if I take this out of its frame?'

'Not a bit, old boy; do anything you like. Why, d'you think you've found something?'

'No, nothing at all!' I snapped, turning the picture over. The back paper was already torn, and it was not difficult to lift another six inches away. The painting was on board, and the board was clearly antique.

'What is it, laddie?' he asked.

'It appears to be Italian or French,' I said. 'It is probably a copy, but at least it is genuinely old. It might be a copy of a painting by Tiepolo or – or Fragonard. Something of that nature. This cheap frame makes it look worse than it is. And it needs cleaning, of course.'

'D'you mean it might be worth a bit of the old folding?'

'It might. Yes, just possibly it might. But I am not in a position to tell you. Anyway, it is the only thing even worth *looking* at in the house. I despaired of there being anything at all.'

'So what do we do with it? Eh? What do we do with it now?'

'Mr Ewart of Sotheby's would be able to tell us more. I take it you would sell it, if it were worth putting up in the saleroom?'

'Ra-ther.' He looked around like a dog casting for a scent. 'There's no liquor in this house. Wilfred, that's the trouble. I'm thirsty as hell. My tongue's too big for my mouth and I want to celebrate.'

'It's far too early to *celebrate*!' I said testily. 'And far too early to drink again. What *is* the time? Four o'clock. What do you want to do with the picture now? You can lock it up, and throw away those two so-called watercolours of the Seine. If –'

'Sotheby's open now?'

'Oh yes, of course. But –'

'How about us getting a taxi and going down straight away? No time like the present. Your man likely to be there?'

'Quite probably. It is as you wish.' To tell the truth I was not at all loth to accept his suggestion, for I was interested myself and would be glad to learn whether my interest was in any way justified.

So we wrapped up the picture in some old sheets of brown paper marked Colindale Laundry and went out and signally failed to find a taxi. So eventually we took the tube to Tottenham Court Road and caught a taxi there, Taylor holding the small parcel as nervously as if it were the crown jewels. I felt apprehensive lest he should be in for a terrible disappointment.

At Sotheby's Mr Ewart was in, and he greeted me with the courtesy of a well-known client and took us up to his room. He unwrapped the parcel and stood the painting on an easel where the daylight fell strongly on it. Sam Taylor bit his nails and I, I believe, pulled at my lip, attempting to look more judicial than I felt.

'Hm,' said Mr Ewart, and then to Sam: 'D'you mind if I take it out of its frame?'

Sam was by now accustomed to this question, but Mr Ewart was far more ruthless than I had been; in a few moments the board was in his hands.

'Yes,' he said. 'Yes, I thought it was Italian. Look, sir, it's signed Longhi in the corner. You couldn't see it for the frame. One can't be absolutely certain without making the necessary tests. But it looks quite genuine to me.'

'Well,' I said, swelling a little. 'That's very satisfactory. I did feel myself that it was a genuine work. Now –'

'Longhi?' said Sam. 'Who the hell's Longhi?'

Mr Ewart looked very pained. 'An Italian, Mr Taylor. Eighteenth century. A contemporary of Tiepolo. One of the best-known of the Rococo painters. Particularly of scenes such as this. A very good example. Do you wish us to sell it for you?'

'Sure,' said Sam. 'If it's worth – any idea what it's worth?'

Well . . . *assuming* that it's genuine – and that we shall know with reasonable certainty by tomorrow – it should fetch upwards of £10,000. Discreetly advertised beforehand, that is. It's very small, of course: but there are very few of these Italian masters on the market.'

'Discreetly advertised', the painting was put up for auction the following month. I naturally went to the auction with Sam Taylor. The bidding was brief and unemotional and stopped suddenly at £26,000. I thought for a moment that Sam was going to be overcome with excitement and that I should have to help him from the room, but he just made it to the nearest public house.

Human nature is very unreliable and rather distasteful to contemplate. Sam never really *thanked* me for my help. He gave a large dinner at the Hanover Club and included me among his cronies, a dinner at which everyone except myself became the worse for drink. My stock in the club as a connoisseur naturally rose, and perhaps he thought that was a fair reward. At Christmas that year he sent me an art book which cost him £3.75. I wrote a thank-you note on the club paper and left it at the desk, thereby saving a stamp.

Human nature is unreliable, yet in some ways it runs true to form. Sam was dead within a year. He had never had unlimited money before, so restraint had always come from an empty pocket. Deprived of that restraint, he drank himself to death.

The money, or what was left of it, passed to his nephew, an indigent bearded young man who taught Biology at a Secondary Modern School.

The Basket Chair

Whiteleaf had his first coronary when he was staying with his niece Agnes and her husband Roy Paynter. He came through it, as of course he fully expected he would. When a healthy man is struck down with a near fatal blow it is as if he has walked into a brick wall in the dark; he is brought up starkly against the realization of his own mortality, and there is nothing to cushion the psychological shock. But Julian Whiteleaf had lived so closely with his own mortality for so long that a heart attack was just another obstacle to be carefully surmounted and added to his list of battle scars. No doubt this attitude of mind had helped him to stay alive when probability was not on his side.

But this was a nasty business, so painful and so disabling. It was hospital for three weeks and then it would be another four at least in Agnes's house before he was well enough to go home. The doctor had been a little reluctant to let him out of hospital, but Whiteleaf badly wanted to leave and Agnes had had some training as a nurse and said she could manage, as Roy was out all day. She was a highly efficient woman.

Although she was his only surviving relative, Whiteleaf had never really cared for Agnes. She was a childless, stocky, formidable woman of forty, who made ends meet on Roy's inadequate salary and found time and money for endless good works. Yet whether it was the Red Cross or the Women's Institute or the Homebound Club, every good deed was performed with the same grim patient efficiency, so that joy was noticeably lacking from the occasion. Far better, Whiteleaf thought – and had sometimes said – if she took a paid job of her own to supplement the family income; but this advice was not appreciated.

So in some ways he would have been happy enough to stay

another week or so in hospital; but as he had opted out of the Health Service some time ago it saved a great deal of money to leave, and anyway he rather thought Agnes liked making the effort to prove her devotion.

Another four weeks with Agnes, mainly confined to his bed, was a daunting prospect. But the time would pass. Whiteleaf was a great reader, and Agnes brought a portable radio up to his bedroom. He would have time to ruminate, time to rest. At sixty-five one became philosophical.

He had had an interesting life, and it bore looking back on. Born above a small bookshop in Bloomsbury, he had been vaguely literary from an early age, but his talents had lain in the unprofitable fields for which Bloomsbury in the 'thirties offered so much scope. Apart from helping in his father's bookshop, he had worked on two Fabian magazines, then had been assistant editor on a Theosophist newspaper which shortly folded up; he had reviewed and done free-lance work, had dabbled in Spiritualism, and then become secretary to the Society for Psychoneural Research. Here he met Mrs Melanie Buxton who financed the society, and had become her lover.

At this stage the war had come and he had found himself a reluctant soldier entering a world which had almost no physical or psychological resemblance to the ingrown, rather intense, fringe-intellectual world he had inhabited before. For a while the fresh air and the hard life did him good. He strengthened and broadened and mellowed under it. But in 1943 he was invalided out, having been twice seriously wounded in the desert and having contracted asthma and a kidney complaint from which he would suffer for the rest of his life.

To his surprise he found himself a rich man. Mrs Melanie Buxton, who was twenty years older than he was, had just died, and she left the bulk of her personal fortune – about £200,000 – to Julian Whiteleaf, 'to help him continue in the paths of research to which we are both devoted.'

Whiteleaf sold the bookshop, which he had also just inherited, and at forty years of age settled down to the existence of a quiet, ailing, dilettante. He never went back to live in Bloomsbury but bought himself a pleasant service flat in Hurlingham and never moved again. There was no one to oversee his interpretation of Mrs Buxton's will, but to fulfil the spirit of the bequest he kept the society in being with a tiny office and a secretary and continued to review books and write articles on paranormal phenomena. So, gradually, he had become something of an authority. Once or twice he helped to conduct inquiries into so-called haunted houses. He continued to dabble in Theosophy. He was known as a fair-minded commentator on the spiritualist scene. He was neither a committed believer nor a scoffing sceptic. Editors of national newspapers, confronted with an unusual book which did not quite fit into any of the recognized slots, would say: 'Oh, send it to Whiteleaf; see what he makes of it.'

He never married. His experiences with Mrs Buxton had satisfied him, and his ill-health after the war was a sufficient disincentive to extreme physical effort.

He joined a good London club and had many friendly acquaintances there or among those with interests like his own; but he had no real friends. He did not feel the lack of them. He looked at life through books. He was a precise, quiet man, sandy and rather small, who spoke without moving his lips. He lived very much within his income and never gave money away, except £20 to his niece each Christmas.

His visits to her were annual and largely a duty. She was the daughter of his sister who had died in the 'fifties, and blood, he supposed, etc. . . . but it was really rather an effort. He would, he knew, have made an excuse to stop the visits before this, had it not been for her husband Roy, who had a responsible but dead-end and underpaid job on the railways, and who, apart from being a nice inoffensive chap for whom Whiteleaf felt some sympathy at having married Agnes, also appealed to the other interest in Whiteleaf's life, which was the steam-engine.

This was the topic of conversation four nights out of the seven that Whiteleaf usually came to spend with them, especially when Agnes was out on some charitable mission; and sometimes at the week-end the two men would go to the railway museum, which was only a few miles away, and study the old locomotives and compare notes. It was a bond. And when he was dangerously ill two years ago after a gall-bladder operation, Roy had come up to London each week-end to see him and had brought up old catalogues and lists of engines from the days of steam, which he had been able to borrow from the local files.

Now that Whiteleaf was convalescing in their house and for a lengthy period, he felt he should pay them something for his keep, and he offered them £5 a week which Agnes accepted – grudgingly, he thought. But it would be a considerable help to them, he well knew, and not to be sniffed at, his weekly cheque. Agnes spent no more time on him than she would have done on her unpaid good works. The doctor called daily and Agnes took his blood pressure night and morning when she gave him his pills. And a starvation diet. His £5 was all profit.

Convalescence is a strange experience. Whiteleaf was used to it, but 'every time,' he wrote in his diary a couple of days after he came back from hospital, 'it presents a new face. It is as if the mind during serious illness concentrates all its energies on survival; but once the crisis is past it relaxes. It even relaxes its normal vigilance and controls – so that strange fancies, wayward concepts, take a hold that in normal times of health they would never begin to do. Nerves are on edge, imagination gets loose, temper frays as if one were a child again. Why snap at Agnes over the fire in my room? She so obviously is doing her best. Why allow oneself to think so much about the basket chair?'

Whiteleaf's diary was the one thing he had kept to all his life. Very often he wrote in it thoughts which later were useful to him when reviewing books or writing articles. He had been glad to get back to it when the doctor's prohibition was removed, and to fill in the empty days. He had always done this after his operations, even calling on the nurses to help him. This time happily there had been no unconsciousness, only great pain and then forced immobility.

'Of course,' he wrote two days after that, 'one wonders how far all paranormal phenomena are explained in this way. And in this context, what does "explained!" mean? "Imagination gets loose," I see I wrote overleaf. But how do we separate illusion from reality? We define reality as something which because it is apprehended by the majority of men is therefore assumed to exist. But does consensus of opinion necessarily prove the positive of any theory of reality? Still less therefore can it disprove the negative. Galileo believed that the earth moved round the sun. His was the scientific eye, perceiving what others could not see. May not the psychic eye perceive another area of truth at present hidden from the rest of us?'

'Is something worrying you, Uncle?' Roy asked that evening when he was sitting with him after supper.

'No. Why?'

'You keep staring at the fireplace as if something didn't please you.'

'Not at all. Nothing is worrying me. But in fact I was looking at that chair on the other side beside the lamp.'

'That one? What about it?'

'It's new, isn't it? I mean new to you? Since my last visit.'

'We've had it about a year. Agnes bought it at a sale. It's a bit of a rickety old thing but it's very comfortable. You'll be able to try it in another week or so.'

'It looks seventy or eighty years old to me.'

'Maybe. But it's *strong*. The frame's strong. Like iron. It's quite heavy to lift. I think Agnes paid a pound for it. About this film . . .'

They returned to discussing *La Bête Humaine*, which Whiteleaf had seen thirty years ago and considered the best film about railways ever made. Roy had never seen it and wanted to. There were copies in France, and being in railways he might be able to pull a string or two. He also knew the proprietor of the local cinema, who, between alternate bingo nights, was always willing to risk a bit of something way-out. He preferred sex or horror films, but if the French film were offered to him to show for a couple of nights without rental charge he would certainly agree to show it.

But it would cost money to bring it over and to put it on. It was no good Roy trying to do anything unless he knew Uncle Julian would bear the cost. Uncle Julian was doubtful, discouraging: he'd want to know a lot more about what he was letting himself in for before he even considered it. They discussed it for a long time and came as near an argument as they ever got, Roy pressing and Whiteleaf hedging away.

After Roy had gone Agnes came in and settled him down for the night. It was diuretic pills in the morning and potassium pills at night, and she gave him these now and saw his inhaler was within reach, threw some slack coal on the fire, which kept it in most of the night but almost extinguished it as a provider of heat, and then stood by the bed, square and uncompromising, and asked him if he wanted anything more.

He said no and she kissed his forehead perfunctorily and left. It was eleven o'clock. He read for a few minutes and then put out the light and composed himself for sleep. The room and the house were very quiet. Roy and Agnes were separated from him by the bathroom and the box room and their movements could not be heard. In the distance a diesel train hooted. It was a lonely sound.

Then the basket chair creaked as if someone had just sat down in it.

TWO

'I think,' said Dr Abrahams, 'you might have stayed in another week. Are you moving about too much?'

'No. Only once or twice a day, with my niece's help, just as you advised.'

'He never has need to stir a finger otherwise,' said Agnes uncompromisingly.

'Well, the electrocardiograms are satisfactory. But why aren't you sleeping?'

'I do well enough when I get off, but it takes an hour or two to – compose myself.'

'He sleeps in the afternoon,' Agnes said. 'I expect that takes the edge off. I can *never* sleep at night if I have a nap after lunch.'

'The breathing all right?'

'No worse than usual. I always need the inhaler a few times.'

After the doctor had gone, Agnes came back and found Whiteleaf writing in his diary.

'You shouldn't do that,' she said. 'It tires you. Dr Abrahams was asking me if you were worried about something. I said not so far as I know.'

'Not so far as I know either. Tell me, Agnes, about that basket chair. Roy says you bought it in a sale.'

Agnes looked rather peculiar. 'Yes. Why? What's wrong with it?'

'Nothing at all. But what sale?'

'Oh, it was that big house about a mile out of Swindon. D'you remember it? No, you won't, I don't expect.'

'D'you mean Furze Hall?'

'No. Beyond that. There was a Miss Covent lived there, all by herself with only one servant. It had thirty-four rooms. Fantastic. She was eighty when she died.'

'What made you go?'

'Oh, it was advertised. Carol Elliot wanted a few things – you know, from down the road – so I went with her. It was an awful old place; she'd let it go to ruin, this Miss Covent; all the roofs leaked, I should think; it's being pulled down. Most of the furniture was junk but it went very cheap. I paid a pound for the chair and a pound for that bookcase in the hall and two pounds for four kitchen mats and –'

Agnes went on about her bargains and then switched to some other subject, which Whiteleaf ignored.

'Did you know anything about it?' he asked presently. 'About the house where you bought those things?'

'The Covents' place? Well, of course, I'd never been *in* before. Hardly anyone had. It was like something out of Boris Karloff, I can tell you. The old lady must have been bats, living there alone. There was some story Carol Elliot was telling me about it but I didn't pay much attention.'

'Ask her sometime.'

'Carol? Yes, I'll ask her. But why?'

'I'm interested in old places. You know my interests.'

'Well, I never heard it was *haunted*, if that's what you mean. Don't you like the chair? I can take it out.'

'No, leave it where it is. I like old things.'

'Well, it's comfy, I can tell you that. I always enjoy sitting in it when I come to see you last thing.'

When she had gone Whiteleaf continued in his diary: 'Recorded and authenticated "possession" of small items of furniture is relatively rare and has no reliable weight of testimony behind it such as the "possession" of houses has. The poltergeist one accepts, because one has to accept it. Beyond that there is only reasonable cause to believe and reasonable cause to doubt. In the case of a chair . . .' He wrote no more that evening.

The following day he began a new entry. 'Is this the hallucination of illness or the clearer perception of convalescence? It is certainly a very peculiar shape. That high rounded back. It is a half-way style, reminiscent of one of the old hooded hall chairs of the 18th century. Why does someone or something appear to sit in it every night when I am trying to go to sleep? And am I right in supposing sometimes that I can hear breathing and footsteps? Odd that in all these years of interest and study this should be the first possibly psychic event that has ever happened to me . . .'

The next evening Agnes said: 'I saw Carol today. It is a funny story about the Covents. Of course she's lived here all her life and we've only been here ten years. She says it was before her time but her mother often spoke of it.'

'Spoke of what?' Whiteleaf asked.

'Well, it's not a very nice story. Uncle. It won't upset you to talk about it?'

'I'm not made of cotton wool,' he said impatiently. 'In any case, how can something that presumably happened years ago have any effect? I'm allowed to read the daily papers, aren't I?'

'Yes, well, yes . . .' Agnes plucked at her lip. 'Well, Carol says they were a young married couple, the Covents, during World War One. He was in the Battle of the Somme and was blown up and hideously disfigured. Apparently spent a couple of years in hospital and they then let him out. I suppose plastic surgery wasn't much help in those days ...'

'No, it was in an experimental stage.'

'So they hadn't done him any good. He was still terrible to look at, and when he came home he never went out of the house but used to sit by the fire all day reading and thinking. His wife used to go out and do all the shopping, etc., Carol's mother says, and that way she met another man and had an affair with him. Somehow or other Captain Covent discovered this, and it must have turned his brain because she suddenly stopped going shopping and everyone thought they had gone away ...'

Whiteleaf felt his heart give a slight excited lurch. 'Interesting.'

'After a few weeks someone got suspicious and they broke into the house and there they were, both dead, one on either side of the empty fireplace. Apparently he'd tied her to a chair and then sat down opposite her and watched her starve to death. Then he cut his own throat. That's what the doctors said. It was a big sensation in the 'twenties.'

'Very interesting,' said Whiteleaf.

'Well, horrible I say. They hadn't any children so the property came to his eldest sister and she took it over and lived there until last year. I tell you the house would have given me the creeps without any funny stories.'

Silence fell and the door downstairs banged.

'That's Roy,' said Agnes. 'I'll get him to shift that chair tonight, just so that it won't worry you.'

'Not at all,' said Whiteleaf. 'Leave it just where it is.'

Agnes shivered. 'Don't tell Roy. He's superstitious about these things.'

Whiteleaf shifted himself up the bed. 'D'you realize I remember the First World War?'

'Do you, Uncle? Yes, I suppose you do. But you'd be very young.'

'I well remember celebrating the Armistice. I was thirteen at the time. It never occurred to me then that I should have to fight in another war myself.'

When she had gone downstairs to get Roy his tea, Whiteleaf

wrote just one sentence in his diary. 'I wonder if this chair, this basket chair was the one Captain Covent sat in? Or was it hers?'

THREE

That night, although he was still not sure about the breathing, he was quite certain about the footsteps. The creaking of the chair as someone sat in it began about ten minutes or so after he was left alone and went on for a little while with faint furtive creaks. They were very faint but very distinct as someone stirred in the chair. Then also quite distinctly there was the soft pad of footsteps, about six or seven, moving away from the chair towards the door. They did not reach the door. They stopped half-way and were heard no more. Presently the creaking died away.

It is surprising what tension is generated by the supernatural. One can write about it. One can attend spiritualist séances. One can even visit haunted houses and still remain detached, scientific, aloof. But in a silent bedroom, entirely alone, with only this wayward wandering spirit for company, Julian Whiteleaf felt himself screwing up to meet some crisis that he greatly feared but could not imagine. It was clearly not doing his health much good or aiding his recovery. The whole thing was strikingly interesting; but he would have to take care, to take great care, to find some means of rationalizing this experience so that he could regain his detachment. Only his diary helped.

'Supposing,' he wrote, 'that I am *not* the victim of a sick man's hallucination and that for some reason I have become clairaudient. (The "some reason" could well be the rare combination of my hypersensitive perceptions during convalescence and the presence of a chair with such an evil aura, amounting to "possession".) Supposing that, then is there any resolution or solution of the situation in which I find myself? Is there any *progress* in this nightly occurrence? Is there a likelihood that I may become clairvoyant too? (And in the circumstances would I wish to be? Hardly!) Why are there only six or seven steps, and why do they always move towards the door?'

That night there were exactly the same number of steps but they were quite audible now, a soft firm footfall, measured but fading at the usual spot.

Whiteleaf never kept his light on, but Agnes had lent him her electric clock, which had an illuminated face, so that when one's eyes were accustomed to the dark one could just see about the room. And tonight a pale blue flame was flickering in the fire, so this helped. But sitting up in bed, Whiteleaf wished there had been no such fire, for the flames conjured up movements about the old chair. He thought: insanity is not evil, yet it so often wears the same guise. Covent must have been insane, driven insane by his own mutilated face rather than by jealousy of his wife. Only an insane man could tie a woman to a chair and watch her starve to death. I must examine that chair more closely. There may even be signs of where the rope has frayed the frame.

It was four o'clock in the morning before he fell asleep.

FOUR

Dr Abrahams said to Agnes: 'Your uncle is not making the progress that I'd hoped for. His blood pressure is up a little and his breathing is not too satisfactory. If this goes on we'll get him back in hospital.'

'It's just as you like,' said Agnes. 'I always help him when he gets out of bed, and we're careful he doesn't overdo it. I keep the fire going all day and night to help his asthma.'

'Of course he uses that inhaler too much: I've told him to go easy on it, but it would be unwise to take it away; he has come to depend on it. One is between the devil and the deep sea.'

'I'll watch him,' said Agnes. 'But he *is* difficult. Strong-minded. He'd fight before he went back to hospital.'

'That's what I'm afraid of,' said Abrahams.

While they were downstairs talking, Whiteleaf was up and examining the chair, as he had done once before when left to himself. As Roy had said, it was a strangely heavy chair for one made principally of cane. The framework was of a thin rounded wood like bamboo but enormously hard. You couldn't make any indentation in it with a fruit knife. There was a number of stains on the seat under the cushion: they could have been bloodstains: impossible without forensic equipment to tell. Whiteleaf had never sat in the chair and did not want to do so now. He felt he might have been sitting on something that should not be there. Only Agnes sat on it, in the evenings, and he had been tempted more than once to ask her not to.

He hastily climbed back into bed as he heard her feet on the stairs.

Later he wrote: 'I get the feeling that someone or something is trying to escape. To escape from the bondage of the chair. (Not surprising, perhaps, in view of its history!) But something more than just that – otherwise why the steps? It's as if the body rotted away long ago but the spirit is still attached to the scene of its suffering and still striving to get away. The footsteps always move towards the door. If they ever reached the door, would something go out? This I could accept more readily were this the actual room in which the tragedy took place. Yet perhaps in the room in which this *did* happen, there *were* only eight steps from the chair to door. Perhaps after the tragedy the chair was not moved for years and this "possession", this spirit, became bound for ever to a routine of "escape" each night. Even so it does *not* escape: it repeats for ever the ghastly ritual. Could it now in this new situation really escape for ever if the footsteps could reach this door? How to encourage them?'

It was the following day that he had the idea. Agnes, with her passion for cleanliness, was scouring his room as she did every day, and when she moved the basket chair to vacuum under it he suddenly called to her not to put it back.

Frowning she switched off the vacuum and listened.

'Don't put the chair back there. Put it – put it just by the dressing-table, just to the left of the dressing-table. I think I fancy it over there.'

She did not move. 'What's the matter, Uncle? Doesn't the furniture suit you? I do my best, you know.'

'You do very well,' he said. 'I'm not complaining, but if you move the chair by the dressing-table it will give me a better view of the fire.'

She stared. 'I don't see how it can. The fire . . .' She stopped and shrugged. 'Oh, well, it makes no difference to me. If that's your fancy. *Where* d'you want it?'

'Over there. A bit farther. That's a good place for it there, I think.'

'D'you want me to move this other chair over? Make more room for the commode.'

'Er – no. No, just leave that. Thank you, Agnes.' He began to say something more but she had switched on the vacuum again.

He didn't really mind because he was counting the steps. At the most the chair was now seven from the door.

'An experiment,' he wrote in his diary. Possibly nothing will come of it. Possibly I shall have interfered with the "possession" altogether. Or possibly the footsteps will reach the door and something will *go out*.'

He spent the rest of the day quietly reading an old book on the Great Western Railway which Roy had brought him. This, he thought, was one of the sagas of our time. The wonderful Castle locomotives that set up records seventy years ago which have never been broken. The 4-4-0's that preceded them. The Cities and the Kings . . . He wished he could concentrate. He wished, perhaps, that he had agreed to pay the expense of having that old film over, even though it dealt with French railways and French engines. They were indeed majestic in their own right. The great snorting locomotives of the Train Bleu, of the Orient Express, with their strange pulsating beat even when they are at rest . . . He wished he could concentrate.

Roy was out that evening at a social affair, Masonic or Rotary or something, so he did not see him. Agnes came up as usual, and, in spite of its uncustomary position, she sat in the basket chair. It was on the tip of his tongue to ask her not to; but again he refrained, partly because he was afraid of her uncomprehending stare, with its half implication that Uncle must be going a bit peculiar, and partly because her having been in the chair had not affected the manifestation on earlier nights.

She stayed longer than normal, talking about some work she was doing for refugees, and he listened impatiently, longing for her to be gone. She stayed in fact until Roy came in, by which time it was nearly midnight; then she gave the fire an unsympathetic poke, thumped his pillow, saw that he had enough water for the night, gave him her perfunctory kiss and was gone.

Roy had come straight upstairs, and the house soon settled. Whiteleaf's heart was thumping. To try to ease it, he began to compose the article he would write for one of the psychic papers on his experiences with a basket chair. One of the psychic papers? But possibly *The Guardian* would print it, or even *The Times*. It all depended upon the end, upon the resolution. It all depended on what happened tonight. In a way it was a triumph, that a man so involved as he had been all his life in paranormal phenomena, should at this late stage *experience* it in the most personal way. To steady himself, he tried to look on it as if it had already happened. He was recounting the most exciting moment of his life. The trouble was it wasn't over yet; he was in the middle of it; and the final experience, if there was one, was yet to come.

The fire was burning a little brighter tonight; Agnes had forgotten to bring up as much slack as usual, and this, with the help of the clock, gave adequate light – though dim. He could see all but the corners of the room. The chair in its new position was not so clearly outlined as it had been by the fire: it looked taller, still more hump-backed, like a man without a head. It cast a faint shadow on the wall behind that did not look quite its own.

The creaking was late coming tonight. He had thought it might not come at all. Always it began with a fairly definite over-all creaking such as would occur when Mrs Covent first sat in it. Then it would be silent except for the faint creaks that broke out whenever she moved. There was no sign of her struggling, as she must have struggled before she became too weak. Perhaps it was her dying that one heard. And the footsteps were the release of her spirit, moving away.

Yet always towards the door. Now they would reach the door. Perhaps – who knew – he would see something go out.

They began. They were slower and heavier tonight. Every step was distinct, seemed to shake the room, measured itself with a thumping of his heart. He sat up sharply in bed, straining to the darker side of the room to see if he could see anything. A flickering flame from the fire, just like that other night, brought shadows to life in the silent room.

The footsteps reached five, reached six and appeared to hesitate. They were at the door. A seventh and then the fire did play tricks, for he saw the door quiver and begin to open. He screwed up his eyes, one hand pulling at the skinny flesh around his throat.

But there was no mistake. He *was* seeing something. The door was literally *opening* to allow something to go out. He could feel the difference in the air. The door was wide and something must be going out.

Then he twisted round in the bed, clutching at the rail behind him, trying to get up, to move away, to get out of bed and scream. Because round the door a hideous deformed face was appearing, with one eye, and the flesh drawn up and scarred, and a gash where the mouth should have been, and no recognizable nose.

It was clear then – quite clear – that moving the chair was not enabling Mrs Covent to go out. Captain Covent was coming in.

FIVE

'It was always a possibility, of course,' said Dr Abrahams. 'The pulmonary oedema was an added complication. But I'm disappointed. He gave one the impression of great tenacity – great physical tenacity, I mean; such men can often endure more than ordinary people and yet recover and live to a great age.'

'Well, I can tell you it gave me the shock of my life,' said Agnes, drying her eyes. 'I came in at half past seven as usual, and *there* he was half out of bed and clutching his throat. He seemed all right when I left him. We were a bit later than usual – about twelve it would be. I never heard a thing in the night. But he'd such an *expression* on his face.'

'He's been dead some hours. He probably died soon after you left him. I think the expression is due to the nature of the complaint: a sudden great pain, shortness of breath, no doubt he was trying to call you.'

'He had a bell there,' said Roy. 'It was on the table. Just there on the table. I'd have heard if he'd rung. I always sleep light.'

'Yes, well, there it is, there it is. His condition had been vaguely unsatisfactory all this last week, without there being anything one could necessarily pick on. I take it you're his nearest relatives?'

'His only relatives,' said Agnes. 'But he was well known in his circle. I think there will be a fair number of people at the funeral.'

SIX

There was a fair number of people at the funeral. Representatives of societies with long names and short membership lists, club friends who had known Whiteleaf for a long time, one or two newspaper men, nominees from charities which had benefited in the past, some of Agnes's friends. It was a fine day, and the ceremony passed off well. After it, after a discreet interval, after a quiet period of mourning, Agnes and Roy burned the diary which had first put the idea into their heads. By discreetly opening it each afternoon while Uncle Julian was asleep, Agnes had been able to keep in touch with the progression of his thoughts.

At the same time they burned a rubber mask of humorously unpleasant appearance which Roy had bought in the toy department of a big store and painted and altered to look more hideous. There seemed no particular reason to burn the mop with which Agnes had bumped nightly on the ceiling beneath Uncle Julian's bedroom. Nor did they bother to burn the basket chair which Agnes had bought in a jumble sale and whose cane had the peculiarity of reacting with creaks and clicks about fifteen minutes after a person had been sitting in it, a peculiarity they had not noticed until Uncle

Julian had drawn attention to it in his diary. It seemed a pity, Agnes said, to destroy a useful chair.

That spring they had their first real holiday for ten years. They went to the South of France for two weeks, Roy had considered giving up his railway job, but for the moment he was keeping it to see how much Uncle Julian's invested income brought in. On the way back from the South of France they spent two days in Paris, and Roy made inquiries about the film he was interested in. Later that year in Swindon he intended to give a private showing to his interested friends of *La Bête Humaine*.

Jacka's Fight

My grandfather was called Jacka Fawle. He used to tell this story, often he would tell this story, and often-times you could not stop him; but it did not matter so much because it was true. He lived into old age, and we children would know if any stranger came by that he would take the first opportunity of telling this story, you could rest assured, so that, hearing it so often, we knew it all by heart and would chime in if he left out a detail. But it was all true.

My grandfather, he was born in Helston in Cornwall in 1853 and went down a mine before he was twelve. At eighteen he married Essie Penrose and in the next twelve years they had eight children, my mother youngest of them all. In 1883 the mining slump came to its worst, and Wheal Marble, where he was working, closed down. So like many of his friends, he thought he would go to America to make his way. There was work there and opportunities there, money to be made. It was a long way and a hard journey, but men wrote home that they were doing well out there. Some even sent home money so that their wives could go out and join them.

Well, it was a hard parting for Jacka and Essie, but there was little chance of her going with him with all the little children crying around her feet. Not that she showed much sign of wishing to go, for, like many women born within sight of the sea, she really feared it and trembled to set foot upon it. So she moved with her young brood of chicks into her father's tiny cottage and bade a tearful farewell to Jacka as he left home. With a Bible in his pocket and a bundle on his shoulder he set off one wet day in March, and they all stood in the doorway in the rain watching while his short sturdy figure grew smaller and smaller trudging down the lane. He walked west on the old coaching road, to Truro, to Mitchell, and thence to Padstow, where he took ship for San Francisco.

It was a terrible voyage – four months it took them around Cape Horn in villainous seas and then all the way up the western seaboard of the New World. Scurvy and seasickness and dysentery and bad food. Seven months passed near to the day when my grandmother opened her first letter from him. It was full of good cheer and good heart and he never mentioned the hardships, for he still hoped she would join him in a year or two. But in fact he had been little enough time in California, casting around as you might say, before he changed his trade. Mines there might be, but much of it was more like prospecting than what he belonged to do. Chance of riches and chance of nothing at all. While building opportunities were everywhere. Houses, churches, factories, all were going up like mushrooms on a damp evening. And bricklayers were in short supply.

So he became a bricklayer, my grandfather became a bricklayer, and his wages were good and steady.

He too was good and steady because he had been reared in the Primitive Methodist Connexion; and many times, he said, in those early years he was thankful for his careful upbringing. San Francisco was a wild and wicked place, where any man could go to Hell for the price of a few weeks' wages. Indeed all California was the same: a lost continent where lust and strong drink and greed and vice were raging. So he made few friends and those were strictly of his own kind. There were other Cornishmen in the city and he tended to be drawn to them because of memories of home. And he attended chapel every Sunday.

Each month, on the first of the month, he wrote a letter home, and each month, regular as a clock, he sent home a small sum of money to help support his family. Each letter ended: 'Hopeing that soon dear wife you will be able to joyne me your ever loving Husband.'

But the months turned into years and she did not join him. The children were all well and all growing, she wrote, but so slow. And Essie *could* not face the sea . . .

If there had been any work at home Jacka would have returned, given up his regular well-paid work and gone home, for he was a family man, and it fretted him that all his children would be strangers to him. Sometimes too he could not help but cast his eye upon another woman; yet by grace he saw this as a lure of Satan and hurriedly dismissed carnal thoughts from his mind. Even his memories of Essie were fading. She wrote him: oh yes, she wrote him, telling him homely details of life in Helston; but she was no handy one with the pen, far worse than he; and the cost of the post was so high that often she missed a month.

All this time he was saving, was Jacka. He lived quiet and he lived frugal and some he sent home and some he saved. But it was tedious work. First it was $500, then it was $800 then $1000. By the time he was thirty-seven, he had saved $3000 and had not seen his wife and family for seven years. Seven long years. It seemed a lifetime. But in all things he was canny, and he kept his money deposited in different banks to lessen the risk. He came to know northern California well, for all his work was not in San Francisco. He worked with Irishmen, Poles, Portuguese, Swedes, Italians, and second-generation Americans. But all the time he stayed true to himself and unchangingly Cornish. He would meet with five or six other Cornishmen every Sunday, and they'd talk of Pasties and Leekie Pie and Pilchards and the damp beautiful landscapes of home.

One day in the early 'nineties one of these Cornishmen, called by the name of Sil Polglaze, he came to Jacka and told him that there was this middleweight boxer come to town, just fresh come from New Zealand but a true Cornishman as ever was; and he was fighting a man called Abe Congle in the Park next Saturday afternoon and how about them going along? Jacka hesitated about this, wondering if there might be sin in it, but it did not seem so, so he said all right, he'd go. Thus he took his first look at Bob Fitzsimmons.

It was a motley crowd that day, no mistake, and nearly all of them shouting for Congle; but Fitzsimmons stunned Congle unconscious in the second round. So it was that all the patriotism in Jacka, lying underneath and scarce acknowledged, came bubbling out like an adit from a mine, and afterwards he pushed his way sore-throated through the crowd and spoke to the Cornish boxer and his wife.

Now Fitzsimmons at this time was twenty-eight, and no figure of a boxer at all. You could laugh, and many did, for already he had a bald patch and had long arms and legs like thin poles quite out of proportion to his great chest and stomach. He weighed scarcely more than 150 lbs, and he had a round red face and his teeth were large and bright like wet tombstones and had stood all the unkindness of the ring. He would have done proud as a comic turn in a circus but it would be foolishness to take him seriously as a boxer. Only Congle did that. Only Congle, still being doused with water like a babe at a christening.

Soon Fitzsimmons was telling Jacka that he too had been born in Helston – in Helston of all places! – and asking all manner of questions about it and whether old so-and-so was still alive, and if the Hal-an-Tow was still danced. I reckon Jacka became his slave for life at that first meeting, and sure enough he was there at the second fight when Fitzsimmons laid low a hard tough negro called Black Pearl. This time it took him two more rounds, but the outcome was just the same. He went in soaking up the punishment which would have stopped any ordinary man and then let fly with his long incredible fists and presently there was a black heap on the ground, and Fitzsimmons was standing there, Jacka said, with his long arms dangling and his white teeth glinting like a bone in his raw red face.

Afterwards, after Fitz left San Francisco, Jacka tried to keep track of him by reading the newspapers, but it wasn't that easy. Fitz went all over the States, but his news value was not high and sometimes the San Francisco papers did not bother to mention when he had been in a fight. Only the big ones were reported, and every now and then through the years that followed Jacka would find an item saying that Fitzsimmons had beaten Peter Maker, or Joe Godfrey or Millard Zenda.

Now although Jacka was a rare one for all things Cornish, he'd made no boast about it, living in such a mixed community, and he was content to be called a Limey when talk of nationalities came up. But Fitz's appearance on the scene had fired his local loyalties with a hot new fire, and while he was not the sort of man to make a show of himself in front of others, he was never above a mention of the wonderful prowess of his friend and fellow townsman Bob Fitzsimmons, and to let it be known what great fighting men Cousin Jacks were when their blood was up. So he became much more vocally Cornish, so to say, and so he found himself sometimes at odds with the Americans and the Swedes and the Irish. Just because he had so much to say for Fitzsimmons they derided Fitzsimmons the more. And so hard words and hard thoughts grew up, half jesting, half serious, and they centred around the name and the figure and the prestige of the scrawny, ungainly, ageing boxer.

When someone brought in the word that Fitzsimmons had put in his challenge for the heavyweight championship of the world everyone except Jacka fairly died with laughter. The great James J. Corbett, Gentleman Jim, six feet one inch in height and 190 lbs in weight, with not an ounce of spare flesh upon him, the best boxer of his age and the idol of the United States, was too superior in every way to be matched with this shambling creature. The challenge was of course refused, and all Jacka's mates told him that this refusal had saved Fitz's life. Quick to defend his idol, out on a limb on his behalf, Jacka shouted that Corbett was afraid and that Ruby Bob was being cheated of the title.

How they laughed! How they lay about and laughed till the tears ran into the bricks and mortar. From then on it was the recognized thing to have Jacka on about it. Any time anyone craved for a quick laugh they had only to mention this challenge and Jacka would be upon his feet and arguing for his friend. I think my grandfather was a good-tempered sort of Christian most of his life, but he often-times lost his temper over this. It changed him a little, made him morose. He never fought anyone because fighting wasn't his way; but he came near to it more than once.

So more years passed. Jacka was growing grey at the temples

and heavier in the girth of neck and stomach. His eldest son was 25, his youngest daughter 14, and he was a grandfather four times over. He had not saved so much money in the last seven years as in the first seven, for he had come to live a little cosier himself, to value a good meal and a glass of beer and a pipe of tobacco at the day's end. But he had saved all the same. In another ten years he reckoned he would have enough to go home, to buy a smallholding somewhere around the Helford River and live out the rest of his life in quietness and peace. By then all his children would have flown; but some of them with luck would not have flown so far, and he and Essie would be able to play with the grandchildren. It was an ambition as yet too far away to look forward to, but there it stood as a reward for a long life of toil. And patient Essie would be there waiting for him still.

Fitzsimmons too had gone on his way, putting all manner of boxers down and out, growing older too and scrawnier but still not quite finished. He was too hard for the young ones – yet. They just had to bide their time, while age and hard knocks crept up on him. So one day the distinguished Corbett found he could no longer ignore this middleweight that no other middleweight could endure the course with. A match was made, arranged, actually fixed for March 17 next, the contest to be for the heavyweight championship of the world, in Carson City, Nevada, the winner to receive a purse of twelve thousand dollars.

And everyone knew for certain who that would be. In vain Jacka defended his idol. They jeered at Jacka, and the good nature had gone out of it on both sides. One big Irish brick-layer called O'Brien was stronger even than most for Corbett – who was half Irish – and offered five to one in any amount and currency Jacka cared to name – if he dared to back his fancy. Jacka refused. In the years in California he had attended chapel whenever he could, and, although his sternest convictions had worn a little away, he still knew gambling to be sinful and he had never indulged in it.

In the weeks before the fight, however, O'Brien continued to goad him; and at last, hemmed into a corner where refusal spelt cowardice, he bet O'Brien fifty dollars at seven to one that Ruby

Robert would win. The money was paid over to the foreman, a big Swede called Lindquist, who was known to be a straight and honest man.

Carson City is only just in the state of Nevada on the other side of Lake Tahoe, and so little more than 160 miles from San Francisco. It was only just off the main railway east, and it was told that the Virginia and Truckee Railroad were laying special tracks so that rich spectators could go all the way on special sleeping coaches, travel overnight and be ready fresh for the contest in the morning. The poorer folk by leaving before it was light could arrive in another special train just the same. Tickets for the fight were $5, and early Jacka bought one. Some of his mates would not pay the money but said they would be able to get in cheaper on the day.

Sitting over his pipe in the evening talking to Sil Polglaze and others of his cronies, Jacka thought much, he said, of the money he had wagered. He stood to lose fifty dollars – but to gain three hundred and fifty. The odds were not excessive, for eight and nine to one were being offered in some quarters. Jacka had the courage of his convictions and so trusted Fitz to win. So *he* stood to win. So he stood to win a considerable sum. It was a sin to gamble; but was this exactly gambling, properly to be so described? He did not feel sinful now he had risked the money. He did not think he would feel sinful if he took O'Brien's stake. He did not think he would feel sinful if he even added to the money at risk.

He would never have done it but for the burning conviction within him that a good Cornishman was better than a good Irish-American. The patriotic resentment he felt towards his mates was as passionate as if he had been called to declare his Faith. And his passion, equally, was not based either on judgment or on knowledge. He had not seen Fitzsimmons for six years. He had never seen Corbett in his life. But he was called on to testify. And the only way he could testify was by risking his money. His hard-earned, laboriously hoarded money. Some of it. Not much, but some. Altogether in the world, if he counted every silver and gold coin he owned and every bank chit, he could muster about $5,600. It was some tidy little nest-egg. How much of it could be put at risk? $300 perhaps? He stood the chance of converting it into $2000. Such a small investment – less than 6 months' saving – to gain so much.

Where most of the bets were laid was in the pool rooms, and these were places which for long years Jacka had avoided as haunts of the devil. But this last four years he had taken to going into Scherz's Rooms with Silvester Polglaze for a quiet game of pool and a glass of beer. No wagers, mind. Just the play. They played for the pleasure and the relaxation. But this was where the wagers for the fight were placed, and the odds were put up on a blackboard, and Jacka licked his lips and saw them shortening, then lengthening again after Corbett gave an interview, then shortening as the time of the fight drew near. Scherz was a Swiss, a tough, hard, cold man but he'd never cheat you. A lot of working men left their money with him because they trusted him before the banks. So this was the place to risk your money if you wanted to risk your money, where it would be safe if you won. Jacka put on $200 at 8 to 1, $100 at 6 to 1, another $100 at 4 to 1; then when the odds stretched out again, he put on a further $300 at 7 to 1.

It was strange, Jacka said, that after he had put the money on, handed over the counter in gold dollars, he felt first a terrible hard nasty sinking sensation of depression, and then after an hour or so a sudden upsurge of hope. No twinges of conscience, that was strange, no feeling that he shouldn't have done it, only an urge to do more. It was like a drug; but it wasn't like the ordinary gambler's drug, when the wins and the losses, the sudden ups and downs of fortune carry a man fluctuating till he loses his stability altogether. There were no losses in this – nor as yet no wins: there was nothing to elate Jacka and nothing to depress him, only a burning conviction that somehow his ungainly hero would come through. A week before the fight he went with two Swedes into the California Athletic Club, and encouraged by them, put on another $500 at 20 to 3. Then at work he took a bet with a man called Sullivan for $200. On the Wednesday before the fight, Jacka went like a thief to one of his banks – the one he trusted least – and withdrew $800. From there, with no one to accompany him and no one to egg him on, he went out and laid his bets.

The last days were an age in passing. Jacka lived in a daze feverishly thumbing through the papers, talking scarcely to no one, refusing even the dangling bait of argument; only stopping in at one bank and then another to draw more money out. Before the fight more than half his total savings had been placed upon Fitzsimmons to win.

On the day all those who were going to the fight had to be up at four a.m. to catch the early morning train. All those leaving off work for the day lost a day's wages and a good conduct mark, but the absenteeism was so great that a whole mass of workers could not be penalized.

It was a long train drawing out of Oakland Station, and a slow one as it wound its way puffing up through the foothills of the Nevadas. Jacka sat with Sil Polglaze and a man called Mark Lothar; Jacka sat in a corner of the hard wooden carriage and spoke to no one. Only his eyes gleamed like one who has seen the light. The train was crowded, and men standing in the compartments shuffled and swayed against each other for four hours until at last it came to rest in the specially built sidings in Carson City.

Here everyone fell out in a swarm: it was as if the train could not have held so many men: they poured from every door and flooded off into the town. The sun was just rising on a brilliant day.

Carson City, the capital city of the State of Nevada, lies in a bowl of the Sierra Nevada at an altitude, so I am told, of nearly 5000 feet, and is surrounded by mountains. It was then a flourishing township, Jacka said, with a population of about 2000 people and had several handsome buildings, including the capitol, a mint and an orphan's home, and a good sprinkling of pool rooms. This morning the mountains were glimmering with snow, and an icy breeze loitered through the town. Dust whorls rose in the streets, and the wooden sidewalks were packed five abreast with men strolling through or looking for food or drifting slowly towards the arena to be sure of gaining good seats. In the gutter mendicants and others stood begging alms or selling favours and crying out for attention. Pretty many of the men who had come to see the fight already wore four-leafed clovers in honour of St Patrick's Day and to show they supported Corbett. Some of the badges were six inches across, and some men wore green shirts and green hats and green ribbons on their sleeves. Women were very absent from the scene.

Food was a big problem, for the eating houses and tents were soon full, and long jostling angry queues formed outside them; but Jacka and his friends had brought meat and potato pasties that Jacka had cooked the night before, and so after a brief walk around the town they tramped off to the arena and got seats. Jacka was much concerned as to which corner the boxers were occupying; Corbett, they found, had been given the south-east corner, so they took seats as near to the northwest corner as they could get. It was a great amphitheatre of a place with the white peaks of the snow-covered mountains all round. You could see the ring from almost anywhere; but although the fight was supposed to start at ten it was scarce dotted with people when they arrived, and they squatted on the grass to break their fasts. After they had eaten they went off in turn, and Jacka, passing a betting booth which had the guarantee of the local bank to support it, could not refrain from slipping in and putting on another $200 as a final token – though here he found the odds had shortened to five to two.

By ten the arena was almost half full, but no sign of the boxers and only one or two officials fussing round the ring. Old pugilists of one sort or another strolled all about, followed by their admirers. Sharkey was there, the only one who had beaten Fitzsimmons – though this, it was generally admitted, was with a foul blow. John L. Sullivan, grey-haired now but as big as ever. And Goddard, and Billy Madden and others. Not far from where Jacka was sitting was a strange contraption on wooden legs which he was told was a kinetoscope. This, they said, would take moving pictures of the fight – or rather many pictures which shown quickly one after the other would give the appearance of movement. It was said this was the first time such an invention had ever been used at a boxing match.

At ten-thirty the arena was three-quarters full, and the sun beat down and the wind had fallen away. This might be March and high in the Nevadas, but it was more like San Francisco in the summer. Everyone had come wrapped up for a cold day and everyone was now sweating. Coats, jerseys, mufflers, waistcoats came off. They lay in piles on the grass and cluttered up the aisles.

Now the famous boxers each made an appearance in the ring and made speeches, most of them challenging the winner of this fight: and they were greeted with applause or derision according to the wayward fancy of the crowd. Then there was a big cheer as Mrs Fitzsimmons came upon the scene. She looked some pale – though normally she was as rosy-faced as her husband – and went down the east aisle to sit in a box beside Governor Sadler and Senator Ingalls. A man behind Jacka, who was a Carson City man and had a stake in the local newspaper, said out loud that Fitzsimmons had told him that win or lose, this was his last fight. He would soon be thirty-five, and not many boxers stayed in the game above the age of thirty, except as human punch-balls. And Mrs Fitz was tired of travelling and longed for a quiet home life.

'Thirty-five, damme,' muttered Sil Polglaze, who had put fifty dollars on Fitz. ' 'Tis old, Jacka. 'Tis a bare five years younger than me, and I could no more fight than ride an ass backwards. It makes you think, Jacka.'

'*You*,' said Jacka, contemptuous. 'You could no more fight not when you was twenty. Fitz is differenter. Fitz'll not let us down.' But for the first time for days the veil of self-hypnosis that was upon him was shaken. This ageing man who talked of retiring – was he the man on whom you risked all your own hopes of retirement?

Muldoon, the time-keeper, was up there now, with Dan Stuart the promoter, Physician Guinan, Manager Brady, Billy Jordan the Master of Ceremonies, Referee Siler, and other big pots. The local man behind Jacka was useful, for he knew the names of them all and pointed them out in a loud voice.

Then suddenly there was a great roar from the crowd, which by now was barely short of 12,000 strong. Bob Fitzsimmons was coming down along the side seats. Martin Julian led the way, then came Fitz, and he was followed by his seconds and half a dozen of other men. Fitz was in a bright pink and mauve dressing-gown and looked just the same bald, red-faced, skinny, thin-legged man Jacka had met six years ago. All the fights he had been in since, all the punishment he'd given and accepted, hadn't altered his face except the skin round his eyes was puffier and he walked a little more with his neck thrust forward as if he was wearing a discomfortable collar. As he passed the box where his wife was sitting he stopped and kissed her, then went on to the ring.

Then before even he had climbed in the great James J. Corbett had appeared from the other side, with his brother Joe at his side and six other men in attendance. The man behind Jacka was giving names to them all, but Jacka paid little attention. His heart was suddenly wanting to fall into his stomach as he saw the difference in physique betwixt the two fighters.

At the roars which went on and on, several thousand more folk outside the ground who had been waiting for a reduction in the price of the tickets, concluded that after all they must pay the proper charge and came pushing and thrusting in, filling up the empty spaces. Few women were to be seen, and those few had peroxide hair and you could hazard a lively guess at their business. To all this Jacka was now blind, as he saw the preparations going forward in the ring. Near beside him the man working the kinetoscope came out to take sightings. One after another, men were making speeches in the ring. The time wanted twenty-five minutes of noon. Then Billy Jordan introduced these two fighters and everyone went mad again. When this was done, the fighters went back to their corners and a silence fell like the day before the Day of Judgment. Overhead was not a cloud, not a wisp, only the brilliant hot sun that made many men drape kerchiefs upon their heads. Fitzsimmons's bald patch shone like a polished saucer. The timekeeper took up his place beside the gong, and behind him stood a guard with a club to stroke down anyone who tried to interfere. The referee was in the middle looking at Muldoon. Muldoon nodded, the two boxers stripped off their gowns and came into the centre of the ring, Fitz thin and gangling with his great chest, looking like a hairless ape, Corbett, far taller and heavier, handsome built, in the peak of condition, proudly ready for the fight. The gong sounded and they were off.

Jacka watched the beginning but says he could remember precious little of the first few rounds. Suddenly the veil was cleft altogether from before his self-opinionated eyes and he saw not two men struggling for a crown but his own wicked wanton recklessness in risking three-quarters of his fourteen years' savings on the outcome of a fight. He felt sick, his bowels rumbled, hammers beat in his head, the blows raining on Fitzsimmons might have been raining upon his own body.

And certainly blows were landing upon Fitzsimmons everywhere. He was lighter than Corbett, shorter than Corbett and *slower* than Corbett. He looked smaller even than his eleven stone four pounds. Everyone knew he had a punch like a mule, but he never was given a chance to use it. The crowd were in raptures of pleasure. Nine in every ten backed Corbett; he was from San Francisco, he was Irish-American, he was good-looking, he was quite the gentleman. Fitz was going to receive what was coming to him.

And Fitz does. After the third round it looks like a massacre. Corbett is boxing like a champion, powerful and fast, landing blow upon blow. Some Fitz partly parries, some he takes full strength on his face and his body, yet he scarcely ever seems to wince or cringe away. Every now and then he will snake out that terrible left of his, but it never finds its mark. His face is red, his mouth bleeding, one eye partly closed – already. It is a strange expression he has upon his face, Jacka says; there is sentiment and tragedy in it, and a sort of fixed grin that bears it all while he still keeps closing in, waiting for an opening, his eyes watchful. There is no temper in those eyes, Jacka says, no resentment, just watchfulness and utter determination that he must not be beat.

In the fourth round there is a lot of in-fighting, with Corbett landing three punches to Fitzsimmons's one. 'Good old Jim!' the crowd screams. 'Good old boy, good old Jim!' while Jacka sits there too paralysed even to shout for his man. Unmarked, Corbett steps away from Fitz, thumping in half arm blows the while, to the face, to the nose, to the ribs, to the jaw. Sometimes Fitz looks like a turtle, his head, red and damaged, half sunk between his great shoulders for protection from the storm.

In the fifth round it appears as if Fitz is done. His lips are swollen, the eye half closed, his nose bleeding, his body crimson all over, part with the blows it has received, part from the blood on Corbett's gloves. He begins to lie on Corbett's shoulder, trying to get a breather, trying to smother Corbett's blows to his ribs. 'Knock his head off, Jim!' they shout. 'Punch his 'ead!' 'Lay 'im out, boy!' It seems endless that round. At the bell Corbett walks smiling to his corner. Fitz turns and plods slowly back to his. They are betting again around Jacka, or offering bets: no one is taking them. Eight to one it is again now. Back to the first odds. Now ten to one. Ten to one, a loud-mouthed check-shirted miner is shouting. Jacka gets up, near sick, fumbles in his pocket, takes out his purse and from it 100 dollars in gold, offers it to Check-shirt. Everyone stares – there is a wild cackle of laughter. Check-shirt thumps Jacka on the back. 'Right, pard, right, it's a deal: settle after the fight.'

In the sixth round it is all Corbett, and he lands a tremendous smash in the second minute that forces Fitzsimmons to his knees and sends more blood spurting from his nose. Fitz climbs slowly up, patient, his great teeth still showing white in a face that no one any longer can recognize. Corbett's body is smeared with blood now, but it is not his own. The seventh round is much the same, Fitz crouching to avoid the worst punishment, and every now and then darting out his terrible blows that still have not lost all their strength.

In the eighth round Corbett has clearly decided to finish it off. Dropping his own skill, he steps in and lands almost as he likes, blows to the neck and the chest and the ribs and the heart. Men round Jacka shout: 'Why don't Fitz give up.? Why don't he quit?' In the ninth Fitzsimmons is down again after a right uppercut that would have put an ordinary man out for ten minutes. He is up on the count of nine, leaning on Corbett, hitting back, weakly but enough to prevent another knock-down before the bell. Corbett is smiling again as he walks back to his corner. So far as you can tell he is unmarked. The check-shirted miner offers Jacka another hundred dollars at 15 to 1. Jacka just stares and shakes his head.

The minute rest has given the seconds a chance again to sponge the blood off Fitz's face, and he comes up looking no different from what he looked six rounds ago. Corbett will need an axe to finish the job, nothing less will do. They fight toe to toe through the first half, and Fitzsimmons seems no weaker for all his terrible punishment. Now he suddenly lands hard and high and often on Corbett, and though Corbett is not hurt, it is blow for blow for the first time in all the contest and a significant change. He goes back to his corner with a more thoughtful look on his handsome face, and you even hear one or two men in the crowd shout: 'Game boy, Fitz!' The eleventh round is much the same, and much whispering after it in Corbett's corner. Divided counsels. There is no doubt Corbett can outbox this indestructible land crab but can he outlive him? Can he by boxing ever tire him out? It is a fight to a finish, and somehow Fitzsimmons must be put down for a count of ten. In the twelfth round Corbett is getting tired and he takes a breather. He boxes comfortably, leading Ruby Robert about the blood-stained ring, landing when he wants but avoiding a fight, while Fitzsimmons patiently pursues him. Suddenly at the end of the round Fitz manoeuvres Corbett into a corner and lands some violent punches to the body.

The bell goes and Corbett's face has changed. You can see no expression on Fitz's at all; it is too badly cut and battered. So to the thirteenth and Corbett comes out with a last intent to finish it. Incredibly it is the fastest hardest round of all the whole bout. Now Fitzsimmons is giving as good as he gets, and the crowd stands up and shrieks and bawls its head off. Toe to toe they fight, and Corbett again gets the best of it. A great blow to Fitz's ribs causes him to drop his hands, and for a moment it looks all over. Corbett swings to the jaw, and by a split second Fitz takes the step back that saves him. Then they are at it hammer and tongs again to the last moment of the round.

So to the fourteenth and Jacka is standing up all through it, jaw slack, eyes staring, like a revivalist who has seen the light. For Fitzsimmons is growing confident, those long thin terrible arms after all his punishment are shooting out like pistons, driving Corbett before them. The crowd are mad with the noise and the excitement. Fitz's blows knock aside the champion's defence, a half-dozen take their toll, and then a withering deadly left just below the ribs and Corbett sags. Fitz's right comes up to the point of the jaw and Gentleman Jim Corbett topples and slides and kneels and falls, and is down and out.

Then all hell breaks loose. Within moments the ring is invaded, officials swept away. Men shout and scream, seconds fight to protect their men. In the middle of it Corbett comes round, dazed and shaken, and thinks the fight is still in progress – he lays out a newspaper man cold with one swing and rushes across to Fitzsimmons and gives him a tremendous punch in the face, which Fitz shakes bloodily off like all the rest. The men pull Corbett away and minutes pass in a maelstrom of fighting and shouting. Somewhere amidst it Referee Siler holds Fitzsimmons's shaking glove aloft, and somewhere amidst it Corbett, still protesting, accepts defeat.

Jacka is trembling from head to foot and his shirt is like it has been dropped in the river. He fights his way towards the ring and near him is Mrs Fitzsimmons fighting her own way, and he catches up with her and kisses her hand, mumbling meaningless expressions of joy. Others are fighting and falling over the chairs, and it is an age before anything like order and sanity is restored. Then the biggest surprise of all for Jacka is that he finds big-mouth Check-shirt waiting beside him shaking his shoulder and wanting to pay him a thousand dollars.

So my grandfather, as a result of a single fight for the Heavyweight Championship of the World, because of his reckless pigheaded belief in a fellow countryman and a fellow townsman (who was no more than a middleweight, and an ageing middleweight at that) and the insane risk he took in backing that belief – made $24,000. So with this and the little extra he had not put at risk, he came overland to New York and thence by sea to Falmouth, and from there by coach to Helston. And there he arrived in triumph and was met by Essie, grown grey and portly, and his five sons, all taller than he, and his three daughters, of whom my mother was the youngest, and his four daughters-in-law and his one son-in-law and his five grandchildren, all waiting for him, all nineteen of them, who with Essie's mother made a round score, and they partook of a splendid tea together at the Angel in Helston and then went out their several ways all over the country, and all twenty of them never met together at the same time ever again.

But Grandfather Jacka, a rich man by the standards of the country and the time, bought a handsome little farm with land running down to the Helford River, and there I was born, and there he lived out a pleasant, useful, quiet and agreeable life for another thirty-six years. And never a stranger would pass the door but what Jacka must tell of how he came to be there and how he had risked so much over a fight in Carson City, Nevada at the turn of the century.

And when it came to my turn, from that fight, thirty-six years later, I inherited three hundred pounds.

But For The Grace Of God

They picked us up about three on the Monday near the Fish Gate. I'm usually the one to run into trouble, but this time it was Gestas's doing. The four soldiers were about their normal duty fetching a political prisoner from Tekoa, some poor devil with a bee in his bonnet and not one of our crowd at all; so much unrest they had their hands full and would have missed us entirely but for Gestas.

We'd barely escaped the night before when they'd come down the narrow street from both sides and trapped our gathering. I'd been on the sill making my speech, and they saw me and came for me, hacking a way through the men and women who got in their way. I'd jumped through the window behind and just got clear, but Gestas had got a spear jab in his thigh that had been paining and festering all today, and maybe that tried his temper. Anyway, as these four soldiers went past he spat, and the wind was blowing and the spittle fetched up on the sandal of the officer; and somehow in no time they'd recognized us and we had a fight on our hands.

Even then, with Dysmas with us, we should have got away, because no one handles a knife better than he does, but at the very worst moment when one of the soldiers was lying skewered on the road with his own spear and another had his tunic ripped up and showing red, what should come round the city wall but a half maniple of the Twelfth Legion escorting one of their high officials back from some country visit.

Had there been people around I could still have melted away amongst them the way I'd done so often before. But this being normal *sexta* time, the few who watched watched from behind the safety of shuttered windows, and soon I was rolling in the dust with the other two.

I'll say this for Rome: they'd have been justified in killing us out of hand; but their damned soldiers have discipline. They knocked us about till there wasn't much life left in any of us, but then we were hauled up and dragged through the dust to Fort Antonia and thrown into one of the deepest dungeons, there to lick our wounds and to contemplate our fate.

Well, there isn't much to contemplate if you've sinned against the Occupying Power. Maybe you'll get a trial, but who defends you against the grievous wounding of a Roman legionary? No one can bring home to you the guilt of the half-dozen you've done to death in the dark; but one wounding is enough. Maybe you'll get a trial, maybe not: the end is the same. You just have to pray that it'll be quick – though you know that it won't.

Gestas took it the worst of us. He knew it was his fault we were lying chained here in the dark. But Gestas was always the tetchy one: up and down like a beetle in a pond; full of fire one minute, despair the next. Not to be trusted. In a war of liberation there are never enough to trust. You have to rely on the others to make up the numbers: the dreamers, the self-seekers, the rash, the boastful, the envious, the shouters who melt away at the first check.

Dysmas was not of these. A big slow fellow – slow except with a knife – slow-thinking, but once he'd made up his mind . . . You wouldn't get a complaint out of him now as we lay in the dark and our wounds throbbed and our bellies emptied and our chins sprouted new beard. Not a leader, he would never be a leader, but a splendid second man: a stay, a support, a comfort even in the darkest hour.

And this was the darkest hour. If I died – as now seemed certain – there was no one else to carry on. I could have wept – and once in the dark did weep – that our fine plans had all come to nothing because of such an idle and foolish gesture. Spittle on the wind. Maybe this was what all men's hopes and ambitions came to.

There was one hope, but it was not much of one. The Passover was near, and it was the custom of Rome to try to put itself on good terms with our people by allowing a free pardon for one prisoner – one Jewish prisoner among the many languishing in these rat-ridden cells. I knew I was much the most valuable prisoner they had – that is, valuable to our sacred cause – but I wondered whether, if a demand was loud enough for my release, whether the Procurator – come from Caesarea for the feast – would accede to it. I had been a hard one to catch, and if set free might give much more trouble. Yet a promise was a promise, and almost certainly many would ask for me.

Then, if that happened, if it really did happen, could I accept it and leave Dysmas and Gestas to a felon's death? If I got the chance it would be my duty to take it, but it wouldn't be an easy choice.

They fed us during those hard days, with foul bread full of weevils, and stale water and an occasional bowl of soup. It just kept us alive. There were ten in one cell, and little room to move. It was hard to count the days because no true light fell in the dungeon. But if you were awake you could just hear the trumpets each morning, and every three hours through the night.

So three days passed, and it was Thursday, the fourteenth of Nizan, and the Passover was near and I thought all was lost. By now many people from outlying districts would be flooding into the city for the feast, and my followers would be diluted and maybe even if they did cry out for mercy for me, their cries would be drowned in the cries of others. No question but Pilate would have my guts if he could – and who was to stop him?

On the Thursday night – no, it must have been some time on the Friday morning – two new prisoners were thrown in. I can't remember what their offence had been, but they had both been burned in the hand, and the moans of one of them filled the cell. The other was more a man of my own heart, and when the bleeding had stopped he tied up his branded hand and told us the latest news. It seemed that Jesus Bar-Joseph was in trouble.

Of course I'd met this fellow a half-dozen times, and twice had been in argument with him – a religious visionary who had come into prominence this last year or so. It was queer, but sometime we'd been mistaken for each other. We had almost the same name, for my name is Jesus Bar-Abbas, and we were of an age and not unlike in looks – at least in colouring and build, though his eyes are lighter than mine. At one time I'd hoped greatly that he would help our cause against the oppressors: indeed, I'd have been willing to stand down as leader in favour of him. I'm not all that much one for religion myself, but you can't over-value it as a means of raising the fervour of an oppressed people, and you had only to go to one of his meetings to see that he left me far behind – indeed anyone I had ever seen far, far behind – as a rabble-rouser. I swear that man – if any – could have thrown out the Roman from our land; but when I went to see him that first time he was a great disappointment.

True, he spoke me fair enough, but everything he said had a double meaning to it, and he turned away the sharp spears of my questions with shifty answers. When I charged him with the need to conquer these Roman devils and cast them for ever out of Jerusalem, he said it was necessary first to conquer our own souls and to cast out the devils within ourselves. When I spoke with contempt of the weakling collaborator Herod and told him I could make him, Jesus, king of all Judea, he said that his kingdom was not of this earth. I thought him sly and a bit of a windbag, and wondered at the time if he was planning to lead his own revolt without me.

I pressed the branded man for more news of this arrest but he had little more to say. It was only by chance, as he himself was being brought in by two soldiers, that he had seen this other procession coming through the town, some twenty strong, led not by Romans but by our own Temple Guard. Twenty men to arrest one man, the prisoner said scornfully; but I knew it wasn't quite like that. The holy man had a great following, and if they had turned nasty, no Temple Guard would have stood a chance. And, for that matter, Jesus Bar-Joseph had a reputation for fireworks himself. Some people said he only had to raise his hand and the heavens thundered.

Well he was caught now – like me, and God help him. The collaborators and the slimy Sadducees had got him. They'd be glad we were both under lock and key. There was no leader of revolt left comparable to him and me – no one else with the *brains*. One by one we had been picked off: caught by the Romans or betrayed by our own folk: John the Nazarite, Simon of Tekoa, Peter of Bethany: they were all dead. After us there was no one.

So the great cause came to an end. I could *not* believe it. Other young Zealots would arise. Perhaps not yet, but soon, to carry the torch of liberty, to fight, not to talk or to preach or to pray, but to fight to the death, as *we* had fought to the death, by foul means if fair were denied us, by the dagger in the back and the poisoned arrow and the thread around the throat – one by one we would pick them off, these vile, forever-damned oppressors, until in the end *they* tired, *they* wearied of the slaughter, and some emperor in far-off Rome decided that enough was enough and drew his legions away to do more profitable and more useful things. This was the end for which any patriotic Jew ought to be willing to die – and for which I very soon, tomorrow or the next day, certainly would die.

There were two or three ways they might choose to dispose of me, but one, the most likely, was the one I dreaded most.

It was a long time that night. There was scarcely room for us all to lie down, and the cold stench of the enclosed place and the groans of the branded men made sleep hard to come by. It was likely to be my last night on earth; certainly it was my last night of hope, for if I wasn't released today, then death was as sure as the next sunset.

So it was with a sinking belly that I heard from one of the gaolers about eight in the morning that Jesus Bar-Joseph had been turned over to the Prosecutor. I couldn't at first think what the Sanhedrin was playing at, invoking Roman Law where its own could run, but whatever the reason I saw my own chance of survival going down the drain. A brilliant fanatic, preaching his doctrines of spiritual purity and that stuff, would be exactly the sort of man Pilate could earn a little cheap popularity by setting at liberty – and do no harm to his own interests. Not the man of action like me. Not the true rebel. And all his set – all Jesus Bar-Joseph's set – would raise merry Hell to get him the pardon.

I wondered what had happened to my lot, whether they were trying to organize something or whether they were at sixes and sevens. I was a popular figure, of course, not only with my own followers but with many ordinary folk, particularly the young ones; but there were quite a few who wouldn't break their hearts if I was hung on a piece of wood on Golgotha. The trouble with a movement like ours – founded as it partly is on terror – is that its sword always has two edges: one to cut down the oppressor, one to discipline the toadies and the faint-hearts in your own folk. So you have enmities both ways.

Down in the cell you could hear nothing and learn nothing, you waited quaking for the next step; and when it came – a while later – it was four guards, and I knew my hour had come. We were called out by name – first me and then Dysmas and Gestas – and we were shouldered together blinking into the startlingly bright light of the shadowed stone passage outside, and then we shuffled along, first along a tunnel, our chains clanking, then up a flight of steps into a tiny courtyard, with the thin spring sunlight beating against a wall. Here after a minute Dysmas and Gestas were taken off in one direction and me in another. A room with a Centurion by the window, holding his helmet and smoothing the plume; one of the soldiers unlocked my manacles, bent to free my ankles. I stood there rubbing wrists and waiting. The Centurion let me wait.

Then he said: 'You are free, dog. Get from here, and, if you are wise, do not show your face in Jerusalem again. The next time there will be no act of clemency to save you . . .'

Well, d'you know, the flood of relief fairly turned my knees to water in a way no prospect of death would have done. To my shame I had to be helped from the room. Then I was led, recovering all the way, through the Praetorium of Pilate's palace and on to a balcony, where a huge crowd of people was milling about below. When they saw me they let out a great yell of joy. *That* was a moment – to feel free again, to be free to join my own, free to plot again and free to fight. Free to breathe the air and smell the sunshine and to live for tomorrow. I came near to blubbering like a weakling and recognized no face in all that crowd, though a voice now and then rang a familiar note in my ears.

I turned to go down the steps, and then saw that beyond the

Procurator and a couple of his lackeys was this preacher, Jesus Bar-Joseph; and God, he was in a mess, his face bloodstained, with a sort of laurel wreath on his head, and blood dripping down his legs and on his shoes, and an old purple cloak round his shoulders. He looked like death. We stared at each other for a second or so, and I guessed then that I'd been right – it *had* been him or me to get the special pardon, but for some reason that I never expected it had come my way. A shiver went down my spine and I thought, out of here before they change their minds, the fools, the damned fools, the thrice-damned fools to give it to me.

I made him a little bow and went down the steps three at a time, and in a few seconds I was being greeted by all my Zealot friends, hugging and kissing me with delight; and in no time I was swallowed up and away. The whole crowd, with me in the middle, began to push and stream out of the square; but just before we got out of sight. I turned and saw them leading the preacher away. And I thought to myself, well, there but for the grace of God go I . . .

It wasn't easy to keep my joy for long that day. They told me that Dysmas and Gestas had gone up the hill with the other Jesus to suffer the expected fate. I bathed and ate and had my cuts and bruises anointed in the house of John of Siloam; and spent the rest of the forenoon with him and four others making plans for the future. We all drank too much, and some of our plans were inflammatory to the point of suicide; but goading us to this, in the back of our minds all the time, was this thought of our two good comrades suffering a horrible death no more than a mile away. It was a special load on my soul for obvious reasons; but more often than not I had more thoughts for the other Jesus who had gone in my place. It didn't seem just, to think more of him than of your closest friends, for he was no friend of mine; but maybe it was the similarity between us, our likeness in looks, the closeness of our names, the feeling that he was now in my place, like another me, as if he was dying in place of me. I tell you, it wasn't comfortable at all.

John of Siloam told me that Judas of Kerioth had laid the information which had led to Bar-Joseph's arrest, and I was not surprised. Some men are born joiners and born betrayers, and Judas son of Simon was such a one. He'd been a Zealot, and among the most eager for action, the most urgent to fight for the freedom of Israel; then things had gone wrong – it was while Peter of Bethany was our leader – and Judas had taken the hump and left us. Soon after this Peter was caught in the Galilean riots and cut to pieces, and, come to think of it now, I would not put it past Judas to have had a hand in the matter and manner of *his* death. Then he had joined the group around the Nazarene, and been hot with enthusiasm for everything they did and said.

That type, I reckon, in a revolutionary movement are the most dangerous bastards of all: it's a sort of egoism in their nasty little souls that turns them sour. They *have* to join and, just as surely, they have to betray.

About an hour after mid-day there was a hell of a thunderstorm – in all my thirty years I remember none like it – and it crossed my mind to wonder whether the other Jesus was such easy prey after all. The stories you heard. Most of them were old men's whisperings such as tag themselves on to any prophet with a following; but there were so many about this chap you almost thought there *must* be some fire where there was so much smoke.

The people I was with stared out at the crawling clouds and the rent sky and whispered among themselves – no rain, not a drop of rain – just lightning and thunder and the smell of sulphur. I thought of Dysmas and Gestas and thought: better the bolt to strike them, put them out of their agony, poor devils; better the bolt to strike on Golgotha.

By the time the sun was down the sky, the storm had passed, but it left no sense of relief behind it. It wasn't like summer thunder that clears the air. And now we are all drunk. Not surprisingly we were all drunk. If you can drink enough it brings forgetfulness. I've a strong stomach but I hadn't the guts to go up there and see my two friends and try to comfort them. I despised myself for it.

But a man came just then to tell us. Simeon of Gilboa. A nasty little rant with a snivelling nose. He'd just come from there. He was the sort who always *was* there, and in a way I hated his bones because of it. They weren't dead yet, he said, but nearly. The other Jesus was dead. He'd died about an hour ago. And Dysmas had made some sort of a pact with him to meet in the next world. He'd been quite carried away by his sufferings and called this Jesus Master, or some such, and Jesus, poor crazed man, had acknowledged it like a king and had promised him a special seat in Heaven. Simeon of Gilboa always had a filthy nose in the cold weather, and all the time he told this he sniffed and snuffled and wiped his nose on his sleeve. So suddenly I could stand no more of it and shoved the wine flagon away so that it toppled over and hobbled red wine like blood on the floor, and wiped my own nose and went to the door.

'Where are you going?' asked John of Siloam, and I said: 'Up the hill,' and he said: 'Then I'll come with you.'

Golgotha's on top of this hill, and a couple of hundred yards north-west of the city wall by the Gate of Ephraim, and seeing crosses and gibbets up there is nothing unusual. I hardly ever remember when there was not something dangling in the wind. Today there was a cold air blowing after the storm, and great clouds still mustered over the Mount of Olives, so that the flat roofs of the city glinted like slates wet by the fitful sunshine. The first thing I saw on the hill was that there were two crosses only. The crowds that always gather for these executions were gone, but a few people were still dotted among the boulders, and we passed a group whispering together, and John wanted to stop and ask, but I grasped his arm and we went on.

Just for a minute I thought: what if he's gone, up to Heaven in a thunderbolt, taking cross and all; that'll be a shock for them; but when I got near I saw the middle cross was lying on the ground, and two soldiers of the Oppressors were standing by it. It was empty. My eyes went to my two old comrades and I saw, thank God, that they were now both dead. They'd been put out of their misery by having their legs broken, but they still hung there like two dreadful plucked fowls waiting for buyers in the market. There was the usual mess of blood and stuff underfoot. They didn't seem to be human any more, that was perhaps the worst thing.

I would have gone up to one of the soldiers to ask what had happened to the holy man, but this time John pulled *me* away and edged me towards a group of our own folk. They told us that two members of the Sanhedrin – of all people – had asked for the preacher's body and were just now putting it in a tomb of their own. I followed their pointing fingers and saw a group of white-clad men clustered about the entrance to a cave-tomb, and not far from them some Galilean women watching.

I had a sense of disappointment. I suppose when you feel the bitter disappointment I had felt this last year since taking over from Peter of Bethany – and especially this last month or so – when you've been through *all* that, and in the cold of the night when you see most truly you can only see ahead of you a long vista of hopeless rebellion – with no strength but men's minds and hearts against all the legions of Rome – then against your best sense you *long* for a miracle; and I suppose at the back of my mind – especially after the last talk with him – had been the crazy hope that this other Jesus *might* have been as good as his word and pulled something off. Come down from his cross and blasted the Praetorium; destroyed Herod Antipas; cut a swathe through the maniples of Rome . . .

Well, it was all nonsense, moonshine, child's thoughts, but I was disappointed just the same. I turned away with John and we stumbled drunkenly back down the hill.

My own family was far away, so I celebrated the Feast of Pesach in Jerusalem with Ezra my cousin and John of Siloam, but at Ezra's house. Ezra was a comfortable warm man, doing well out of the occupation, but I'll say this for him, he never wavered in his support of the Cause. There were ten of us sat down that next day in the afternoon to eat, and after Ezra had blessed the cup of consecration we had our meal of bitter herbs and unleavened bread and pascal lamb. Ezra, dipping his first morsel of bread in the *haroseth*, handed round a sop to each one of us, and when we had all taken a piece he said: 'To Jesus our leader, mercifully saved to us this day, thanks be to God!' Then we all sang the *Hallel* before beginning the feast.

Well, of course it's a time for rejoicing, and I was glad and thankful to be there, and who wouldn't be; but I couldn't really enter into the spirit of the thing. I had refused to go with Ezra to the Temple with the lamb. I'd shut my ears to the trumpets. I had spent all the morning of the Sabbath lying on my pallet in the upstairs room.

That night when the bazaars were open again I wandered with Ezra listening to the people. Many seemed already to have forgotten the executions, and I was angry at their cheerful mien. Those who did speak of it spoke mostly of the death of the holy man, because I think it was felt that Dysmas and Gestas were patriots fallen fighting for their country and this was a crime against the nation; but the slaughtering of this prophet who had done no harm and had cured the sick and – some said – raised the dead, was a crime against God. But it was only the Galileans who were really bitter, and it was in my mind to make capital of this, since there were so many in town, but Ezra would have none of it. 'No speeching tonight. You've been in enough trouble.'

But when you're in the mood I was in, you can't rest. I bought some myrrh and aloes at one of the stalls in the spice market, and Ezra said: 'What are those for?' And I said: 'For Dysmas and Gestas – I'll go in the morning.' And he said: 'Leave it be; they are in the felons' grave; if the soldiers catch you ...' 'Why?' I said, 'there's no law.' 'No, but they'll seize the least excuse, and you're in no state to hide your thoughts.'

On the way home who should join us but Simeon of Gilboa again, still wiping the snot on his sleeve, with news that Judas of Kerioth was also dead. It was said he'd done it himself, but I knew him better than that. Traitors never betray themselves: it's the one and only thing you can trust about them. The holy man might be involved in all this mystical forgiveness – I'd seen his eyes yesterday morning – but not all his followers were of the same persuasion. One or other of them had seen to Judas. It was also said that the priests had moved in haste at the last because they had been told that an uprising was planned during the Passover while all the Galileans were in the city. I only wished it had been true. I still could not get it straight – why, having been to such pains to get him killed, the Sanhedrin, or some members of it, should have such care for his body. It didn't make sense. It was a mystery that rubbed raw in my mind.

That night I slept badly, and with wild and terrible dreams. I woke in the very deep of the night and remembered that second meeting I had had with the other Jesus.

It had been while I was still hoping – now that Peter of Bethany was dead and so many Galileans killed by the Romans – that Jesus Bar-Joseph would be goaded into throwing in his lot with us. We had been alone for a few minutes, even Simon Peter out of the way; and to try to entice him, I'd listed how many things there were between him and me – things we had in common. The same given-name, the same purposes, the same age and size; but he had smiled and shaken his head. Brother, what a smile: it could have led a nation out of captivity. But all he said was: 'My friend, your mission is of the sword. What would you gain if you gained all Israel?' This seemed plain nonsense, and I said so. Then to challenge him again I said: 'You speak of being Son of the Father. Well, that is my name too. Bar-Abbas means Son of the Father; have we not a common cause?' But he turned it away again by telling me that I was really Son of the Fatherland, which of course is exactly what I have always claimed and got us no-where. What other meaning could there be? Then I looked at him and thought I perceived his other meaning.

'Some say you claim to be the Son of God.'

'I claim nothing.'

'Then what are you?'

'The Son of God.'

'If that is not a claim . . .'

'Truth is not a claim, Bar-Abbas. The stars are in the sky, the moon will rise, the seasons change; these are not claims, Jesus Bar-Abbas.'

I was turning away when he added in a gentle voice: 'We are

all sons of God, my friend.' I scowled at him, seeing another sly evasion, and he added: '*You* are the son of God: all men are the sons of God. All men bear within them the spirit of the Father. All men, Bar-Abbas, are born of the flesh and the spirit. They draw the temple of their body from the flesh of their mother on earth, and the spirit that inhabits the temple they draw from their Father in Heaven. This is a truth, Jesus Bar-Abbas, just as the stars are in the sky and the moon will rise.'

That night of the sixteenth Nizan as I lay in the dark on my pallet in the dark of the night, I thought of this for a long time. I remembered then I had said to him: 'So you are as other men?'

'No . . . I am not as other men.'

'In what way do you differ?'

'Not in the body.'

It had seemed the same old argument round in circles.

'In the body and the spirit lie corruption and incorruption.'

'And when you die?'

'I shall ascend into Heaven. As we receive at birth, so we give at death: the body to the mother, the spirit to the Father, as we received them.'

There had been more of this stuff until Andrew of Bethsaida came in to break it up. I couldn't remember it all, restless there in the dark, lying in the dark, months later, now the prophet was dead. He had said, what else had he said: 'But no man shall live in the Father except through me.' What did that mean? 'If you love not your enemies as yourself you may not enter the Kingdom of Heaven.' This was insufferable nonsense, and I had stormed out.

I could rest no longer now, so got up and quietly dressed, thinking there were signs of the dawn. But it was only the cloudy moonlight, the Passover moon we had scarcely seen because of a week of heavy night cloud. I felt I must go out and smell the air.

The sound of Ezra's two children; deep breaths in the night; creak of a board, hand brushing the wall; foot in the straw; out in the windy dust of the street I pulled my girdle tight against the chill. The anointing spices in one deep pocket, short staff in hand, dagger under belt.

227

The gates would be closed as yet, but I knew a way. You turned down an alley opposite the Shushan Gate and opened a door and squeezed through a long-dry drain and you came out between two rocks on the other side of the wall. From there it was five minutes' walk.

But it seemed darker outside the city; the great clouds like a tent and the moon hiding and the wind blowing keen in your face. I stumbled once or twice on the boulders, and once a goat stared up at me like a white devil, standing on the limestone path in front of me, long faced and soulless.

As I got to the top I could see that all the cross-beams of the crosses were down; from here the felons' grave was over the brow; and that *must* be a hint of dawn in the east, since the moon was now setting. I found the graves all right. They were only lightly filled in – a scattering of dry earth to keep the flies away, and in one shallow hole a knee and foot showed. I squatted beside it and shoved the earth away from where the head was likely to be, but the head I uncovered was a strange one and had been rotting there a week. I looked round and saw with disgust that there were eight or ten such graves, all in the same state. I hadn't thought that so many others had died of the same complaint and so recent; to find my friends meant a long and nasty search.

I sat for a time thinking, watching the dead light grow. Then I stood up. Friendship – well, it can go too far – and no good it would do them anyway. But there was one I could pay last respects to. Though not a friend. Never a friend. 'Just as the stars are in the sky and the moon will rise . . .'

I shambled round the grisly skull of the hill and came to the cave-tomb from the east. The dawn was at my back. There was a great stone against the opening; but it was a different, more dignified resting place than a felon's grave. It had dignity. What any patriot deserved. Much more than I should ever have had. I put my back against the stone and my feet against the wall and slowly heaved it away. It was a weight like the weight of the world.

When I'd done I wiped the cold sweat off my face and went in. They had laid him on a wooden trestle in the centre of the cave, and they'd swathed him in white clothes. The cave was low and I had to bend to go in farther. I must say I felt peculiar bending over him: you know, it was as if I was bending over another part of myself: as if the spirit in me had died and lay mummified in the compass of this dead rock. For a little I forgot the spices in my pocket; just for a little I had to see this other face. I dragged the cloths away, and it seemed to me suddenly that the cloths were not cold. I touched the face, and although it was cold I thought to myself that it was not cold *enough*. It was not cold enough for dead.

God, it was as if an earthquake had happened inside me. I didn't think – not properly reason, that is – I didn't think, but through me like a spear went words like: not dead – not dead but liveth – done to death by Sadducees – buried by Sadducees – but what now – what contrivance was this? – not dead but liveth – by whose grace does he live?

It didn't ever make even as much sense as that; only *one* thought really came through – get him out of here – out of the cold of the tomb, out of the cold of death into the warmth of the living earth and the sun. Not caring about spirit or any of that side, not at the moment the spiritual; just life in the human body.

So I grabbed the body round the waist and carried it to the mouth of the cave-tomb. It was heavy with a *dead* weight, but I carried it just as easily as one carries the living. When I got to the entrance I saw that day had half come on us while I was inside, but still grey with cloud. The swifts were flying against the light of dawn. I stood with the weight on my shoulder looking round the hillside, trying to think what to do next. And then, in the silence, I heard a footstep ...

... I leaned against the opening of the tomb and let the burden slide from my shoulders. I stood there frozen like a stiff one myself in the half light, and then a woman came round the side of the boulder. I just knew her, by her long black hair, even in that light. One of Jesus Bar-Joseph's closest friends.

We saw each other more or less at the same second. I reckoned she had had much the same idea as myself, because she carried a bag that was probably spices and oils; but she dropped this on seeing me.

'Mary,' I said, 'Mary of Magdala,' and took a half-step, and then looked towards the burden I'd let slip down among the stones.

I think she couldn't have seen this, because she suddenly collapsed to the ground herself and said only one word: 'Rabboni!' Rabboni: that means Master. I knew then that she'd made a mistake, and I mumbled: 'No, Mary. Look again. But I believe your Jesus lives nevertheless ...' But before I could say more she had scrambled to her feet and was running away across the hillside like someone was after her. 'Mary!' I shouted. 'Mary!' But there was no stopping her.

It was quiet after that, and in the full dawn even the wind was quiet. Jerusalem was just below us on the side of the hill, smoke beginning to rise from some of the houses. To the right the Mount of Olives; beyond that the valley leading to Jordan. I bent and struggled the body of the prophet on to my shoulder again. It seemed to sigh as I picked it up.

With this on my shoulder, with this burden, I turned away from Jerusalem and began to tramp heavily downhill towards the road to Bethany. If Jesus Bar-Joseph was really still alive, this was the only safe place for him, not anywhere in Jerusalem. At Bethany he'd have a chance to get his wounds anointed and he could rest and stay hidden. I walked to the bottom of the hill, and then saw a group of pilgrims just emerging from the city gates on their way home after the feast. If I was seen it would mean trouble.

A hundred metres from the road, at the foot of the hill, there is a cave, another cave; so I turned in there and laid the prophet down on the ground, well towards the back where there was a stretch of fine gravel. And I crouched near the front to watch the pilgrims past. They were very slow in coming, walking with two asses, an old man bringing up the rear. But if there was hope for the prophet there would be need, and urgent need. I went back, into the shadowy back of the cave.

I looked at his face. I remembered it well. I looked at his face as if it was my face. Suffering had taken the lines away – or maybe they'd never *been* there. It hadn't the lines mine had. Everything on mine showed, I sometimes thought: the danger, the combats, the scheming, the knife thrusts. His hadn't got those lines. It was a face that had lost touch with earth. It was still like mine, but with all the evil gone. It was maybe like every man's with all the evil gone. It was pale with the pallor of death and at the same time the pallor of purity.

The skin of the forehead was badly scratched, the hair matted over it. I pushed the hair away. The skin was cold, the mark of the scratches black, like writing on a scroll. I touched the skin again. It was cold – but was it cold enough? Had my sense of touch cheated me in the greater coldness of that other cave? Some of the wrappings of the body had fallen away in the tomb, but I pulled aside the rest and felt for the heart. There was no sign.

I squatted on my haunches and looked out and watched the pilgrims go past. But there would be others. Today of all days this road would be constantly peopled with pilgrims leaving the city. If he *was* dead I couldn't take the body back, because I'd surely be seen now and I'd be condemned for defilement – by my own folk not by Rome. If I was to go on with the fight for our national freedom, I couldn't afford this sort of blot on my reputation, that I'd taken the body of this holy man out of his tomb. If I left him here he might be found, or he might never be found.

But if he was *not* dead . . .

I thought I heard a sigh, and swung round in a flash to look at the body. It hadn't moved, yet I felt as if something was about it – a ghost, or the ghost of a spirit, or the spirit of a man or the spirit of a god. I put my fingers again on the forehead, and this time it *was* more cold. I'll swear there was a difference, as if the slight warmth of the day was showing up the utter coldness of the tomb. It was as if the last life was moving away, had moved away, had left while I squatted there muttering in the half dark.

A hell of a sadness came over me. I felt as if I'd lost something personal to myself – as if I'd lost the best that was in me, the best that was in all men. I knew now that in that moment when I'd thought him alive I'd wanted above all for him to live on. I'd wanted to carry him over my shoulder, wounded but triumphant, down the slope to Bethany. I wanted him to recover to lead our people, all people maybe, out of the valley of oppression and servitude, out of the valley of the shadow.

Just for a while I forgot my hatred of our oppressors, and my ambition to lead our nation out of its own servitude. It was as if I'd got my ideas crossed there in the cave, and for a while even national liberation wasn't important measured against the importance of the man who had just gone.

Confused as I was, I felt I would have died in his place, instead of him in mine, if he could have gone on leading people the way he had been leading them, towards a new life.

Again I was full of a sense of *disappointment* – only this time it was much worse, much, much worse. I had thought I could bring him alive to Bethany. I had thought I was going to do that and now I could not. Maybe he *had* been alive when I found him – the last spark lingering – but now the last spark had gone out.

I began to weep. Believe it or not, I sat down on a stone there in the mouth of the cave and blubbered like a child. I wept for myself and for my generation and for generations yet unborn. For there, it seemed to me, with or without the grace of God, went we all.

Lightning Source UK Ltd.
Milton Keynes UK
UKHW01f1832040618
323694UK00003B/666/P